Dreams Become Reality
by Megan Johnson

Published 2015 by The Light Network
Copyright © Megan Johnson

Printed in the United States

Interior layout by Christi Koehl

Edited by Keidi Keating

ISBN: 978-0-9966403-5-0

Dreams Become Reality

Book 1 of The Dreams Trilogy

By Megan Johnson

"Maybe dreams really are more than just our imagination."

I'd like to dedicate this book to all of you who want to pursue your dreams. Your dreams can be achieved as long as you work hard and never give up.

Acknowledgments

My parents for supporting me through the writing process.

Your Book Angel for agreeing to republish this book and work with me on making this a great series.

My family in Cincinnati for supporting me and believing in me.

Megan Johnson

All I see is darkness, but I smell something burning. I slowly open my eyes, still half asleep. I glance at the clock on my desk. It's 3:15 a.m. I look over, and there's a man lying next to me. I've never seen him before, but I begin to shake him to wake him up. I almost forget there's a fire because I'm taken aback by the handsome man with bright blue eyes in my bed.

The smell is starting to get more intense. My fire alarm goes off. We both jump out of bed, and I put my slippers on. I look under my door and see the reddish-orange glow of flames. The man checks the doorknob, and it's hot. We realize we can't get out that way. I look out of my second-story window and do a double take. I thought I saw a figure standing across the street, but when I look again, there's no one there. I quickly change my focus back to escaping.

I call 911 on my phone. We have two choices: wait for the firefighters to get here, hopefully in time to save our lives, or attempt to jump to the tree outside my window and climb down.

We decide to take the window. The tall, muscular man goes first and puts his hand out for me to take. It takes me a few seconds to get the courage to jump to him. Suddenly, the fire roars through my bedroom door. One, two...then there's nothing but the fear of death. I'm falling through the ceiling to the first floor. I realize my time here on Earth is almost gone. All I see is orange around me. The flames start burning my skin like a thousand pricking needles pricking. All I can do is scream.

I wake with a start and take a deep breath. Touching my skin and looking around my room, I realize it was just another dream. I'm sweating and breathing heavily. The dream seemed so real that my skin feels overly heated.

These dreams are something I deal with almost every night. Do you ever have dreams that feel so real you can't tell whether it really happened or whether it was just a dream? Well, I go through that all the time; it's part of my daily routine. There are many times when I really have to think about something to figure out if it actually happened. It kind of sucks.

I have a hard time getting myself out of bed and ready for the day after that disturbing dream. But I try to suck it up and focus on the day ahead. The man in my dream was very attractive, so maybe that's a good sign.

I co-own Sweet and Spice, a coffee and pastry shop in downtown Charleston, South Carolina, with my best friend, Sarah. We came up with the idea when we graduated from The College of Charleston together. We wanted to create a place that served great coffee and food and also provided a place for people to sit, read, relax, and do work in a stress-free environment. We found a great spot on historic East Bay Street in the heart of downtown, and our parents helped us out with the start-up costs. The shop is full of floor-to-ceiling windows so people can enjoy the harbor view, and we have a patio out front. We filled the interior with tables and benches painted bright yellow, green, and purple. Each wall is a different color that brings its own funk to the place. Our customers love it.

I get to the shop at 7:00 a.m., like I do every day during the week, and start the opening process. Sarah follows right behind me.

"Good morning, sunshine, did you have any dreams last night?" Sarah knows about my dreams, and she asks me about them pretty much every day, although I don't tell her about all of them.

"Good morning, and yeah, I did have a dream. A pretty scary one." I tell her in detail about the fire, the man, and how I died in the dream.

"Wow, that is freaky, Linda. I don't know how you get through your days after dreams as surreal as that. But on the bright side, maybe that was the man of your dreams!" she adds in an attempt to cheer me up.

"Yeah, maybe," I say, faking a smile. I can't shake the feeling that this dream means something more. My arms still feel as if they are burning.

After the morning rush has died down, my younger sister walks in. "Hey, sis. I came to get my coffee fix before class this afternoon.

Lord knows I need the caffeine! I'm so over this semester, and there are still two months left!"

My sister can be overdramatic sometimes, but I love her. "Oh, suck it up, May. Once you have to start paying bills and living completely on your own, you'll wish to go back."

"Yeah, yeah, you always say that. Can I have the white chocolate mocha, please?" May is about five foot nine with long brown hair, and she's as skinny as a stick. But she has a sophisticated style and knows how to show her figure off to its best advantage. She's always smiling and can put anyone in a good mood with her fun and lively personality.

As I make her coffee, I tell her about the dream from last night. She tends to worry about the effect my dreams have on me.

"The dream from last week and now this one? Are you sure you're okay?"

"I'm fine. Keeping busy with work and talking to you and Sarah helps a lot."

"All right. But you know I'm only a phone call away if you need me."

I smile and give her a hug and a kiss on the cheek. "I know, and I love you."

After May leaves, Sarah says, "You didn't tell me you had another one of these dreams last week."

That dream had seemed like something right out of the news headlines, and I hadn't wanted to talk about it, but I know Sarah won't let up, so I recount it for her. "I was standing in front of New Town High School and saw a man in a long brown jacket walk in. Then I heard a bunch of gunshots and screams. When I went over to see what happened, I woke up."

"Do you think all of these dreams have some kind of hidden meaning?"

"I don't know. They seem so real, like they could happen in real life. But that would be crazy, wouldn't it? I mean, that's something you see in movies or read in books. People who can see the future in dreams? It sounds like a science-fiction movie," I say as I sip my coffee.

"But you do hear stories of people having a sixth sense. What if this is yours?"

Sixth sense? That's a scary thought. I mean, how would I be able to live a normal life? My stomach starts to turn with nerves.

I shake my head. "No way, it's not possible." A customer walks in, and I move to the counter to assist them, hoping Sarah will drop the conversation.

As Sarah and I are cleaning the countertops and putting out fresh pastries, something on the TV in the corner catches my attention. I turn up the volume to listen to the breaking news story.

"Holy shit, Sarah, listen to this."

A video of New Town High School is playing as the reporter says, "Sources say a man in a brown coat walked into the school and was confronted by the office secretary, who tried to stop him from entering a hallway lined with classrooms. That's when the man pulled out an assault rifle and started shooting. Ten people were killed and fifteen injured—"

I quickly turn off the TV and sit down, trying to catch my breath. I feel light-headed. "I saw that before it happened." A rush of fear takes over my body, and I start to shake.

Sarah rushes over with a glass of water. "Are you okay?"

"Not really. I mean, there's no way this is a coincidence. The same guy in the brown coat and the same school? This is the first dream I've had where things actually came true. Maybe I really can see the future. This would explain why my dreams seem so real."

Sarah rubs my back as she listens to me.

"My dreams growing up as a kid never came true. They used to be intense and lifelike, and I'd wake up in a panic, but I always knew they were just dreams. But now the dreams feel like something more." I pause, looking for another explanation. "This is the first one that came true, so maybe it's just one dream, and it won't happen again." I'm trying to see a bright side, but I know deep down inside that this is just the start.

"It might be, but if it's not think of how many people you could help or lives you could save."

My eyes widen as that implication sinks in. "Yeah, but talk about the pressure that puts on me! How would I even handle a situation like that?" My voice rises, and the handful of customers in the shop look over at us.

"Okay, okay, relax," Sarah whispers as a customer heads to the counter.

"Go check them out. I'll be all right."

I put my head down on the table, trying to get some sense of what is really going on. What if this, right now, is a dream? What if I wake up and none of this is real? I chuckle. *Yeah right, I wish.*

Sarah comes back, and she's got a smile on her face that makes her blue eyes seem even bigger. "Hey, this means you may actually meet the man of your dreams, the one from the fire dream!" I know she's trying to help, but it's not working very well.

"Yeah, but what about the fire? I mean, how do I know when it's coming, or how to prevent it?"

"At least you'll know to hurry out of the house if there's a fire. And the guy across the street, have you ever seen him before?"

"No, and I can't seem to get the dream out of my head. Now I've got to deal with both of these dreams." I rub my arms as the burning sensation returns.

"Just try to stay busy today. Maybe that will help."

"I will. Thanks, Sarah."

I try to fall back into the familiar routine of the shop as we prepare for the lunch rush, but the whole time I'm thinking about being too scared to fall asleep tonight.

What else am I going to see in my dreams?

Chapter 2

It has been a week since the fire dream occurred. If I've had any dreams since then, I don't remember them. Nothing out of the ordinary has happened.

It's Wednesday morning, and I'm walking to the shop when I remember my sister's birthday is this Saturday. She'll be turning twenty-one, which means I'll be taking her to a nightclub. I text May with a plan for Saturday:

"Hey, sis, I want to take you to Pavilion for your birthday. The rooftop bar overlooking the harbor will be the perfect place to celebrate your twenty-first birthday. Plan on being at my house at seven for dinner, then we'll walk over. I can't wait!" I add a smiley face.

She must be up for class already because she texts me right back. "Sounds amazing! I'll see you then! Love you."

As I walk to the shop, I see Sarah has arrived just ahead of me. We say our good mornings and get to work.

Our shop is jam-packed during the breakfast rush. We are fortunate to have a lot of loyal customers, and they keep us hopping, making more coffee and pastries. I'm wiping down the counter when the door opens again, and I look up, unable to believe my eyes.

As he walks through the door, everything seems like it's in slow motion. He's tall and muscular with smooth caramel skin and dark hair. And those eyes—bright blue and beautiful. I'm in some sort of trance and I can't take my eyes off him. Then he smiles, and my heart starts pounding. His pearly white teeth light up his entire face, and I'm melting. My body is tingling, and all I can think about is him picking me up and setting me on the counter for amazing sex. As he walks closer, my legs begin to buckle, so I quickly straighten up and lock my knees.

"Hi, I hear you have good coffee here," he says in a deep, raspy voice. I know I need to respond, but I can't seem to open to my mouth. *Linda, snap out of it and talk to him!*

My wits finally return. "Well, not to be biased, but we do have the best coffee in Charleston." I'm smiling so big my cheeks hurt.

"My buddy told me about this place, and it's on the way to the hospital, so I figured I'd stop by and try it."

"I'm glad you did. We love meeting new customers. So you're a doctor?"

"I'm an orthopedic surgeon at MUSC."

"Oh, nice, I'm sure you stay busy."

"I'm on call a lot, so I can get phone calls at any time of day. It can get overwhelming, but I love my job."

"That's great. What would you like to have this morning?"

"Hmm, the Milky Way mocha sounds good. I'll have that."

"Coming right up," I say, smiling as I start making his drink.

"So do you own this place?" The sound of his voice gives me butterflies.

"Yes, along with my best friend, Sarah." I point her out, and she gives us an over-exaggerated wave.

"Seems like you have a successful business."

"Yes, fortunately. The location really helps. We get locals and tourists alike." I hand him his mocha.

"Thank you." He takes a little sip. "Wow, this is very good. I'll have to come back."

I smile and say, "I hope you do. Next time, you can try the white chocolate pumpkin spice latte. It's a great seller."

"I think I will," he says with his hand out for me to shake. "It was nice to meet you…"

"Linda."

"Linda," he says in that deep, intense voice.

"It was nice to meet you as well…"

"Luke."

"Luke," I say. I don't want to let go of his hand. We stand there awkwardly, staring at each other and shaking hands.

"Well, I better get to the hospital. I have a knee surgery to prep for."

"Good luck with the surgery, and I hope to see you in here again."

He smiles and walks out the door.

I look over at Sarah, and put my hand over my heart, and mouth. "Oh my God!"

She's by my side in an instant.

"Holy sexiness!" she says with a laugh.

"I know, right! He's so hot, and his voice is so manly. What I wouldn't give for him to come back in and grab me and kiss me." Then it dawns on me. There's something very familiar about him.

"Shit," I say out loud, my tone changing from excited to wary. "He was the man in the bed next to me in that dream."

"Wait, are you sure?"

"I couldn't be surer." We both stand there, staring into space. My mind is blank because I don't even know what to think of all this. "So he is literally the man of my dreams. We're going to have a serious relationship if he's sleeping with me in my dreams, right? I'm not sure how I feel about this. I don't like knowing what's coming."

"I can't believe any of this is happening. For your dreams to be coming true, I can't imagine how you feel. I'm sorry. I don't know what else to say." Sarah has a half smile on her face, but I can tell she's concerned for me.

"I'm just glad you're here with me now."

We get back to work, but I can't focus well for the rest of the day.

I tend to stress too much about everything. I'd always had a hard time dealing with stress until I got into running and working out. I was never really overweight, but after joining a gym, I lost twenty pounds in the last year. I'm happy with the way I look now, but the real benefit has been the way exercise helps relieve some of my tension.

"You look deep in thought," Sarah says.

"How can you tell?"

"You squint your eyes, which causes your forehead wrinkles to show."

"You're saying I have wrinkles?" I say jokingly as I laugh.

"You know that's not what I mean," she says, dragging out the emphasis on the *e* sound.

"I know, I'm just messing with you. I was thinking of running after work to get my mind off things."

"You've been running a lot; I need to join to you. I could use your motivation."

"You can join me anytime."

Our last customers of the day are leaving, and we start the closing down process. I walk the last customer to the door and lock it behind her so I can start cleaning the floor. I'm surprised when someone knocks on the door. I look over at Sarah with one eyebrow raised. "I'll get it."

I gasp when I see who it is. "Oh my God, Sarah, it's Luke!"

"Well, answer the damned door!" she shouts. I close my eyes and take a deep breath. My heart is pounding with excitement.

"Hi, Luke, come on in."

"Hey, I'm sorry, I know you're closing down. I wanted to catch you before you left."

"It's not a problem." I'm so nervous my voice is shaking.

"I was wondering if you'd like to go to dinner with me sometime?" My mouth drops open because I'm taken aback by the question. But I guess, in a way, I saw it coming.

"Yes, I'd love to!"

"What about this Friday? I can pick you up after you close."

"Friday sounds great."

"I thought maybe we could walk over from here to Fleet Landing? The weather should be perfect for eating on the waterfront."

"That sounds wonderful."

"Great! I'll be here to pick you up around five thirty. Will you be done with your cleaning by then?"

"Yes, I will. I'm looking forward to it." We smile at each other and exchange phone numbers.

"I'm looking forward to it too. I'll see you Friday." I watch him walk out the door and realize that my nerves calmed while I was talking to him. I felt comfortable with him.

"Ahhh!" Sarah screams. "I'm so excited for you! Your first date in a looong time."

"You're right, it has been a long time. Last time I went out with a guy was with you-know-who."

"Oh, don't go bringing that asshole up. You seriously need to get over him. Yeah, you thought Tyler was the love of your life, but he cheated on you. And the man of your dreams just asked you out!"

"I know, but it's hard, even if it has been awhile." Sarah rolls her eyes and sighs.

"I'm excited for this date though. I wish it was Friday now! This will be the longest two days of my life."

"Mm-hmm, you better be excited."

After closing up the shop, we both head home, and I decide to go for a run to clear my head. Luke keeps popping into my mind, but then, so does the fire. I stop running and shake my head. *Stop thinking about the fire. You just met what seems like a good guy, so enjoy it.*

After three miles of running, I feel refreshed. I shower and make chicken for dinner and enjoy a glass of wine. I'm tired, so I crawl into bed to read until I fall asleep. Just as I'm closing my eyes, I hear my phone ping. It's a text from Luke: "Just wanted to say good night and I can't wait till our date Friday."

I instantly smile and text back, "I can't wait either. Good night." I put my phone down and close my eyes, drifting into sleep with a smile on my face.

***

I'm at Pavilion Bar for May's twenty-first birthday. May looks beautiful. Her long brown hair is curled, and she's wearing a tight dark purple dress. My long black hair doesn't need any curling because it's curly on its own. I'm wearing a teal dress, which brings out my green eyes. May and I take a Fireball shot at the bar. When I put the glass down and glance over at the other side of the bar, I see a man. He's wearing dark clothes, and he smiles, a terrifying crooked smile. His bottom jaw seems abnormally long, making the gap between his bottom and top teeth open. His smile is off center. I look into his cold black eyes. I'm fixed in his glare. I feel disgusted and terrified of this man, and I'm not sure why. The feeling he gives me when I look at him is horrifying. The neon lights in the bar make him look dirty. He looks like a killer.

He gets up from the chair while he's still looking at me. He walks up to a girl with a French braid that falls midway down her back. She's wearing a tight black dress with red heels. He starts whispering in her ear. I wish I knew what he was saying. They walk out of the bar together. Why in the world would she follow him? She was way too tall, slim, and beautiful for him.

"May, I'll be right back. You stay here."

"What? Where are you going? Is everything okay?"

"Y-yeah it is, I'll be back," I say with hesitation. I quickly walk out of the bar to try and find this man. From the way he looked, I couldn't imagine the girl would have gone with him so willingly. I look to the left and see the girl stumbling as she walks. The man is holding her by the arm. I try to keep a safe distance so he won't know I'm following him. There are a few people walking down the street, but no one else seems to pay any attention to what's going on. He makes his way over to an alley leading to the harbor. It's a dark area that the streetlights don't quite reach. He puts a hand over the girl's mouth and takes out a knife with the other.

"NO, stop!" I yell as I run toward them. He looks at me and smiles and begins to stab the girl over and over. I quickly take out my phone and dial 911.

"A girl has been stabbed over by the harbor near Waterfront Park." I hang up the phone and look up as he's throwing the body into the water. I'm too late. I don't have any weapons on me. I was too afraid to try and stop him.

He turns around and stares at me and then begins to run toward me. I run and call out for help. Then I trip over the uneven sidewalk and fall to the ground.

I wake up holding my chest, breathing heavy. I close my eyes and try to calm myself down before I have another panic attack. I'll be at that bar in two days; what if I see that man there? I scream out loud because I hate this. I hate these dreams, I hate that I'm seeing murders and dead bodies. I hate that I'm seeing things in the future. "What's wrong with me? Why me?" I yell out. My body is shaking, and I can't keep my hands steady enough to pick up the phone. I just want to call May as she'll help calm me.

I take deep breaths to relax and am finally able to hold the phone to all May. It's five in the morning and I'll be waking her, but I don't care. I need her. My heart is still pounding as I wait for her to pick up.

"Linda? It's five in the morning. What's going on?"

I begin to cry, my voice shaky. "I had another dream, a bad one, and I think it might come true."

"Okay, big, deep breaths. Just try and relax. Tell me what happened."

After I take a deep breath in and out, I tell her everything.

"Wow, maybe we should call the cops?"

"And tell them that I dreamed of someone getting stabbed?

They'll think I'm crazy."

"Okay, but if we see him at the bar, then I think we should. Especially if we see him walk out of the bar with the same girl."

"God, I hope it doesn't come true. I hope we don't see him and this is just a nightmare."

"I don't want it to be real either. I'll come by your shop today. I'll need some coffee before my 8:00 a.m. class."

"Good. I'll be glad to see you. I love you."

"I love you too." I hang up the phone, throw it on the bed, put my face in my hands, and cry.

Chapter 3

I feel a little better after letting it all out. I've got to pull myself together before I go to work. I get up, shower, and listen to some upbeat techno music to get myself in a better mood. I make coffee, eat some oatmeal, and watch the news until it's time to go to work. I think about Luke and our date tomorrow, which puts me in a better mood.

It's a beautiful spring morning, and the walk to work is peaceful. I love the atmosphere of downtown Charleston. The beautiful, colorful buildings and homes like the ones on Rainbow Row, the tall antique lampposts, all the family-owned shops and restaurants, and of course the scent of the ocean close by.

As I walk in, I see Sarah, who's standing next to a handsome man. My first impression of him is all muscle and no brains. He's one of those muscular and fit guys who carries protein bars around with them wherever they go. I know I'm not supposed to judge a book by the cover, so people say, but I can't help myself. He has brown hair in a buzz cut. All I can pay attention to are his wide shoulders and huge arms.

Sarah comes up to me excitedly, walking so fast she's practically skipping, and the smile on her face is immense. "I'm so glad you're here. I have someone I'd like you to meet." She grabs my hand before I can respond and drags me over to him.

"Linda, this is Bobby, and he's our new helper." My mouth drops open in surprise.

I hold my finger up and say, "Excuse us for a second."

I pull her close to me and try to whisper, but I'm so angry. "What are you doing making decisions like this without me? What can he even do of any significance for our shop? You can't just hire someone because they're nice to stare at." Judging by the way her eyes widen, she was expecting a different reaction from me.

"Whoa, I didn't mean for this to make you mad. You're right, I should have come to you first and discussed it, but I think he could bring something good to our shop. I went to high school with him, and we ran into each other the other day at the gym. He's a chef, and I thought it'd be a good idea to add lunch to our menu. With a wider range of offerings, we could bring in more customers."

It *is* a good suggestion, but I'm still angry that she decided on it without my consent. "You mean he can actually cook? He's not just here to flirt with you or become eye candy for our lady customers?"

"He's a legit chef and he has great ideas. Just give him a chance."

"Well," I say reluctantly, "if his food can bring in enough business to cover his salary…"

"Yay! This is going to be so great!" She's way too excited about this.

I get up and put out my hand for him to shake. "Hi, Bobby. I apologize for being rude. I was just surprised that my partner made such a big decision without me." I offer him a conciliatory grin. "What lunch ideas do you have?"

We talk for a while, and he does have a lot of great ideas, so we officially hire him.

"Welcome to our staff, Bobby. Glad to see what you can do."

"Thanks. I'm going to get back there and whip up some samples, and then I'll make a lunch menu."

Sarah looks at me and winks. "I told you so!"

"Yeah, yeah, don't make a habit of this though!"

About two hours later, Bobby comes out with a tray full of different lunch menu items, just enough for us to get a taste of each. I have to admit, the food is amazing. I think it'll bring in more customers.

"This is awesome, Bobby! So glad to have you on board!" He smiles and goes back to make more food.

May walks in with her backpack, looking cheerful. She always makes me feel better when I'm down. "Hey sis, how are you today?"

"I'm doing okay, still a little shaken up, but I'm better." May nods for me to follow her out to the patio so we can talk.

"We don't have to go to Pavilion for my birthday Saturday. I don't want this to affect our night. I know we'll both be constantly looking around for that man and girl."

"I can't do that. If this dream really is going to come true, I need to be there to stop it before it happens. I'll never forgive myself if I don't show and that woman dies."

"All right. But I'm worried about you and these dreams. They're starting to overtake your life. You can't even enjoy yourself because of what you see."

"Well, you don't really know what it's like. Yeah, it sucks, but I still enjoy myself. I'm learning to live it with. If these dreams end up being true, then maybe I could work with the FBI and help stop murders before they happen. Think of all the people I can save." I get a small adrenaline rush after saying that. I imagine working with the FBI and being a hero. A smile starts to appear on my face.

"I guess that would be a neat job. Just be careful, that's all I ask."

"I will. Oh, and by the way, I have a date tomorrow night!"

"What! With who?"

"You're never going to believe this: it's the man from my fire dream. He walked into the shop yesterday. I swear doves flew by him as he walked in. I almost couldn't stand because I was taken aback by how sexy he was. Anyway, he came back later and asked me out to dinner."

"The man from your dream? Wow, the dreams are getting more real. But I'm happy for you. I better get to hear all about it on Saturday."

"You will, now let me get you some coffee."

Soon enough, closing time comes around, and I head home. I'm getting more and more anxious by the minute.

I'm so anxious I can't sleep. I keep tossing and turning through the night. I finally drift off only to wake up at 3:00 a.m. I tell myself to relax and go back to bed.

Next thing I know, my alarm is going off at 6:00 a.m. I slept a dreamless sleep.

I have to dress better for work than I normally do since Luke is picking me up after. I decide to wear a long dress. The top is white with a flower design that covers the entire upper body. A brown belt separates the top from the sheer royal blue skirt that's loose and flowing. I brush my teeth and put on my perfume. I eat a quick breakfast, and then I'm off to work.

"Wow, you look great! Luke is going to drop his mouth when he sees you," Sarah says when I walk through the door.

"Thanks. I am so nervous!" I say as I tie my apron over my dress.

"Don't be. Once you guys warm up to each other, I'm sure you'll feel comfortable with him."

"I hope you're right."

I keep looking at my watch throughout the day, anxious to see Luke walk in. I don't stop moving all day. Soon enough, it's time to close down. I hear the bell on our door as someone walks in, and I know it's Luke. I take a deep breath and turn around to see him.

He's in beige pants with a navy blue sports blazer and a white collared shirt underneath. When I look at him, my body becomes hot and starts to tingle. He gives me a feeling that I've never felt before. As if it's just me and him and no one else in the world. I can't hear anything going on in the background when I look at him; I'm fixed on him. Then he smiles, my stomach turns, and my heart starts beating faster.

"Hi, I hope I'm not too early. Do you need to finish closing down the shop? I can wait here until you're done."

Again, I'm frozen, but I snap out of it quickly. "No, it's okay. Sarah and Bobby can close down for me."

"Yeah, we've got it. You two have a great night!" Sarah yells from the back.

"All right, let's head to the restaurant, then," Luke says as he takes my hand. I feel bad because my hands are sweaty. I'm so nervous. But he doesn't seem to care. "Would you like to get a table outside at Fleet Landing? It has a beautiful view of the harbor," Luke says as we continue to walk hand in hand.

It's such a beautiful spring evening. The weather is in the seventies; the perfect night for an outside date.

"That would be great. I was nervous for this date," I admit to him.

"Don't worry, I was too. I was afraid you were going to turn me down when I asked you out."

"I was surprised you asked me, but I'm glad you did."

"Me too," Luke says with a smile. We arrive at the Fleet Landing and are seated at a table outside on the deck.

"Wow, this is a wonderful view," I say. "I can't believe I haven't been here before."

"It's not as good as the view right in front of me," Luke says.

I put my head down so he can't see the blush in my cheeks and smile. "Thank you."

"So to be honest, I haven't been on a date in a while. My work at the hospital keeps me pretty busy, but when I saw you, I had to ask." I'm surprised by his comment. He's so good looking, and hello, he's a doctor, so I figured he would have been on many dates.

"Well, I haven't either. Ever since my last relationship ended, I've just been focusing on myself and my shop."

"Did your last relationship end recently?" *Oh boy, I don't know if I'm ready to discuss this.*

"Umm, it was probably eight months ago. Long story short, he cheated on me, and I left him."

"I'm sorry to hear that."

"So do you know what you're going to have yet?" I say, anxious to change the subject.

"Nothing better than their fresh catch. The Atlantic salmon sounds good."

"Mmm, good choice. I'm leaning toward the flounder." The waiter arrives to take our wine and food order.

"So do you have family in the area?" Luke asks when he leaves.

"Yes, actually most of my family is here in Charleston. My parents live in a small town on the outskirts of Charleston, about thirty minutes away. My sister goes to the College of Charleston, and my grandparents, aunts, uncles, and cousins all live around the area. I was born and raised here, and I don't ever want to leave. I think it's a beautiful place to live."

"That's nice that your family is close by. I wish that were the case for me."

"Where's your family?" I notice his smile falters a bit and a look of hurt passes through his eyes.

"I'm not very comfortable talking about my family, but suffice it to say there were major issues with my parents growing up, and I spent a lot of time with friends. After I graduated from Johns Hopkins, I went to medical school at the University of South Carolina in Columbia. Then I did my residency here at MUSC, where I got my job, and I've been here ever since. I love this area and wouldn't want to go back to Maryland."

"Well, it seems like the family issues made you stronger. If it were me, I might have broken down and had a hard time continuing with school, or doing anything for that matter."

"I told myself that I'd never become my father, so I focused on my career and my future."

"Well, you have a great attitude on life." I want to know more about his father, but now isn't the time to press the issue. I'm impressed with what I know of Luke so far. He seems very well put together, and he's a strong-willed person.

"Thank you. Did you graduate from college around here?"

"Yes, I graduated from the College of Charleston with a degree in business. After Sarah and I graduated, we opened up our shop."

"That's pretty neat, opening a shop with your best friend right out of college."

"Yeah, owning my own coffee shop was a dream of mine. You had a lot of school to go through. How old does that make you?"

He smiles. "I'm thirty-three."

"Oh, an older man," I say as I grin.

"Older is better; we're more mature." He winks as he says that, and my heart starts to beat fast again. He seems to have this effect on me, making me nervous all the time.

"That's true," I say, and we laugh.

Our food comes, and it's delicious. "Do you have any close friends that are in town?" I ask him between bites.

"Yeah, I have a few buddies at work that I like to hang with, but my closest friend is Jeff. He works at the hospital as a nurse practitioner; he was the one who told me about your coffee shop."

"That's nice. I'm close to Sarah and my sister, May."

We each have two more glasses of wine as we talk about the things we like. We have a lot in common—football, food, movies, and music, and we can't stop smiling at each other. I'm starting to feel comfortable with him and getting good vibes.

He gives the waiter his card to pay the check. "Look at that beautiful sunset," he says to me.

It is beautiful over the harbor. The orange-pink sky reflects off the water, saturating everything in an amazing glow. "How about we walk along the harbor and enjoy this sunset?" he asks me.

"I'd love to." I smile at him as we get up to leave the restaurant. We walk hand in hand, enjoying the views of the sunset, the water, and historic Charleston. This night couldn't have been any better.

We walk to Waterfront Park and stop in front of the beautiful Pineapple Fountain. He turns to face me, and I know what's coming. My heart begins racing so fast I think it's going to pop out of my chest. He takes my hands and says, "This is has been such a great evening. I hope we can do it again."

I smile and say, "I'd love to see you again." He leans in and kisses me. His lips are soft. My body starts to tingle. Our kiss becomes more intense, and I wrap my arms around his neck. Our bodies move closer together as our tongues intertwine. Then I suddenly remember we're in a very public place. We pull back, look into each other's eyes, and smile.

On the walk back to my house, we stop to end the night with some tasty ice cream.

When we get to my house on Tradd Street, he walks me to my door and kisses me again. The kiss is soft and tender. "I'll text you tomorrow. Maybe we can set up another date this week," he says.

"I'd love that." I smile, and he gives me one last quick kiss before I open the door and step inside. I shut the door and lean my back against it. I close my eyes and smile. What a perfect first date. I'm already anxious to see him again.

Later, as I climb into bed, I think about my sister's birthday the next day and going to the bar, but then I see the man with the crooked smile, and darkness begins to take over.

***

I am standing in a kitchen in a big house. I walk around in amazement at the size of this place. I walk into a hallway that's big enough to drive a car through and start to hear whispering. I quietly walk over to a closet; the door is slightly open. The whispering is louder here, so I stop and concentrate. It sounds like a little boy, and he's talking to himself. I figure a young kid talking to an invisible friend is somewhat normal. Most children go through invisible-friend stages. Then I start to understand what he's saying, and it becomes abnormal.

"But, Mary, she's my mommy. I don't want to kill her," the little boy says. My eyes become big, and I start to panic. The boy and this woman, whose voice I haven't heard yet, are talking about murdering his parents. I hear footsteps upstairs. I look up and duck behind a wall around the corner of the wooden staircase.

The closet door opens, and I peek around to see a boy, only a boy. There's no woman. Oh, great, a psycho little boy who hears women's voices, I think to myself. Then I hear the boy walk into the kitchen. I hear what sounds like a drawer opening. It sounds like he's grabbing silverware from the clanking of the steel.

Oh my God, he's getting a knife. I have to figure out a way to warn the parents. But if they see an unknown girl in their house telling him their son is going to kill them, they'll call the cops on me. But I can't let them be murdered. What should I do?

I hear the boy walking up the stairs. I look around the corner again and see a butcher knife in his hand. I follow, not too close behind but enough to try to stop what is going to happen. I don't get a look at which room he walks into. I look into the first room I come to when I hear, "Tommy, NO! What are you doing?" It's a female and she screams. I run into the room the screams are coming from and see the boy.

He's standing over his mom pulling the knife from her body. There's blood splattered on the yellow wall and the white-striped satin bed sheets. "Oh my God!" I shout.

The boy turns around. He has sandy brown hair, brown eyes, and patches of freckles on his cheeks. He smiles and starts walking toward me. I run out the bedroom door, down the curving wooden stairs and out the front door. I'm dialing 911 to report the murder when I look to the door and see the boy standing there with a bloody knife and an evil grin. Darkness takes over.

I open my eyes and realize it was just a dream. I sit up in bed, freaked out, and turn on the light. It's only four in the morning. I don't know if I'll be able to go back to sleep. I go into the bathroom and splash some water on my face. I look at my pale face and green eyes in the mirror and say, "You're not crazy."

I get back in bed and think. Luke pops into my mind. I'll have to tell him about my dreams at some point if this becomes serious. I mean, I did see him coming. If we sleep together and I wake up with a panic attack, he's going to want to know why. What if he's freaked out by the fact that I saw him in a dream before I met him? What if he doesn't believe me? Well, we've only had one date, so maybe I'm getting ahead of myself. I put my hands over my face and sigh.

I have a long night of birthday celebrating ahead of me. I close my eyes and force myself to sleep.

Chapter 4

I wake up at around 9:00 a.m. and look at my phone. Luke texted me. I instantly get a smile on my face. "Good morning, beautiful. I was wondering if you'd like to do something today?" What a great text to wake up to, especially after a rough dream night.

I send a reply: "Good morning to you too! I wish I could, but I'm celebrating my sister's twenty-first birthday at the Pavilion Bar tonight. How about tomorrow?" After I send the text, I get out of bed and put on some coffee.

It's only a few minutes later when he texts me back. "Tomorrow is perfect. How about dinner and a movie? I'd like to cook for you." A chef and a gentleman! I'm not used to this treatment.

I look up movie times on my phone and text him back. We both love scary movies, so we decide on the newest horror flick, and afterward, he's going to cook me dinner. I feel like I'm back in high school, getting this giggly and excited over a text from a boy.

I go for a long run downtown to pass the time and relax before I shower and start to get ready. I put on my favorite teal dress. I preheat the oven and start to make brown sugar spiced chicken. I'm also steaming fresh broccoli and cooking sweet potatoes. May loves this meal.

May walks in my front door. "Mmm, something smells amazing!" she says excitedly. She walks into the kitchen and gives me a big hug. "I'm so excited for tonight. I've been looking forward to it all week!"

"Me too! Dinner will be ready in about thirty minutes; how about a cranberry and vodka to start off your twenty-first birthday?"

"Oh yeahhhh," she says. May looks beautiful. Of course I

already knew what she was going to wear. In my dream she wore what she's wearing now: the dark purple dress. Her brown hair is curled with a strand of hair pulled to the side with a bobby pin. I begin to get a bad feeling in my stomach.

May sees the struggle in my face. "You're doing the thing with your eyebrows again. What's going on inside your head?"

"You're wearing the exact same outfit you had on in my dream."

"So you're worried because I have on the same outfit that will mean that everything else in the dream is going to happen exactly the same? Can you try not to worry about it? I want to enjoy my twenty-first birthday. I know it sounds a little rude, but I've seriously been waiting for this all week."

"Yeah, but you also know what we are walking into as well."

May rolls her eyes. "But I'll try, just for my baby sister."

A smile grows on May's face. "Thank you! Shit! I almost forgot, tell me about your date with Luke!"

I tell her everything that happened and how we're seeing each other again tomorrow.

"Sounds like it's starting off good, sis! I'm happy for you!"

"Thank you, I'm excited about Luke." I was going to tell her about the dream I had last night, but I don't want to put another damper on her night.

After a good dinner and two cranberry and vodkas, we're ready for the bar. Good thing it's a pretty night out because we have a lot of walking to do. We walk with our arms locked, talking and laughing all the way to the bar. It's packed tonight.

We head over to the bar and order some drinks. So far, no girl or creepy man. I can't help it; it's going to be in the back of my mind whether May likes it or not.

We dance for a while, sit down, have some drinks, then dance again. While I'm on the dance floor, a woman catches my eye. She's wearing a black dress and red heels. *Fuck*, I think to myself. *There she is.* I start looking all around the bar to see if I can find him. I walk over to the bar because, if my dream is correct, he'd be on the other side.

May follows behind me. I go up to the bar and look across and can't believe my eyes. There he is, in his dark clothes. He's just as dirty and creepy as he was in my dream. His crooked smile and messed up jaw makes him look like a serial killer. He continues to smile at me. He picks up his drink, and I can see dirt under his fingernails.

May grabs my arm. "Is that him?"

"Yes, it's him." I look at her and say, "We're going to have to call the cops soon."

"I can't believe your dream is coming true."

"Me neither." I look back over, and the man is gone. "Shit, he's gone. We have to go now!" In a panic, I look all around to see I if I can find the woman in red heels, and I can't.

We run out of the door and look to the side, but I still don't see them. "How could we be this far behind already? I'm calling the cops now. May, you stay here. I don't want you around this guy. Wait here for me to get back."

"You're not going alone!" she yells.

I call the cops as I run to the alley near the harbor where he took her in my dream. "Hello, there has been a stabbing over by the harbor near Waterfront Park!" I hang up the phone and start running toward the park. I arrive just in time to see him throwing her body over the harbor wall.

"No!" I scream out loud. How can I be late? I could have stopped this! The man turns toward me and starts walking closer. I hear the sirens in the distance. The sound scares him off, and he runs away.

I fall to my knees and start to cry. I can't believe I couldn't stop the murder. I can't believe my dreams are truly coming to life. My life is never going to be the same.

The cops pull up. "Ma'am, are you okay? We got a call that there was a stabbing in this area. Do you know anything about it?"

"I'm the one that called it in." The cops look around, stunned because they see nothing.

"Did you see the stabbing?"

"No, but I saw the man dumping the girl's body right over there into the harbor." The first cop nods for the other cops to go check it out.

"So you saw him throw the body over, but you didn't see him stab her?"

Shit, how am I going to get out of this one? I should have thought up a better story, but I was so shocked I didn't think clearly enough.

"Yes, that's right."

The cop raised his eyebrow in suspicion. "Then how do you know she was stabbed?"

"Uh," I can't think of what to say. "I saw the knife lying on the ground over there with blood on it." *That was a good comeback!*

"Mm-hmm," the cop says, nodding his head up and down. He doesn't seem to buy it. "Well, if you can stay for a few minutes, I want to get your exact statement."

"Uh, okay, sure."

May comes up and hugs me. "Are you all right?"

"Yeah, I need to give a statement before we can leave."

I tell the cops that I saw the man leave with the girl and thought he looked suspicious, so I followed them. I lost them for a little bit then found him dumping her body into the water. Then he ran when he heard the sirens. I give him my description of the guy, and they send me on my way.

May is going to stay the night with me. When we get home, I go straight to bed. It's a long time before I finally fall asleep.

When I wake in the morning, I go downstairs and turn on the news. I figure something will be on there from last night. Sure enough, there is. They found the body of the woman in the water and warned everyone that the killer was still on the loose. They showed a description of the guy on the news and said if anyone sees someone like him to call in right away. They mentioned a witness but didn't give my name.

May comes up behind me and puts her hand on my back. "I'm sorry, Linda. I'm so sorry this is happening to you."

"Thank you. I can't believe I can see things before they happen. I don't know if I should call it a gift or a nightmare." I start to turn off the TV when I see something that catches my eye.

The reporter is recounting a story about a boy who murdered his mother. The reporter says the boy heard a woman's voice in his head telling him to kill his mother, and he's now in a mental institution. I drop my head and begin to cry.

"I had that dream two nights ago," is all I say to May. She doesn't say a thing; she just wraps her arms around me.

I have to pull myself together. "I have a date with Luke this afternoon."

"Are you sure you want to go after everything that has happened?"

"Yes, I want to get my mind off things, and Luke does a good job of that."

"All right, I'll head out and let you get ready. Let me know how it goes. Love you."

"I will. Love you too." I sit on my couch in silence for a few minutes. I gather my thoughts and tell myself everything will be okay.

I keep myself busy with cleaning, and before I know it, Luke is knocking on my door. The butterflies start rioting in my stomach again.

"Hey, come on in," I say when I open the door.

He kisses me on the lips as he enters. "How was the birthday celebration last night?"

"Uh, it was eventful."

"I saw on the news this morning about the murder that happened nearby. The guy was at the same bar you were. I'm glad you're okay."

Do I want to tell him I was the witness? I don't think I can yet.

"Yeah, thank goodness nothing happened. It's scary to know that a murder occurred so close to where we live."

"It is. You ready for the movie?"

We walk to his car, and I smile when he opens the door for me. "Thank you. I'm not used to men opening car doors for me."

Before he shuts the door, he says, "Well, you might as well get used to it," and he smiles and walks around the other side.

***

"Well, that was intense! How about a good dinner to calm things after that movie?" Luke asks. The movie ended up being very scary. I think I might have squeezed his hand too tight at times. But we enjoyed it.

"Sounds wonderful to me!" He drives me to his place. He pulls into the drive of a beautiful home on Montagu Street. It's a redbrick structure with white balconies.

"Welcome to my home sweet home," he says as he opens the front door. The house is clean and well kept. It has beautiful hardwood floors and beige walls, nice leather furniture, and everything matches!

"This is very nice, and it's spotless. I'm impressed."

He laughs. "Well, thank you. I hope you'll be just as impressed with my cooking."

"Oh, I'm sure I will be. What are you cooking?"

"I was going to grill some steaks since it's so nice out."

"Sounds great!" He shows me around his house before he starts to cook. When he gets to the bedroom, I imagine us on that big bed, naked.

We go back into the kitchen, and he pours each of us a glass of wine and starts to prep the steaks. He opens up more about his family to me. I'm glad he feels comfortable enough to tell me. "When I was about eleven years old, my mom decided to divorce my dad. To this day, I still don't know the real reason she left. But when she left, she left everything behind. I haven't heard a word from her since. My dad started drinking. The more he drank, the more he forgot about me too. He didn't bother to come to any of my school activities or sporting events. I had to cook for myself. Every time I came home from school, he was already drunk.

"When he got an eviction notice, he started to pick up his act and work again. He ended up saving our house. Things became better over the years. Then when I went to college and he was alone, he started drinking again. I was so sick of it by the time I graduated that I wanted to be away from him. That's when I moved here and finished med school. I haven't talked to my dad since I left."

I'm surprised by his story. Considering the way Luke carries himself and how successful his career is, I'd never have thought that he had a rough childhood.

"I'm so sorry. That's awful. Did you ever try to contact your mom to see why she left?"

"Yeah. The older I got, the more I tried to find her. Anytime I got a number and called, she never answered. I think she was messing around and didn't want the responsibility of a family."

I put my hand over his. "I'm sorry."

"Thanks. I've gotten over it through the years, but it still hurts."

"I'm sure it does. I don't know how anyone could truly get over something like that."

We eat our dinner and talk more about why things happen in life and how everything happens for a reason. The steaks are so good. They have a smoked, peppery flavor.

After cleaning up, we decide to sit outside on his balcony and watch the sunset with some wine. The more I get to know Luke and the kind of person he is, the more I like him.

"So this ex of yours who cheated, how long did you guys date?"

"We dated for two years. I thought he was the one."

"Well, I'm glad things didn't work out because I'd have never had a shot with you," Luke says to me. I look over at him and smile. His eyes are fixated on me, and I can't look away. Luke gets up and takes my hand, and I stand up in front of him. We stare into each other's eyes for a moment, and then he kisses me.

I know what's about to happen. I usually don't take it this fast, but I can't help myself. I want him so badly I can't wait another minute.

Our kiss grows deeper, harder, more intense. He presses me up against the glass door. My breathing starts coming in pants, as does his. He reaches behind me to open the door, and we're still attached at the lips as we go inside. His hands roam all over my body, and it feels so good. He takes off my shirt, and I take off his. Luke picks me, and my legs are wrapped around his waist as he walks us into the bedroom, kissing my neck.

I quietly moan to show him I enjoy what he is doing, and then I whisper in his ear, "I want you, Luke, all of you."

He looks me in the eyes and carries me to the bed. He lays me on the bed, kissing my stomach, and makes his way to my breasts, where he takes off my bra. He rubs his hands all over my body. He slowly makes his way to the zipper of my jeans. I moan again to encourage him. The feeling of his body on mine is incredible. He's strong and warm, and his touch is soft yet rough at the same time.

He pulls off my jeans and panties. He kisses my thighs, my stomach, then up to my lips. I push him over so I can take his pants and boxers off. I like what I see. His body is tight and hard. I rub my body against his as I kiss his perfect lips. We slowly grind against each other, our bodies moving in sync. Then he flips me over, and he's inside me. I throw my head back in pleasure. Soft sounds escape my lips, growing louder as he thrusts faster and faster. He moans and kisses me. Our bodies are slick with sweat. We're both breathless, but he doesn't let up, and I can feel myself moving closer to the edge. I close my eyes and cry out his name as I come. I grab the sheets tightly as he thrusts one last time and shouts with his own climax.

We lie there, entwined, not moving, gasping for breath. The feeling I have in that moment is powerful. My entire body is tingling. He kisses me softly and moves off and to the side, gathering me close. I kiss him lightly on the lips and then lay my head on his chest as we both catch our breath. "Wow," is all I can say.

He kisses me on the forehead. We lie there for a while, naked, comfortable, and satiated. Then he says, "Do you want to stay with me tonight?"

I look up at him. "I'd love to."

I put on one of his t-shirts and he puts his boxers on, and we lie in his bed and watch a movie. He holds me close. I feel safe in his arms. My eyes become heavy, and I drift into sleep.

***

I am standing on a bridge over a river. I have no idea where I am or what river I'm standing over. Oddly, there's no traffic, not a single car. It's dark out; maybe that's why there are no cars. I become very scared because I'm alone in an unknown place. I look at my phone to see the time. It's two thirty in the morning. I begin walking down the bridge to see if I can figure out where I am.

I walk to the end of the bridge and turn to get a good look now that I'm back on land. It's the Ravenel Bridge that spans the Cooper River. I follow the exit ramp into Charleston. After a couple of blocks, I find an old, beat-up brown station wagon sitting on the side of the road. I see a figure inside, and I slowly approach.

"Hello, are you okay in there?" Why I care or why I decide to check this out, I'm not sure. I know better; I should just walk away.

I hear no answer, so I move closer to see who the person is and what I can do to help—and I freeze. I recognize this man. He opens his eyes and smiles. I know that wicked smile. I glance in the back of his car where I see a girl lying down with tape over her mouth and her hands tied behind her back. Mascara is running down her cheeks. Her eyes are wide with terror. Her shirt is ripped, and she's missing a shoe.

"Oh no!" I yell.

"You can't save this one either. No cops coming this time," the man says in a deep, eerie voice.

"What do you want from me?" I ask.

"What I want is you." He smiles and looks me up and down.

I feel like I'm going to get sick. "Leave me alone," I say, and then I begin to run.

"You won't be able to get far," he says menacingly.

I don't care, I just run as fast as I can. Then I hear him start the car. I pull out my cell phone to dial 911.

"I'm coming for you," he yells as he speeds up the car. I can't dial in time. I keep running and looking back. The car gets closer and closer, and then it hits me like a ton of bricks.

I fall to the ground. I see his dirty black boots from under the car as he walks around to me. He has knife in his hands when he stops in front of me. "Finally, you're mine, and there's no one here to stop me." He laughs.

I shut my eyes and scream.

Chapter 5

I wake up in a panic. Luke wakes up right away.
"Are you okay?" He rubs my back as I calm down. I know I have to tell him about my dreams.

"I just had a bad dream."

"Do you want to tell me about it?" I put my head down and start to cry. He puts his arm around me. "It was just a dream, and dreams aren't real. You're safe now."

I pull out of his embrace. "That's just it, my dreams are real."

He turns his head and narrows his eyes in confusion. "What are you saying?"

Oh boy, here goes nothing.

"I was afraid to tell you because I didn't want you to think that I'm crazy. I was going to wait until we'd spent more time together and this became serious."

He takes my hand in his. "I thought last night was pretty serious. You can tell me."

I sigh and tell him everything, from the dreams of my childhood to my most recent dreams that have come true.

"I can see why you would think that I'd think that's crazy, but I don't. I believe in psychics and weird things happening that we can't explain. I believe in fate and that everything happens for a reason. I think you have a special gift. Other people may never understand it, but you do."

A wave of relief washes over me. "I thought you were going to end things with me after you found out."

"I wouldn't do that. I like you and think you're a special person. Now you're even more special than I thought." He smiles at me and kisses me.

"I'm thinking I should call the cops. Let them know about the girl in the car."

"Do you know what river and bridge it was?"

"It was the Ravenel Bridge over the Cooper. On the Charleston side. That's a busy bridge, but it was deserted in my dream."

"Maybe there's construction going on during the night and no one can pass."

"That would make sense, though I didn't see any construction in my dream. When should I call the cops? I don't know when the girl will be there or even when or where he kidnapped her."

"I guess the only thing you can do is go there before two thirty and keep an eye out. When you see the car, call the cops. But you're not going by yourself. I'll be right behind you."

"But you weren't with me in the dream; I was alone."

"Well, at the time of the dream, you hadn't told me about your gift. Now that I know, I want to be a part of it and help you. Maybe we can change the outcome."

I'm so relieved that he not only believes me but that he wants to help me. But he needs to know what he's getting into. I take a deep breath and tell him what else I've been holding back. "The stabbing at the harbor the other night…I was the witness. I saw the murder happen in my dreams. But I was too late to stop him from killing that poor girl."

He hesitates before he responds, as if weighing his words. "You're not responsible for what happened to that girl. What you have is a gift. You weren't able to help her, but that doesn't mean you can't help in the future. Maybe we can figure out a way for you to control the dreams so you can see more details."

I'd never thought of that before. Is it possible that I could somehow manipulate my dreams to my advantage?

Luke gets up and kisses my forehead. "I'll make us some breakfast."

"I think I could get used to all of this cooking," I say with a smile.

***

After a day spent walking around downtown, window shopping, and watching the sunset over the harbor, we get a pizza from Mellow Mushroom and take it back to my place.

We still have a couple hours to go before it's time to head to the bridge, so we put on a movie. I don't make it twenty minutes into the movie before I'm straddling him on the couch. I can't help myself. I want him all the time. I can't keep my hands off him.

He picks me up off the couch and carries me upstairs to my bedroom. It doesn't take long for both of us to get naked. He picks me up and backs me against the wall. I wrap my legs around his waist, and then he's inside me. He feels so good, and I cry out at each thrust. Then he spins around and puts me on the bed, where I roll him over and climb on top of him. I rock against him, faster and faster as my release nears. I love looking down on him from this angle. His head is thrown back against the pillow, and his eyes are squeezed shut. His hands grab my hips as he starts thrusting up to meet me. We climax at the same time amid a chorus of gasps and shouts.

I roll off of him and let out a big sigh.

Luke laughs and says, "Well, that's a good way to pass the time."

***

We leave my house at one thirty, hoping to see something before it's too late. Luke is confident that we'll be able to help this time. But I'm silent on the car ride over. *What if I'm wrong? What if there's no car and no girl tied up? What if I'm too late and she's already dead?*

Luke puts his hand over mine. "I can't imagine how scary this is for you, but I'm here for you."

I smile. "Thanks. That means a lot." We pull off to the side of the road a few blocks before the entrance ramp to the bridge. He takes my hand when we get out of the car, and I move closer to him. My stomach is in knots. It's a dark night, and I have no clue what we're stepping into. This murderer is crazy, and I could be walking right into his trap. But the stars are shining brightly, the crickets are chirping, and the cool breeze carries the smell of the ocean. It's a nice night to be a savior.

We get to the base of the bridge and there are no construction signs and no traffic.

"I find it weird that there are no other cars. I know it's late, but still, you'd think we would have seen another car or two by now," Luke says.

"You're right, it is strange." An ominous feeling comes over me. My heart starts to beat fast, and my stomach begins to turn. I feel like I'm going to have a panic attack. I tighten my grip on Luke's hand.

We walk onto the bridge ramp. About fifty yards ahead, I see the car. "Luke, look, there's the car off to the side just like in my dream." It's a beat-up brown station wagon. I pull out my phone and call 911.

We walk up to the car, and there's the woman on the backseat, but no sign of the man with the crooked smile. I begin to panic. "Luke, that means he's somewhere out here, probably watching us, waiting to make his move." I suddenly can't seem to catch my breath.

I open the door to check on the woman while Luke keeps an eye out for the man. She's barely alive. She can't move because her ankles and arms are tied, and makeup is running down her face. Her legs are dirty, and she's missing a shoe. Her black dress is ripped at the top. I try to remove the gag without hurting her. "It's going to be okay; the cops are on their way."

She doesn't respond; she just nods her head and lays it back down on the seat. I walk toward Luke feeling light-headed.

Luke helps me sit down by the car. "It's okay, the cops will be here soon, and you'll be safe."

"How am I safe when he's out there? In my dream, he wanted me because I almost stopped his murder by the harbor. Now he's playing with me, dragging me out here—only he's nowhere to be found. He wants me scared, and he has accomplished that."

"Tell the cops you saw the same man again. Maybe they can put a bigger search out for him."

"I will, but this guy seems smart. I feel like I'll always be looking over my shoulder until they catch him." Just then, the cop cars and ambulance pull up.

"The lady is in the car; she is beaten badly," I say to the cop.

They cut her out of the ties and put her on a stretcher. The cop comes toward me, and I know he wants answers.

"Miss, can you tell me your name and what you saw?"

"My name is Linda Brown."

"Linda Brown, as in the lady who was a witness to the murder by the harbor the other night?"

"Wow, word travels fast around the police department. Yes, that's me." He narrows his eyes and nods.

"Interesting. Okay, Linda, what did you see?" I told him I saw a man run from the car that matched the description of the murderer from the other night.

"And how did you find this car randomly sitting out here?"

the cop asks.

"We stumbled upon it as we were walking, and that's when we saw the man run away from the car."

"And that's not your car parked down the road a bit?"

Shit, I forgot they can look up license plate numbers.

Luke stepped in. "Linda was feeling a little carsick and wanted to get out and walk to get some fresh air."

"Right. Getting fresh air on a deserted bridge at two in the morning? There are some holes in your story, and it's awfully coincidental that you're involved with both murders."

"Involved? I'm not involved, I just happened to witness both of them," I say with anger. The cop stares at me and doesn't say a word. *Great, he probably thinks I'm a nutcase.*

"We've got one of the best detectives in the state on his way here. You can be sure he'll get your story straight."

"Are you detaining her, officer?" Luke asks, an edge in his voice.

"Not at this time. But don't leave town. We'll be in touch soon."

I shake my head as the police officer walks over to the ambulance. I turn to Luke. "This detective will never believe the truth. He'll think I'm crazy."

"You never know, maybe he will believe you. People in the FBI deal with crazy stuff all the time. Let's get out of here while we still can." Luke takes my hand, and we walk back to the car.

We're both quiet on the ride home. While I get ready for bed, Luke checks the locks on all the doors and windows. I'm so tired I fall asleep nearly as soon as my head hits the pillow, Luke's strong arms wrapped around me, making me feel safe...for the moment.

***

The next morning, after the breakfast rush, a man walks into the shop. He is handsome, with a nice smile, dressed in black slacks, a gray shirt, and a black jacket, but he looks like a cop to me. He has dark brown hair and brown eyes. He is tall and built. I would guess he is in his early to mid-thirties. He has a single freckle on his cheekbone that I notice because it's shaped like a leaf. He comes up to me at the cash register. "Are you Linda Brown?"

"Yes, I am. And you are?"

He puts his hand out for me to shake, "I'm Detective Tom Walker, FBI. I'm investigating the incidents that occurred this past week and would like to talk to you about them."

"I've already talked to the local police. I really don't want to tell the story again."

"I know it's hard for you, ma'am, but this seems to be a special case, and I think I can help." He's polite and seems sincere, but he also speaks in a tone that reminds me he could haul me into the station if I don't speak to him willingly.

I sigh. "All right, let's go out on the patio and I'll tell you what happened."

I tell him everything, though I leave out the part about my dreams. I can tell right away that he's not buying it.

"There are some holes in this story. Why did you follow them? What would make you think something would happen? How did you know she was stabbed? Yeah, you saw a knife and assumed, but still, you didn't actually see it happen. Are you telling me you just get 'bad feelings' about things?"

He knows something's up. And I know it's going to look pretty suspicious if I have another dream and end up as a witness to another crime. *What the hell, I might as well tell him. What's the worst that can happen?*

I take a deep breath. "This is going to sound crazy, and I promise I'm not crazy. I had a dream last week. In my dream, I saw a man leave Pavilion with a woman, stab her in that alley, and throw her body into the harbor." To my relief, he doesn't seem skeptical; he seems intrigued. His thumb and finger are on his chin as he listens to me talk. I tell him about the second dream at the bridge.

"I knew there was something special to this story," he says. He moves his head closer to me so no one could hear what he has to say. "I can see things before they happen in my dreams as well."

There's nothing that could have shocked me more than what he just said. My mouth falls open, and I sit back. I can feel my eyes widening as I stare at him. I don't know what to say. I finally find my voice. "Are you serious, or is this a joke?"

"I'm serious. That's why, when I heard your story and all of the holes in it, it seemed familiar to me. I know what it's like to see things before they happen. It's scary, but it can be a good thing. Working with the FBI and having the talent I have helps stop crimes before they happen. This is why I've been so successful."

"Wow, I didn't know there was anyone else like me. I thought I was crazy."

"You're not crazy; you have a gift, which is why I came to you today, to see for myself. Do you know how successful we'd be if we work together?"

"But I didn't get there in time to save the girl. I messed up. I'm just getting used to knowing I can see the future. How can I be sure that I'll be right?"

"Once you know you can see the murders before they happen, you start paying more attention to particular details in your dreams. The more you have them, the easier everything gets." A spark of excitement grows within me. Working with the FBI and helping people, being a savior to so many…can I really do this?

"So what do you say? Do you want to work with me and be my partner?"

"What about my shop? I love it here and don't want to give it up."

"You can still work here. We'll simply keep each other up to date on our dreams. If you see a murder in your dream, call me right away, and we'll take care of it. With both of our talents, we can solve many cases and save many people."

I sit there cracking my knuckles. I do that when I get nervous or excited. Finally, I say, "All right, I'll do it."

Tom smiles and shakes my hand. "Welcome aboard, partner. As soon as you have a dream, call me, no matter when."

"Okay, I will." He gives me his card before he leaves, and I sit there thinking about what I just agreed to. I never thought my dreams would become a gift. But I get excited thinking about helping people. Having someone like Tom, who knows what I'm going through, makes it easier to accept my gift.

Sarah comes out from the back the second the door closes behind Tom. "Okay, who and what was that about?"

"He's an FBI agent. I agreed to be his partner."

"What?" she shouts.

I explain the whole story to her.

"Are you sure this is a good idea? You're going to become very involved in these cases, and some of it might be pretty disturbing. You don't have any training to cope with that kind of stuff."

"I'm sure. These dreams have already been disturbing, and I'll be dealing with it from here on out, so why not do something about it? Why not turn the dreams around to help people? And with the FBI, no less."

"I get that. I just worry about you. But you know I'll always support you."

"I know, and thank you." I smile at her. "Let's get back to work."

Chapter 6

A month flies by without any dreams of future crimes. I don't know whether that's a good thing or a bad thing. I haven't had a chance to work with my new FBI partner. But Luke and I have been going strong, and the shop has kept me busy. Bobby's lunch menu is a big hit. I'm in the back of the shop baking some blueberry muffins when Sarah walks in. "Linda." She doesn't speak again until I look up at her, and the look on her face puts me instantly on alert. "Tyler is here to see you."

My heart drops into my stomach, but the sick feeling quickly turns to anger. "He's got some nerve to come into my shop and ask for me." Sarah holds her arms out and shrugs her shoulders. I wipe my hands and throw the towel onto the counter before I storm past her into the dining room.

Tyler's face lights up when he sees me. "Linda! How's your beautiful self been?"

Bobby and Sarah raise their eyebrows, look at me, and hurry into the back. Tyler's brown hair has gotten long and shaggy, and he's put on some weight since I last saw him. But I see he still wears his Nike Air running shoes. He'd never wear anything else. I'm happy to note that I feel nothing at the sight of him after so long. Nothing but disgust, that is.

"What are you doing here? I told you I never wanted to see you again."

"Linda, listen to me for a second, just hear me out."

"Nope. I'm not even going to give you the time of day. Leave."

His smile fades, and he closes his eyes and puts his head down. He looks up me again and very quietly says to me, "I want you back. I know I messed up. I know I hurt you. I didn't realize the good thing I had until I lost it."

I start to feel nervous, and a part of me feels bad for him, but then I picture him with the tall, blonde, big-breasted woman I caught him in bed with.

"Yeah, you messed up, all right. I loved you and would have done anything for you. I still get sick to my stomach thinking about you and her. But I've moved on. I don't want you in my life. Please don't come back here, Tyler."

He looks at me with puppy-dog eyes that might have worked on me in the past, but they don't now. "I'm sorry. I had to at least give it a shot. I hope you find someone who treats you the way you deserve to be treated. I'm sorry for hurting you."

"I've found someone who treats me right. Goodbye, Tyler." He walks away slowly and then stops at the door to look back at me one more time. I quickly look away until I hear the door shut behind him. When I look back, he's gone.

"I can't believe he showed up here," Sarah says as she reaches my side.

I look over at the door, picturing him standing there and looking at me one last time. "I know, I can't either."

Just then, my phone pings with a text from Luke. "Be ready at 6:30 tonight. I'm taking you out for dinner at Poogan's Porch." My face instantly lights up. He always seems to know when I need a pick-me-up, and Poogan's Porch has the best shrimp and grits in town. This man certainly knows the way to my heart! Thoughts of Tyler fade away as I spend the rest of the afternoon thinking about how lucky I am to have Luke in my life.

***

I spend a little extra time getting ready that evening. Even though we see each other nearly every day, I still get just as excited to see him as I did on our first date. I can't get enough of him.

He walks in while I'm putting the finishing touches on my makeup. "Hey beautiful," he says. In his hands is a bouquet of beautiful pink and orange roses.

"They're gorgeous! What did I do to deserve this?"

Luke kisses me. "I wanted to do something nice for you."

"Thank you! I love them." I put the roses in water and we head out to the restaurant.

I love the unique, homey feeling at Poogan's Porch. It's a relaxing place to eat a good meal—if you can get a reservation. I don't know how Luke pulled it off on such short notice. We ask to sit outside since the weather is so lovely.

I don't really want to talk about Tyler with Luke, but I don't want to keep any secrets from him either. "I know this isn't the best way to start dinner, but Tyler came into the shop today."

"Tyler, as in your ex Tyler?" His voice is flat.

"Yeah, he wanted another chance with me." I tell Luke about our encounter, and I can tell he's upset. He doesn't speak much, and he looks at me blankly while I tell him. "I told him I met someone who treats me the way I deserve to be treated."

Luke puts his hand over mine. "Thank you for being honest and telling me. I don't blame the guy though. He did lose something great, but he can't have you back."

"He never will." I smile and squeeze his hand, and he changes the subject.

"I had to do a shoulder surgery today. A seventeen-year-old girl was texting and driving and got into a car wreck. She ran a red light and got t-boned, had to repair her rotator cuff."

"Oh, that poor girl; texting and driving is so dangerous. I wish there was something more society could do to get people to stop."

"Me too. Oh, and my buddy Jeff wants to meet you. I was thinking I could cook for you both at my place soon."

"Sounds good to me. I'd love to meet him."

After we finish our delicious meal, we head back to my place. We're both tired, but that doesn't stop us from having another round of mind-blowing sex.

Afterward, I lie in his arms and fall fast asleep.

***

I'm at my coffee shop, but it's around 11:00 p.m., and we're never open that late. Nobody is in the shop with me. I close up and am about to start my walk home when I see a Husky puppy walking down the street.

"Well, hey fella, what are you doing out here at night all alone?" The puppy comes up to me and licks my hand. He begins to whine and walks away. I follow the puppy because I want to take him home if he has no owner. He goes to the Dumpster behind my coffee shop and begins jumping up and clawing at it. I open the Dumpster and immediately feel sick to my stomach. There's a dead body inside, a young woman about my age with dark brown hair. She has a tight red skirt on and a black tank top that is ripped. She's covered in

blood. I can't see her face clearly, but it looks like her face is covered in scratches or stab wounds. I call 911 as soon as I stop shaking and take a breath.

I stay for questioning when the police arrive and tell them how I found the body. They look in her wallet and find her ID. Her name is Gloria. I'm glad I found her body so she can be laid to rest, but this is the first time I've ever seen a dead body, and I'm in shock. I feel like a zombie because it's hard for me to move my muscles. I'm shaky and begin to wonder how she was murdered and why her body was in my Dumpster.

"Do you need a ride home, miss?" the cop asks me.

"No, I just live a couple blocks over. I'll be fine." I walk around to the front of my shop. I need to sit down and find the strength to walk home. I look across the street, and that's when I see a man in all black, wearing a ski mask and holding a knife, standing under the streetlight.

I begin to panic. I get up and start running. I feel like my body weighs a ton of bricks. I'm breathing too heavy to continue running. I hear the footsteps coming closer. I turn around to look, and he tackles me to the ground.

The loud buzzing sound of my alarm wakes me up. I get up fast and hold my heart. It's racing, and I wipe sweat from my forehead.

Luke wakes up. "What's wrong?" he asks as he rubs my back.

"I need to call Tom. I didn't get enough details from this dream, but maybe they can prevent it from happening."

"What happened?"

I hold up my finger. "Give me a second; you can hear the story as I tell Tom."

"All right," he says with a sigh. He lies back against the headboard and crosses his arms. I don't think he likes that I want to tell Tom first, but he's my partner and he understands what I'm going through.

Tom picks up on the third ring. "Tom, it's Linda. I just had a dream."

"Tell me everything you know." I tell him every detail that I can remember.

"Tom, it's the same man from my other dreams. His smiled showed through the mask, and I'd know that smile anywhere."

"We'll keep an unmarked car parked near your shop and have

men making rounds to see if they can find the woman with the description you gave me. Maybe we can save her before she gets attacked. We'll start tonight."

"Okay, and if I see anything suspicious while I'm at work today, I'll call you. Thank you, Tom. I feel better now that I got to talk to you about it." As soon as I say that, Luke rolls his eyes. "I'm glad you called me, talk to you soon."

I turn my head to face Luke. "I told you that Tom understands because he has dreams as well. Don't get upset."

"I'm not upset. I'm just frustrated because I want to understand and know what you're going through so I can help."

"You do help me, by being here with me when I wake up. You're here to comfort me, which is exactly what I need." Just then, Luke's phone rings.

He gets out of bed quickly while he's talking. I can't hear him say much, but I figure it's an emergency at the hospital. He comes out of the bathroom with his toothbrush in his hand. "I've got to go. Motorcycle accident. This guy's fibula and tibia are broken and sticking out of his leg. He's lost a lot of blood." He kisses me on the forehead and runs out the door.

I sit there, close my eyes, and picture the girl in the Dumpster. Tears start to form. I hope we can save her. Then it dawns on me. When I took out my phone to call 911, I saw the time. I didn't pay much attention to the date because I was occupied with dialing. But I think I remember seeing Thursday.

I call Tom and tell him.

"Good to know. We'll have men scouting the area starting at 8:00 p.m. There can't be too many girls in a red skirt and black top."

"I want to be there too. If I see the man with the crooked smile, we can finally catch him."

"You can stakeout with me in my car. I'll pick you up around seven forty-five."

"Great, see you then."

I begin to think that I'll get to see the action right in front of me. I feel an adrenaline rush—a mix between fear and excitement. I'll get to see the murderer get caught tonight, hopefully.

***

While I'm at work, I keep a constant lookout for anything suspicious. Sarah can tell that my mind isn't all there because I'm not talking much. I'm too focused on what's going to happen tonight.

"Hey, are you doing okay?" Sarah asks as she walks up to me behind the counter.

"Yeah, I just have a lot on my mind right now." I decide not to tell Sarah about the body in our Dumpster because I know it'll scare her.

"All right, whatever you say." She sighs and walks away. I can tell by the look she gave me when she walked away that she's upset that I'm keeping something from her. But it's for the best that I don't tell her until afterward.

As I'm cleaning the countertop, my phone rings. It's my mom. "Hey, honey," she says in her soft voice. "It has been a few days since we talked. I'm checking in to see how you're doing."

With May's support, I'd finally found the courage to tell my parents about my dreams coming true a couple of weeks ago, and they took it pretty well, all things considered. "I'm good. Business is booming, and Luke and I are becoming more serious."

"How's it going with the FBI?"

"Tonight is the first case we're getting to work on together."

"Well, that's exciting. Are you sure you're up for dealing with the crimes you're going to see?"

"I'm mentally preparing myself. I know it's going to be hard at first, but I see these crimes in my dreams anyway. I know what's coming."

"Well, good, then. I'm happy for you, honey. Now, when do we get to meet Luke?" I laugh because I've been waiting for her to ask.

"Whenever you want. I know we haven't been dating that long, but I have a good feeling about this one."

"How about you two come over for dinner at our place this weekend? I'll cook one of your favorite meals."

"Okay, how about Saturday, say six o'clock?"

"Sounds perfect, honey. I love you and see you then."

"Love you too, Mom," I say before I hang up.

My parents are the perfect picture of what love is, at least I think so. They were high school sweethearts. My dad was a football player, and my mom was a basketball player. They're both very athletic and tall. They seem to grow more in love with each other every year. Dad still opens doors for Mom, and they still flirt like they are twenty years old. I look up to them and hope one day I'll have a marriage like theirs.

It is almost time to start closing down when May walks in. "There's a man outside asking for you."

"Who is it?"

"I don't know, I've never seen him before, but he has a creepy vibe to him."

I take a big gulp and feel like I swallowed a marble. "What does he look like?"

"I don't know, there's nothing really special about him except that he looks like he has something funny going on with his jaw."

I start to panic. I stare at the door without saying a word. I walk toward the door slowly, but May stops me with a hand on my arm. "What's wrong?"

"I...I think it's him. The man from my dreams." My legs start to shake as I realize I'm about to confront the man who has been after me in my dreams for the first time. I pull my phone out and call Tom. "The man from my dreams is here asking for me. He's right outside my shop."

"Don't go out there. Lock the door and stay inside. I'll be right there."

But I don't listen to Tom because I'm stubborn. I want to see him. I want to confront this man who has been tormenting me in my dreams. It's still daylight out so there's no way he would attack me. I want to know why he's doing this and what his motive is.

"I don't think it's a good idea for you to go out there," May says, stepping in front of me.

"I agree. Let's just lock the door and stay inside until Tom gets here," says Sarah.

I'm assuming Bobby overheard our conversation because he comes out from the back with a gun in his hand. "He better not try anything."

I'm not listening to anyone. Their voices sound like I'm underwater. I'm imagining what it would be like to talk to him and see his dirty face, yellow teeth, and crooked jaw. I go to open the door. My heart is racing; my hands can barely grasp the door handle because they're sweaty.

I open the door and see nothing. I quickly glance left and right and across the street, but he's gone. "Shit, he's gone," I say as I walk into the shop.

"He was there a minute ago," says May. "This is part of his game. He's playing with me."

I flip the OPEN sign to CLOSED, and we all sit around a table. I have to tell them what's going on tonight now that he showed up at my shop. As I finish telling them the story, Tom knocks on the door.

"Where did he go? I walked around the shop and down a few blocks before I came in, and there was no sign of him."

"He was gone before I could even see him. May saw him outside, and he specifically asked to see me. When I walked out, he was gone."

"Well, at least we know he's in the area. We've just got to make sure we find Gloria before he does tonight."

"May, Sarah, and Bobby I don't want you all anywhere near this place tonight. I don't want to put you in any danger."

"Don't you worry, I won't step downtown at all," says Sarah.

"Please be careful tonight, and Tom, watch over her," May says. Tom nods in agreement. We stay behind as they all leave the shop.

"Do you want a ride home? It's not a good idea to walk home since he is close by."

"Yes please."

I'm silent during the two-minute drive to my house. We sit in the car in front of my house before I get out.

"I know tonight is scary for you. It's your first encounter with a case like this. I won't let anything happen to you. I promise my men and I will catch this guy." I start to feel a pinch of warmth inside, a comforting feeling.

"Thanks, Tom." I turn to open the car door as Luke pulls his car into the driveway. "I'm glad Luke is here. I want you to meet him."

Luke walks toward Tom's car. "Luke, this is Tom, the detective I told you about. Tom, this is my boyfriend, Luke Jackson."

They shake hands. Tom smiles at Luke. "It's very nice to meet you, Luke."

Luke isn't smiling so much. "It is nice to meet you as well." Then it dawns on me that I never got to tell Luke what was going on tonight.

"Tom and I are working together tonight, hoping to save

the girl and catch the man from my dreams." Luke raises his eyebrows.

"Oh? What exactly is the plan?" Luke asks. Tom fills him in.

Luke shakes his head. "I don't like the idea of Linda being there. What if you turn your head for a second and the man attacks her?"

"She'll be in the car with me the whole time and will stay there. She's just there to ID the man and the woman. She'll be safe, I can promise you that."

"I still don't like it. She'll be in danger."

"Luke, honey, I want to do this. I want to make sure this guy is caught so I can walk around without being scared. So I can enjoy my days without fear. I promise everything will be okay."

He shrugs his shoulders. "All right."

"I'll see you tonight." Tom gets in his car and drives away. I can feel the tension with Luke.

"I know this upsets you that I'm working with the FBI, but I want to do this, I want to help people. You have to trust me going forward with this. Tom and I will more than likely be spending a lot of time working together. I'm doing this because I want to help save lives. I want to do something good with my gift. You're the one who first gave me the idea."

"I know you like helping people. You're a caring person, and the FBI is lucky to have you. I'm not necessarily worried about you and Tom. I'm worried for your safety. I don't want anything to happen to you. I want to protect you, and knowing that I can't and Tom will be the one protecting you irritates me."

"You do protect me, babe, every day. If working with the FBI is going to be a part of my life, then it's going to be a part of your life as well. I need you to be supportive. I can't worry about you getting upset every time I'm involved with a new case. I want to be able to talk to you about the cases without an attitude from you. If we're going to be together, it's something you're going to have to get used to. I can't have these dreams and stand by doing nothing."

Luke sighs. "You're right. I'm sorry for getting upset. I do trust you, and I'm happy that you're excited about working with the FBI. It'll just take a little getting used to, but I'll support you one hundred percent."

I kiss him on his soft lips. "Thank you."

***

"You ready for this?" Tom asks when I open the door a couple hours later.

I shrug my shoulders. "As ready as I can be."

"I'll be waiting up for you. Please be careful," Luke says. He kisses me, and then Tom and I walk out the door. A rush of anxiety comes over me as we walk toward his car. My first planned encounter with the FBI on a murder case. I have to swallow many times to keep myself from throwing up. I pop a piece of gum into my mouth, hoping the mint will soothe my stomach.

"So here's the plan. We're going to scout out the area and watch for this girl to walk into a restaurant or bar. We'll keep an eye out for the man as well. If we see the woman, we'll ask her to come with us. I'll take her to safety, and then we'll come back for the man."

"And if we don't see the woman?"

"Then we're going to have to wait it out until we do see something. I have men walking through the restaurants and bars as well to see if they can find her." I'm relieved when he says that.

While we sit and wait, we begin to talk about the job and how I'm going to get more involved. "If a case comes to me, and I need help finding a missing person or murderer I'll call you, and we'll sit down and talk about the case. You're going to try and dream about the case to see if you can find any information out."

"You mean, like, control my dreams?"

"Yes."

"I don't know if I can do that. I'm just getting used to seeing clips of things happening. How would I control my dreams?"

"You've never tried to dream about something or put yourself in a certain situation?"

"No, I haven't."

"Then how do you know you can't do it?"

"Okay, say you give me a case and I dream about it, then I give you the details of when and where it's going to happen or where the missing person is. Do I get to come with you on the cases like I am tonight?"

"Yes, that's exactly what I want you to do. It all depends on how dangerous the case is, but more than likely you'll need to come with me so you can ID the people involved."

I take a big, deep breath in as I take in all the information. "I can do that. But why can't you just try to dream the situations?"

"I've tried, but I can't control my dreams."

"Then what makes you think I can?"

"We won't know until you try."

A few hours pass with no sign of anyone. I'm growing more and more anxious, and Tom must be able to tell because he says, "Linda, I want you to know that nothing bad is going to happen to you tonight. I won't let it. I'm here to protect you, and that's what I'm going to do."

I face away from Tom and a small smile forms, but I don't want him to see it. "Thank you."

Just then, I see a woman with a tight red skirt and black tank top walking into a restaurant a few doors down from my shop. "Look, Tom, I think that's Gloria."

He radios one of the officers to follow her in. A few minutes later, the officer comes on the radio, "Tom, we lost sight of her; she isn't inside anymore."

"Keep looking," Tom responds.

"I'm going to take a look around. Stay inside the car." I nod at him.

After about twenty minutes of constantly scanning through the windows, I start to get scared. There are a lot of people walking around tonight, which is good. But to know there is a killer out there looking for me isn't such a great feeling. And Tom still hasn't come back, which is starting to worry me.

I look out the front windshield when I see a figure walking my way. I start to panic when I get a clearer view. It's him, the man from my dream, and he's in all black and has the mask on. *Get up and out of the car*, I tell myself. He starts to pick up his pace, and I can see something shiny in his hand. I know exactly what it is: a knife.

I get out of the car and run. I hide behind another parked car and call Tom. He answers right away and I whisper to him, "He found me; he's chasing after me. I'm hiding behind a car now."

"Stay calm. Look around you and describe the buildings you see. I'm coming back toward the car now."

"I see a big blue two-story house. I'm surrounded by homes. I'm on Elliott Street, behind a red Volvo"

"Okay, I'm running that way now."

"Please hurry." I slowly look around the car to see if I can see him. It is dark out now, and all I can see are street lights. I don't see any movement. I sit behind the car and lean my head back, closing my eyes and taking deep breaths. *Everything is going to be okay. You're okay,* I tell myself.

I hear footsteps coming my way. I get up and run. "Wait, Linda, it's Tom."

I stop. "Oh, thank God," I say as I let out a big breath. "Did you see the guy?"

He shakes his head in disappointment.

"What about the girl?"

"No, we haven't seen her either. There's one place left we need to check."

I look at my phone. "It is eleven o'clock."

"If we get to her in time, there's a chance she could still be alive. If she's even there, it's our last chance."

He radios his officers, "Meet us at the Dumpster behind Sweet and Spice." We get there just as the other officers arrive. The Dumpster is closed.

"Here goes nothing," says Tom. I'm walking close behind him when I see something dripping from the dumpster. I grab Tom's arm. I brace myself for what I'm about to see when he opens that Dumpster. Tears start to form in my eyes, and he opens it.

Gloria is there, covered in blood. Her skirt is pulled down to her ankles, and her eyes are open, but then we see her blink.

"She's alive! Call the ambulance now," yells Tom. She coughs up blood. I can barely see her skin; blood engulfs her face and upper body.

"It's going to be okay, ma'am. Help is on the way." He turns to the officers. "Get CSI down here now and start dusting for fingerprints."

I hear the siren of the ambulance coming closer, and I see the red lights in the distance. *Thank God she's alive, but where's the man with the crooked smile?* I get chills thinking about him chasing me.

The paramedics bring the stretcher. They carefully lift her up, but she's coughing up more blood and having a hard time breathing.

The forensic crew arrives as Tom walks me back to the car. "Thank you for your help today. Without you and your dreams, this girl wouldn't have made it out alive."

"I don't think I helped at all, and he's still out there."
"You did help, and I know how scared you must be, but we won't stop until we find him." I nod.

He drops me off at my house, and as soon as we pull up, Luke is out the door. "Are you okay? How did it go?"

"Well, the girl is alive, but the killer got away. He started to chase me, but I don't think his intention was to catch me, only to scare me."

"What?" Luke is pissed. He turns on Tom. "Your men didn't catch this lunatic?"

"I don't know how he got past us or how we got away, but I'm going back to talk to my guys now and figure out what went wrong. But like I told Linda, we will find him."

"You better because he's out for Linda. Who knows when or where he will attack."

"I understand. I know you'll do what it takes to protect her, and I'll do the same. Just make sure she doesn't go anywhere alone. And, Linda, if you have any dreams, you know what to do."

"Yeah, I got it." I yawn. I'm exhausted after this night of worrying and panicking.

"If you need anything, don't hesitate to call," Tom says as he walks to his car.

Luke wraps his arms around me. "I'm so glad you're safe. I won't let anything happen to you. I'll stay with you every night." I feel safe in his arms, knowing he'll be right by my side.

"Thank you."

"Let's get you inside. I'll draw you a bath so you can relax." That's exactly what I need: a bath and some sleep.

Chapter 7

Tom leaves me alone for the next few days because I'm still shocked with everything that happened. There hasn't been a sign from the killer, but I'm sure he's out there waiting to make his move. Today is the day that Luke is cooking for Jeff and I. I'm excited to meet his best friend, the only real brother he has ever had.

Luke drops me off at work. He won't let me go anywhere alone. "I'll pick you up at closing, and then we'll head over to my place and get dinner started. Jeff is going to meet us there around seven."

"Sounds great. Good luck with your surgeries today." I kiss him and then head into work.

I'm putting out all the fresh pastries for the day when I hear my phone go off. It's a text message from Tyler.

"Linda, please give me another chance to talk to you. I miss you."

I sigh out loud and show the text to Sarah.

"Gosh, does he not understand what it means to leave someone alone?"

"I'm just going to text back and tell him to leave me alone, and that I'm in a happy relationship. Hopefully, he'll get the point."

"Let's hope so."

Around one thirty, Tom walks into the shop. I'm excited to see him, and I'm not sure if that's a good thing or a bad thing.

"Hey, can I borrow you for a second?" he asks. I nod and follow him outside.

"What's up?"

"I need your help on a case. I know you probably would like a few more days to heal after the last incident, but this can't wait."

"I can help. Tell me about the case."

He puts his black briefcase on the table and pulls out some files. "An eight-year-old girl went missing in Wannamaker County Park yesterday. The mom claims to have turned around for a second, and she was gone. We talked to people that had been at the park that day, but no one noticed anything out of the ordinary. I need you to put yourself at this park around 11:00 a.m."

He shows me a picture of the little girl. She's wearing a pink polka dot dress that falls to her knees. Her long brown hair is held back with a matching pink headband, and she has the sweetest smile.

"This poor girl," I say as I shake my head.

"With your help, we can find this girl alive."

"I've been researching lucid dreaming techniques online, and I'll try to dream about it tonight. I'll give you a call tomorrow morning."

"Great, thanks. It will help to really picture yourself at the park and concentrate on the day and time. If you've never been to the park, take a quick trip up there or look it up online so you can get a good idea of what it looks like. Envision yourself at that park as you close your eyes," he says as he puts his paperwork back in his briefcase.

"I've been there before with Luke, so I know it pretty well."

"Perfect," he says as he gets up quickly; he seems to be in a rush.

"How about a coffee to go on the house?"

"You read my mind; I'd love one. I really enjoy working with you. I know it hasn't been that long, but you're such a caring, compassionate person, and I really respect that."

I blush at the compliment. "Thank you, I enjoy working with you as well," I say with a smile. He follows me back inside to grab his coffee and heads out the door. I watch him walk away.

Sarah must have caught me staring at him. "You know, he's pretty cute," she says.

"What's that supposed to mean?"

"Ohhh, nothing."

"Come out and say it, Sarah, I know you want to," I say with a little attitude.

"It's just that he's really good looking, and you'll be spending a lot of time with him. Do you think he'll come between you and Luke?"

"Of course not! Yes, Tom is an attractive guy, but it's strictly business. Plus, I'm beginning to think that Luke is the one."

Sarah's eyes widen, and she smiles. "Really? I knew it! I can tell by the connection you two share, and the way you talk about him all the time."

"He's meeting my parents this weekend."

"Oh, big step! I think your parents will like him."

"I hope so. If my parents and May don't approve, that's a deal breaker." We laugh and get back to work.

The rest of the afternoon flies by, and Luke walks in just as I'm putting away the pastries for the night. "Hey beautiful."

"Hey, babe, I'm almost done."

"No rush, take your time."

I put everything away, take off my apron, and walk up to him for a kiss.

He takes my face gently in his hands and kisses me deeply. I'm dizzy and breathless when he finally pulls away.

"Well, it's nice to see you too," I say as I smile.

He smiles back. "You ready now? I want to freshen up a bit and get the hamburgers and hot dogs started on the grill."

"Mmm, sounds good!"

It doesn't take but a few minutes to get to his townhouse. I help him carry in the groceries he got for dinner.

"I need to take a quick shower." Luke looks at me with a sexy grin and asks, "Do you want to join me?"

I walk up to him and put my arms around his neck. "Do you even have to ask?" He picks me up, my legs wrap around his waist, and he carries me into the bathroom.

He turns on the shower, and we undress each other. We step into the warm spray of water, kissing, our wet bodies sliding together. He pushes me up against the shower wall and I brace one leg on the edge of the tub.

With the warm water hitting our bodies, he enters me, moving in and out fast and hard till my body is tingling. I feel like I'm floating. My fingers dig into his back, and I scream as I climax.

When we finish, I wrap my arms around his neck, and we kiss softly under the water, our bodies slowly swaying back and forth. He grabs a loofah, puts some body wash on it, and starts washing my body, paying special attention to my breasts. Then it's my turn. Watching the water and soap run down his tight, six-pack abs makes me feel hot, and I get turned on again, but we don't have time for another round. As he turns off the water and grabs a towel, I stare at his hard, strong body and smile. He turns around and winks at me.

We get dressed and start prepping for dinner. Luke bought corn on the cob, hamburgers, hot dogs, and red potatoes. We pop open a couple of beers and fire up the grill.

Just as we're putting the meat on the grill, Jeff appears in the patio doorway.

"Hey, bud!" Luke says as he walks out.

"Hey, hey, something smells good," Jeff says. He's about medium height, dark skinned, and dressed in preppy Hollister clothes: khaki shorts, tan sandals, and a button-up plaid shirt. He's pretty handsome. He's got a narrow, square chin, big brown eyes, and a smile that could take any woman's panties off. He's definitely a chick magnet.

He looks at me. "Is this the famous Linda I hear about all day, every day?" he asks with a smile and puts his hand out to shake.

I shake his hand and smile. "It's nice to meet you, and I hope you're hearing all good things!" We all laugh.

"Trust me, nothing but good things." We fall into easy conversation as Luke grills up the burgers and dogs. There's nothing like grilling on a beautiful summer day. We eat on the patio, and the more beer we have, the more we start talking about our pasts, and they tell me stories about their college life together.

"I'm a big NFL football fan," I say.

"Oh yeah, brownie points there! She's a sports fan," Jeff laughs. "But here's the make or break question. Who's your favorite team?"

"My team is the Carolina Panthers."

"All right, all right, not too shabby. I'm a Dallas Cowboys fan. I'm originally from Texas, and my heart still lies with that team."

We sit out on the patio talking, drinking, and watching as the sun sets. I'm comfortable with Jeff, and I can see why he and Luke are so close. They have a lot in common, and Jeff seems to be a trustworthy person. I know Luke, and I can't see him being friends with someone who wasn't.

"Sounds like you two were quite the partiers in college."

"Who isn't nowadays?"

"True. With all the hard work I put in, the times when I went out with my friends made it less stressful."

"Amen to that," says Luke. He holds up his beer and we tap them together and take a sip. We have a few more drinks and realize how late it's gotten.

"Hey, I don't want you driving back, so how about you take my couch to sleep on tonight?" Luke says to Jeff.

"Thanks, man. Now no funny business while I'm staying out here," Jeff says, and we laugh.

Luke and I get into bed. All the food and beer has made me sleepy. I lie in his arms, close my eyes, and drift into sleep.

***

I'm in my shop with Bobby and Sarah, closing up for the day. We all say our goodbyes and walk to our cars. It was raining that morning, so I had driven to work. I'm parked in the back, and Sarah and Bobby are parked on the street. I probably shouldn't park in the back because that's where the Dumpster is and I always think of the woman we found there. The back of the shop is secluded with the one spot to park and the Dumpster.

I think I hear footsteps behind me. I look back, thinking I'm just being paranoid since it's still light out. But there he is, the man all in black with a ski mask. Before I can scream or run or do anything, he slams me up against my car, and my head bashes into the window. I fall to the ground; I can feel myself blacking out. When I try to open my eyes, I can see the guy kneeling down and staring right into my face. He pulls out a knife and says, "I finally got you." Then I pass out cold.

I wake up in a cold sweat, screaming. Luke rolls over and hugs me. "You're all right. I'm here. It's going to be okay. You want to tell me about the dream?"

"I think I know when and where this guy is going to attack next."

"Who's he going to attack?"

"Me."

***

"I think I'm going to take off work today and keep an eye on you," Luke says as I'm getting ready for work.

"You don't need to do that. Your patients need you. Tom and the other cop he's assigning will be there to protect me." After my dream, I called Tom, and he promised to put extra surveillance on the shop.

"I really don't like leaving you alone. I'm coming to your work before you close, so I can make sure nothing will happen."

"I won't be alone. Bobby and Sarah will be there. And if at any time I feel scared or threatened, I will call you. Besides, it rained that morning in my dream and I drove to work, so I don't think it will happen today. And when the time comes, I want this to actually happen so the cops can catch him. Then this will all be over. If you're there and he sees you, he might not go through with the attack."

He raises his eyebrows. "So I'm supposed to wait and hear if my girlfriend gets attacked or not? I'll be too anxious all day, worrying about you."

"It'll be okay, Luke, I promise."

He shakes his head and sighs. "How about I come and sit in my car down the street? It'll be like I'm not even there. That way if something happens, I can still get to you quickly."

"If that will make you feel better, then fine." He leans in and kisses me on the lips.

"I'm going to put some coffee on and make breakfast. Take your time getting ready. I'll wake up Jeff, and then I'll drop you off at work."

We have a wonderful breakfast of veggie omelets with mushrooms, green peppers, onions, and spinach with bacon and sausage. When we're finished, Jeff leaves to go to the hospital. "I'll see you at work soon, and, Linda, it was very nice to meet you. Luke is one lucky man, and I'll kill him if he does anything to screw it up."

I smile. "Thanks, Jeff. It was nice meeting you too."

I look at Luke when he's gone. "Well, I've got his approval!"

"Yeah, you do. He'll probably talk about you all day today."

Luke drives me to work, and as we pull up to the shop, I see that Tom is already parked across the street. "Please be careful today. I'll come as soon as I can and park down the street and sit there until it's over."

"I will. Have a good day at work." He kisses me hard, almost like he doesn't want to let me go. I get butterflies in my stomach. I don't want to let him go either.

Once inside, I decide to tell Sarah and Bobby what's going on.

"I don't want you both to be here if this goes down. I don't want to put you in any danger. This is our one good shot to catch this guy for good."

"We can't just leave you here alone. What if the guy comes earlier?" Sarah asks.

"I won't be alone. Tom and another officer are outside watching, and Luke will be down the street waiting. Please, just take the day off. I can handle the shop on my own today."

She's reluctant, but she finally gives in. "Well, at least let us help you get everything set up for the day, and call us tonight so we know you're okay."

"I will, and thank you guys."

It's a long day at work. After the lunch rush dies down there's only one customer in the shop on her laptop. I walk over to the windows and stare out into space, thinking about everything.

My life has changed so much within the span of a couple months: meeting Luke, my dreams becoming reality, working with the FBI. It's crazy how things can change so quickly.

I'm so lost in thought that I lose track of time, and when I turn around, I realize that the girl left, and I'm alone. I look down at my watch. It's 4:50 p.m. My heart starts to beat faster. "Well, here goes nothing," I say out loud.

I start closing down the shop. As I'm cleaning the counters and putting everything away, my hands start shaking. I can barely hold on to anything. I'm terrified of what could be about to happen.

I put my hands on the counter and lower my head, forcing myself to take deep breaths. *It's going to be okay; you're going to be okay. It didn't rain today, and you didn't drive to work. Today will not be the day.* I repeat this over and over as I finish closing up. As I make my way to the door with the day's trash, my legs start shaking. I have to sit down for a few seconds to gain the strength and courage to walk out that door.

I step out and lock the door behind me. I scan the street, and all around me I see normal people walking on a beautiful day in downtown Charleston. I don't see anyone dressed in all black. *There's no way he's going to attempt to attack me during the day.* I walk around back to the Dumpster. My hands are sweating, and I feel like I'm going to throw up. I turn the corner and stop to look around; I see nothing and no one. Then I hear something near the Dumpster. It sounds like metal scraping against metal.

My heart pounds and aches with fear when I see the man in black with the ski mask step out from behind the Dumpster. No one can see us right now behind the building. My knees begin to buckle. I want to run, but I can't move. He brings out the knife from behind his back in slow motion.

"I've finally got you. It's been a long time coming," the man says in a deep, rough voice. He has a smoker's voice. He smiles. I can see the crooked jaw outline through his mask, and his teeth are yellow and have black spots between them. He looks like a killer out of a Texas Chainsaw movie.

He moves closer and holds up his knife. My life flashes before my eyes.

"Hold it right there." Tom's voice comes from behind me, and I've never been so relieved in my life. I turn my head to look and see him pointing his gun at the man. The man tries to make a break for it, but Tom tackles him to the ground. The man falls face-first, his head smacking off the pavement. Tom grabs his arms and pulls them behind his back as he puts him in handcuffs. Finding the courage to face my tormenter, I walk up to him and say, "Not what you expected, huh?"

"Don't worry, this isn't over," he says with a sickening smile.

"Yeah, it is, buddy." Tom jerks him up and shoves him into the back of his car, positioned right at the top of the alley. I can't believe I didn't hear him pull up. He comes back to me and puts his hands on my shoulders. "Are you okay?" I nod and then look behind me.

"Where's Luke? He said he'd be here."

"I don't know; I haven't seen him," says Tom. His tone softens. "But I was here for you." I raise my brow in surprise, not sure what to think about that. In a way, I kind of like it. *Don't think that. Luke isn't here, and I'm worried, but Tom seems to make things feel a little better.* I decide not to respond to his comment, and he quickly changes the subject.

"I'm going to take this guy into the station. Are you going to be all right walking back home?"

"Yeah, I feel better now that this asshole is caught. Thank you."

Tom drives off, and I walk home. I dial Luke's number, but it goes straight to voice mail.

This is weird. He promised he'd be here, and with something this big, I thought for sure he would be. Knots form in my stomach, and I suddenly remember the dream with the fire and Luke next to me in bed. I still haven't told him about that, and my dreams have been coming true, so when is that dream going to come true?

I walk home and get in the shower. My phone is on the bathroom counter so I can hear it ring if Luke calls, but he doesn't.

I walk slowly downstairs with a sick, uneasy feeling in my stomach. I sit on the couch and turn on the TV. I sit and watch the pictures move, but I don't pay any attention to what's on. I keep thinking about Luke.

After another thirty minutes, I begin to think I should call Tom. Just then, Luke walks in the door. I run up to him and throw myself into his arms. "Where were you? And where have you been? The guy did show up today, and we caught him, but you weren't there."

"I got held up in back-to-back emergency surgeries. I didn't get a break at all to call you." He kisses me on the forehead and hugs me. "I'm so sorry. I'm so glad you're safe."

"I was worried sick about you."

"I know and I got here as fast as I could. I didn't think today would be the day since I drove you to work and it wasn't raining. I'm so sorry I wasn't there for you. Tell me what happened."

I tell him the story, but inside I'm upset. I know I shouldn't be because his work can get crazy, and he doesn't get many breaks, but he was supposed to be there. I was counting on him. I can't help but feel as if he's let me down.

Chapter 8

The next few days go by without any interruptions. It's Saturday, the day my parents get to meet Luke. On the drive over, I decide I'm going to tell Luke about the fire dream tonight. He has the right to know I saw him coming and to know about the fire before things get even more serious between us.

We pull up to my parents' house. I can tell Luke is nervous. I take his hand and give it a squeeze.

"Just be yourself, and they'll love you."

We walk up to the house, and before I can even knock, Mom opens the door with a big, cheerful smile. Her long dangly earrings are swaying in her excitement. Her brown curly hair is all made up nicely. I figured she would do that; she always gets excited when my sister and I come visit. I have to bend down to hug my mom, who's about half a foot shorter than me. I give her a big hug and see Dad right behind her. I have to stand on my tiptoes to hug Dad. He's six foot three and built like a tank. "Mom, Dad, this is Luke Jackson. Luke, these are my parents, Barbra and Wesley."

"It's a pleasure to meet the both of you. I hear are great things about you," he says as he shakes their hands.

"It's nice to meet you, Luke; we've heard great things about you as well," Mom says, smiling.

We walk into the foyer and past the living room. "This is a lovely home you have here," Luke says to my parents.

Mom looks over and smiles at me. "Why, thank you. You are too sweet."

We walk into the dining room, and to my surprise, May is sitting there at the table. "Oh my gosh, what are you doing here?"

"You think I'd miss out on your boy meeting our parents? No way! Plus I have yet to meet him myself," May says as she smiles.

"I should have known you would be here."

"Always one step ahead of you, sis. After all, I'm the younger and wiser sister."

"Ha! Yeah right! More like the immature and crazy one."

Mom chimes in as usual. "All right, you two, we have a guest."

"Sorry, Luke. This is typical sibling rivalry."

"No need to be sorry. I think it's great that you have a special bond with your sister."

"Let's eat before we get too comfortable sitting and talking. Your dad and I cooked lasagna, fresh green beans, and homemade garlic bread."

"Wow, now I know the place to come and get a good meal," Luke says, smiling.

"Oh yeah, my parents are great cooks."

As we eat, Mom and Dad give Luke the third degree. They ask about his work at the hospital and his education. Then Dad asks him about his family.

I put my hand on his arm, trying to convey with a look that he doesn't have to share anything he doesn't want to.

He nods and tells them the short version: that his mom walked out on him, and his dad had a drinking problem, and that's why he moved away.

"I want to make sure I raise my family right," he says. Mom and Dad immediately perk up when they hear that. I can see them picturing grandbabies already.

I decide now would be a good time to bring up what has happened in the past week with my dreams and the FBI.

"Gosh, honey, you've had a rough couple of days," says Mom.

"I have, but I wouldn't have been able to get through it if it weren't for Luke, and I'm very thankful for that, and the fact that this creep is finally behind bars."

"I worry about her, but I'm here to protect her, and that's what I'll continue to do," Luke says.

"I know your mom and I feel much better knowing that Luke is there with you," Dad says as he turns a big, toothy grin on Luke. His dark eyes and dark hair seem to brighten when he smiles. He's likes to come across as being hard and tough, but he can become a big teddy bear in a second.

"He's got my approval!" May says in a screeching, high-pitched voice.

"Oh boy, am I glad. I mean, what would I have done if my baby sis didn't approve of my boyfriend?" I wink at her.

She blows me a kiss and shoots up a playful middle finger.

After dessert and a couple of after-dinner drinks, Luke and I decide to take our leave. "It was a pleasure meeting you, Mr. and Mrs. Brown. And you, May," Luke says as he shakes their hands one by one.

"The pleasure was ours," Mom says. "Please feel free to stop by anytime, you two."

I look over at Luke as we walk to the car. I'd already fallen for him, but seeing him interact so well with my family—telling jokes and stories, laughing—it's as if he fits right in, and I'm even more convinced that he's the one.

"I had a great time tonight, and I love your family. I've always wished I had a family as close as yours."

"I think they loved you as well. You fit right in! I'm so happy we decided to take this step."

"He kisses me before he opens the car door for me and slips me a little tongue. It never fails, I always get butterflies. And I hope my parents aren't watching from the window.

When we get home, we're both feeling pretty tired, so we lie in bed and watch a little TV. I've tried every night to focus on the little girl in the park, but so far I haven't had any luck. I know our chances of finding her decrease with every day that passes, but I still hope I can dream about who took her and lead Tom in the right direction to find her. As I picture her and the park in my mind again, the world around me begins to fade to black.

***

I'm at a park, sitting on a bench by myself, looking around, watching the children and families play. All of a sudden, I see the little girl walking into the woods by herself. No one else seems to notice. I want to make sure I get a good look at the man who takes her. She keeps looking around, as if she's trying to find someone or something. I go up to her and say, "Hi, are you okay?"

"Yeah, I'm just trying to find this man."

"What man? Your father?"

"No, a man who told me that if I come into the woods, he'll give me candy and presents."

"Oh no, sweetie. What did this man look like?"

"He was wearing jeans, a red t-shirt, and a red baseball cap."

"Okay, that's a good job, sweetie. Was he dark skinned or light?"

"He was light, and his smile seemed different."

"Different? What do you mean different?"

"Well, he was missing some front teeth."

"It's a good thing I found you. Didn't your mom ever tell you not to talk to strangers?"

"But I wanted some candy and presents. And aren't you a stranger?"

I laugh. "Yes, I am, sweetie, but I won't hurt you. I'll help you find your parents."

"Okay," the little girl says with a frown. She's adorable in her pink polka dot dress and matching pink headband. She takes my hand, and we walk back to the playground. I see a young, slim, and gorgeous lady who's crying and asking if anyone has seen her daughter. She spots us walking toward her and runs to us, scooping her up. I can see where the girl gets her beautiful long brown hair.

"Honey, what are you doing walking away from the playground? I told you to not leave my sight."

"I'm sorry, Mama, there was this guy who told me he had candy." The mom looks up at me and starts to cry again. I begin to explain to the mom that I saw her daughter walking and brought her back here. I didn't see the man anywhere, but I'm sure he was waiting nearby.

"We should call the cops and let them know there's a man at the playground trying to lure little children," says the mom. "Honey, what did this man look like?"

The little girl answers shyly and gives the same description she gave me.

"Honey, that's great. You did a good job."

Her mom turns to me. "Thank you so much for going after my daughter. I can't believe I didn't pay attention. You may have very well saved her life."

"No need to thank me." The mom looks at me with a half-smile, enough for her dimples to show. I can tell she's worried; I'd be scared after that incident as well. The sun is shining so bright, I shut my eyes for a second against the glare.

I slowly open my eyes, as if I was still looking into the sun. Luke is still asleep. I get up and grab my phone and head down to the kitchen to call Tom.

It's five in the morning, and he yawns as he says hello. "What's up?"

"I had a dream about the little girl in the park."

"That's great! Tell me about it."

I give him details, time, and description. "But in my dream, I saved her before this creep got to her. What does that mean? If he has her now, how are you going to find him?"

"You can't save everyone." I nod my head but don't respond. "And our dreams aren't always accurate, like the one you had about being attacked on a rainy day. But this could still be really helpful. My men and I will go to the park and stake it out to see if we find a man matching that description, or anyone who may have remembered seeing him. We will find the girl, Linda. You've done your job, and now it's up to us. Thank you."

"Will you keep me posted? I won't be able to sleep until I know that girl is safe."

"I will, I promise."

Tears begin to form. I really get attached to these cases, and it makes it so hard to continue to do this work, but I do like helping people. It's a love-hate relationship.

I go back to the bedroom and climb into bed. Luke rolls over. "Is everything okay?"

I tell him what just happened.

"You and I both know how good Tom is at his job. They will find the girl and the man. You did a great job."

"Yeah, but it was too late. I wish I could have seen the dream before the girl went missing."

"You didn't know anything about the case until Tom asked for your help."

"That's true."

"Worrying about it isn't going to help either."

"I can't help it."

Luke kisses me on the lips. "Just try. They will take care of it." Luke doesn't understand the pressure, the pain, and the adrenalin rush these dreams and cases bring me. "Why don't you try going back to sleep? It's early and it's Sunday. You should sleep as much as you can."

"I'll try." I roll over onto my side and look at the clock. I stare deep into the light and think of the little girl. Then I close my eyes and hope and pray she is safe.

I wake up to the smell of smoked bacon. I head downstairs to find Luke making breakfast.

"Good morning, beautiful."

"Good morning." I kiss him and pour myself some coffee.

"I was thinking we could go to Wannamaker County Park today," he says. "I know this case is killing you, and you want to help find the man rather than sit here."

"You're right. I can't sit here and wait. If we see the guy today, we can get a hold of Tom and put an end to this."

"Sounds like a plan. Eat a good breakfast, and then we'll head on out."

"Thank you, Luke. I guess you know me better than I thought."

He smiles and shows his pearly white teeth, "Well, we do spend every day together. If I don't know you and your habits by now, then I wouldn't be a very good boyfriend, would I?"

I laugh. "I guess you're right."

"Plus, I told your family I'd protect you, which is what I'm going to do. I support you and the decisions you make. I want to try and understand what you're going through so I can help as much as I can."

"You're doing fine, babe." I take a bite of the crisp, peppery bacon. He makes the best bacon.

***

I don't even bother to tell Tom what we're doing because he'd try to talk me out of it. When we get to the park, it's full of kids and happy families. It makes knots in my stomach to know this man is preying on these children, who are so full of life and joy.

Hearing the children's laughter brings a smile to my face. I'm going to catch this guy if it's the last thing I do. These children need to be safe. Luke and I sit on a bench and observe. There are kids swinging on the swings, sliding down slides, running around playing tag. It's a beautiful sight.

All of a sudden, I feel a soft touch on my shoulder, and I jump as I turn around.

"Tom, you scared the shit out of me. Don't sneak up on me like that."

"Sorry, sorry, I didn't mean to. What are you doing here? Wait, I already know this answer." His hand is still resting on my shoulder. "Linda, I told you we'd take care of it."

"I know, but I couldn't sit around and wait."

"How did I know you were going to do this?" he says, smiling and shaking his head. Luke looks pointedly at Tom's hand on my shoulder and back up to Tom's face. Tom quickly removes his hand. "Well, any sign of this guy?"

"Nothing yet. We haven't been here that long."

"I have a few of my men walking around the park keeping an eye out."

"Good, then we have plenty of eyes, so he shouldn't be missed. I don't even know if this man is going to show up today, but at least we're here in case he does."

"I'm going back to the search. I'll leave you two be." Luke and I nod in farewell.

About an hour passes, and we don't see anything. Luke and I don't talk much, and I wonder if he's engrossed in the search or if he's thinking about Tom's hand on my shoulder.

I spy a young girl in jean shorts and a cute yellow flowered tank top walking into the forested area with no adult. I jump up and point her out to Luke.

"That girl is walking alone into the woods. That's what happened in my dream; he tried to lure her into the woods so no one could see him."

"Let's go." I send Tom a quick text, and Luke and I make our way to the wooded area, but there are so many kids and people around that it makes it hard to keep track of the girl.

We speed up. When we enter the woods, there's no sign of her. "There's no way he got to her that fast," I say in frustration.

"Shh," Luke says. We hear ruffling through the leaves.

I turn around and see the man with missing teeth, holding the girl by her mouth so she can't scream. He has a knife to her throat.

"Please don't hurt her," I say in desperation.

He smiles an evil and ominous grin.

"And what are you going to do about it?" His voice sounds gross; it's so raspy and he coughs at the end of every sentence. He smells of smoke and sewage.

"Just let the girl go." Just then, Tom comes up behind us with his gun pointing at him.

"I'd listen to the girl if I were you."

"And I'm supposed to be threatened by the gun?" The man

moves his head back and laughs. "I'm much smarter than you think. You think you're going to shoot me? I'm holding this precious little girl." He tightens his grip, and the girl whimpers.

"Be careful, I have a clean shot right to your head," says Tom.

The man picks the girl up and holds her in front of his body as a shield. "How about now?"

This man is playing some sick game, and it's making me nervous. The intense adrenalin rush that's going through my body right now makes me feel weak. Not knowing the outcome of this situation is killing me.

Then the creep closes his eyes and starts counting back from five. Tom, Luke, and I quickly glance at each other, wondering what's going to happen when he hits zero.

Tom is still pointing his gun at him and we are all silent.

"Three, two, one!" Then he throws the young girl at us and begins to run.

The girl and I fall to the ground, and Tom quickly runs after him. Then I hear a gunshot. Luke takes off toward the sound.

I look at the little girl. "Are you okay, sweetie?"

She nods her head. I stare into her beautiful, innocent, teary blue eyes. "It's okay, you're safe now."

Tom and Luke are walking toward us with the man in handcuffs between them. He's limping. Looks like Tom shot him in the leg. I see the blood soaking through his pant leg.

Thank God he's caught. I feel instant relief.

"Will you two take this girl back to the park and try to find her parents? I'll send an officer over to talk to them about what happened. I'm taking this guy into the station."

Luke and I start to walk back with the girl. She won't unwrap her arms from around my neck, so I carry her. "What do your parents look like?"

"I'm here with my older brother. I'm scared."

We walk around the park until she spots her brother lying on a bench, asleep.

She forces her way out of my arms and runs up to him, shaking him awake. "Harry, wake up."

He quickly gets up in a panic. "What is it? Are you okay?" She starts to cry.

"Actually, she's not okay, and if you hadn't been sleeping and were actually paying attention to your little sister, then you'd know."

"Oh my God, what happened?" I tell him the story and he begins to cry. He looks to be only about seventeen. "I'm so sorry, baby girl," he says as he brings her into his arms and hugs her tight.

"I promise I won't ever let you out of my sight again." He kisses her on the forehead.

He then looks up at me. "Thank you for saving her. I owe you everything."

"Just watch out for her closely and take good care of her." I see one of Tom's officers approaching. "You're going to have to talk to the police. They'll probably have to call your parents."

He nods his head, and more tears begin to fall.

Luke and I head home, waiting anxiously to hear from Tom. "Now if only Tom can get answers from this creep so we can find the girl in the polka dot dress."

"I'm sure he will."

When we get home I go straight to the couch and lay down. What an intense day it has been so far.

A few hours pass before Tom calls.

"Tom, give me answers."

"Well, we got the location of the warehouse where he takes the children, and we found the girl."

"Oh, thank God. Is she alive?"

"Yes, she is. This creep had a room decked out in teddy bears, candy, and pink flowers. She's lucky. We found a few bodies in trash bags hidden in a closet. We got there just in time to save that girl."

I start to cry. "Those poor children."

"I'm sorry you have to hear that, but the girl is safe and back with her family. Thank you for your help, Linda."

"Thank you for finding her and saving her."

"It's my job. Now it's up to a judge to decide his future. But it's not going to be a pleasant one."

"It better not be. That bastard deserves to die."

"Couldn't agree with you more. I'll talk to you later. Get some rest."

There's something about his voice that soothes me. "Thank you."

I hang up and rush into Luke's arms. "He killed children. How could a man do that?"

"He isn't a man, he's an animal."

"The girl from the park is safe."

"I'm so glad to hear that. Now we can relax and put this behind us."

"Yeah, and wait until the next case."

Luke cradles my head and holds me.

Chapter 9

A few months have passed and fall is just around the corner, my favorite time of the year. Luke and I decided to move in together. Since Luke was renting his townhome, he moved into my house. This is a good starter home for us. But now that we're living in my house, my thoughts turn more and more to that dream I had months ago about the fire. It's going to come true, but I'm not sure when. I still haven't told Luke about it, but I can't put it off any longer. He needs to know.

Luke is making breakfast before work and I need to tell him now to get it off my chest. "Luke, there's something important I need to tell you. I've been keeping it from you because I wanted to make sure we were going to stay together. Now that we've moved in together, it's time for you to know."

His eyebrow rises in suspicion. "Okay, what's wrong?"

"I had a dream months ago that this house was on fire. In my dream, we were lying in bed and awoke to the smell of smoke. We had to climb out of the window and jump to the tree outside my bedroom. You jumped first, and when you tried to pull me onto the tree, I fell through the floor into the fire."

"Oh my God."

"Wait, I'm not done. I had this dream…" I sigh. "Before I even met you."

"So you dreamed about me coming into your life before I actually did?"

"Yes. I didn't want to tell you because I didn't want to scare you off. I probably should have told you earlier, but I was worried you'd freak out and leave me."

"Well, I think it's kind of cool. I mean, this is your gift, seeing the future, and you saw me. It makes me feel more confident about us."

"But what about the fire?"

"We've dealt with all your other dreams. We'll do what we always do and take care of it. I won't let you get harmed in any way. So if there's a fire, I'll get both of us out alive, I promise."

I'm so relieved and so lucky to have him in my life. "I feel so much better now that I've told you. Can we go upstairs after we eat and make an escape plan for when this happens?"

"Of course. You're always thinking ahead."

I think about that for a minute. "I wonder if we could possibly prevent the fire."

"We could, but you don't know when the fire will happen or how it'll start. We'll have to keep our guard up and watch out for suspicious signs."

"I hate waiting and not knowing when things are going to happen. How are we going to be able to sleep knowing we'll be waking up to a fire at some point?"

"It's scary, but there's not much else we can do but wait."

"You don't seem too frightened by it."

"Well, both of us can't be too scared. I have to stay focused so I'll be ready when it happens."

His words and confident attitude comfort me.

"So, in your dreams was I as good looking as you thought?" he asks with a wink.

I smile. "Oh, you're so much sexier in person." I kiss him hard. "When I saw you walk into my work that day, I thought I'd exploded inside. I wanted to take you on that counter in front of everyone."

"Oh yeah?" he says with a sexy grin. "I found you pretty attractive myself. I had to come back that same day to ask you out. You still feel that way about me?"

"Oh, baby, I do."

"Mmm, that makes me feel good." He wraps his arm around me and pulls me hard against him. "But I know how you can make me feel even better." I laugh as he sets me on the counter and proceeds to bring the fantasy I told him about to life.

***

Just as we open the shop, Tom shows up. I've been spending a lot of time with Tom. I don't think Luke likes it very much, but he supports me anyway. I've been having dreams often, at least once a week, sometimes more. And so far we've solved them all.

We're an effective team.

"Hey, I'm glad you're here. I need to talk to you," I tell him as I walk out from behind the counter.

"All right, let's go outside."

I tell him about the fire dream. "For some reason, I'm having more trouble seeing this dream than any other dream."

"There isn't much we can do about it other than wait. You haven't had anyone harass you in a while and you're not in any danger now."

"Yeah, but you should know this better than anyone. Serial killers don't just leave the picture; the man I saw standing across the street in the fire dream is probably planning something big."

"Well, you're right about that. Just keep a close eye out, and I'll do the same."

"Do you have another case for me to work on?"

"No, actually, I just wanted to see you." He's looking at me with a hopeful expression I've never seen from him before. "Seeing you," he pauses for a second and takes a deep breath, "seems to make my days better."

My stomach drops as I realize the direction this conversation is about to take. "Luke and I just moved in together," I blurt out before he can say anything else.

He suddenly goes very still. "Oh, really?" He clears his throat and looks away as if he's embarrassed. When his eyes meet mine again, there's a flash of something there—anger, jealousy? But it's gone in a moment. He pushes back his chair and says, "Well, that's great. I'm sorry for bothering you today. I'll call you if anything comes up." And just like that, he's up and walking down the street to his car.

I sit there in confusion, not entirely sure what to think. We've been spending a lot of time together, and he's charming and handsome, but I'd thought flirting was just part of his personality. And he's known all along about Luke. Could I have really missed the signs that he was interested in me as more than a professional partner? Did I inadvertently lead him on in some way? Will things be awkward between us after this? Before I can get far with that line of thought, a group of customers comes through the door, the start of our lunch rush, and I go back in to help. I stand behind the counter, gratefully falling back into the routine of busily filling orders. But I continue to replay the scene over and over in my head the rest of the afternoon.

Luke walks in as we are closing. I have my earbuds in while I'm sweeping, and he comes up behind me and puts his hand on my shoulder. I jump with fright. For some reason, the thought of Tom pops into my head.

I pull out my earbuds. "Gosh, you scared me!"

He's laughing. "Sorry, why are you so jumpy?"

Oh gosh, do I tell him why? Do I tell him what Tom said?

"Um, no reason. Can't be too safe these days, never know who or what's going to appear."

"Are you all right? Still thinking about the fire dream?"

"Yeah, I guess I am."

"How about I get your mind off it? Let's grab a bite to eat somewhere, your choice."

I smile. "Sounds like a wonderful plan. How about 82 Queen?"

"In the mood for a more expensive taste, I see." He winks. "That sounds good."

"Great!" I say excitedly. "But I want to go home and change first." Luke opens the door and I turn around to lock up. I take a deep breath before I turn back around to Luke. *Okay, pull it together. Stop thinking about Tom and enjoy the night with your boyfriend.*

***

The evening starts out nice; we order wine and Luke tells me about his successful surgeries that day. Then out of nowhere, Tyler struts up to our table. He's dressed like a gentleman for once in black slacks and is sporting a confident smile, as if we should be impressed by his new look and the new girl on his arm. She's tall, blonde, and big breasted, wearing a tight dress that's low enough for the world to see her goodies. *Great, first the whole Tom thing, now Tyler has to show up.*

"Well, isn't this a small world?" Tyler says with a cheesy grin.

"Well, what do you know? It is a small world. Too small," I say. I begin to feel a little hot; this is an uncomfortable moment for me.

With a short, agitated tone, I introduce them. "Luke, Tyler. Tyler, Luke." They nod and leave it at that.

"So, Linda, how have you been?" Tyler asks.

"I've been great. My business is going great, Luke and I moved

74

in together, life couldn't be better," I say with a cheesy grin. All this time, Luke is staring at Tyler with a stony face.

"Oh, you guys moved in together?" Tyler's eyebrows rise. "Don't you all think that's a little fast?"

"No, I don't. We're doing just great. Thanks for your concern."

"Well, isn't that just lovely," Tyler says sarcastically. "My date and I better get going. I don't want to keep her waiting. She's insatiable." He leers at her and struts away with her still hanging on his arm. I think he was expecting a different reaction, a jealous reaction from me, maybe?

"Wow, he sure is a good pick," Luke says, smiling and shaking his head.

I laugh. "What in the world was I thinking?"

We finish our Carolina crab cakes and wine in peace after that.

Meeting my ex face-to-face must have affected Luke more than he let on because when we get home, he makes love to me fiercely, almost as if he's trying to prove to me—or himself—that I belong to him. He falls asleep right after, but I lie in bed reading for a while.

My phone pings. It's late, so I figure it's Tom texting me about a case. To my surprise, it's a text from Tyler: "I miss you and still love you. Seeing you again tonight convinced me of that, and somehow, I will get you back."

I stare at the phone in shock and annoyance. *How many times do I have to tell him no?* I delete the text because I don't want to risk Luke seeing it. He'll just worry anyway, and it would cause tension between us. What he doesn't know won't hurt him. Eventually, Tyler will get the picture...I hope.

I turn off the light and pull Luke's arm around me for comfort. He snuggles in close to me. I close my eyes and wait for sleep to take me.

***

I'm in a park at night, walking by myself. I glance at my phone to see the time and date. It's Saturday, 1:55 a.m. I'm trying to figure out where I am, when a loud scream pierces the night. I jump, startled, but I run toward the screeching scream. As I get closer, I can hear a woman yell, "Help me!" Then I hear grunting. I call 911 on my phone as I search for the woman.

I tell the cops what I hear; they tell me to stay on the line so they can track where I am. I'm trying hard to find her, but it's dark out and all I can see are bushes and park benches. Then I hear more grunting. I walk quietly up to a bush, and then I can't believe my eyes. I see a man in gray sweat pants and gray hoodie on top of a girl on a bench. Her face is pressed into the wooden slats, and her blue skirt is around her ankles. His hand is pushing her head into the hard wood.

"Hey, get off her! The cops will be here any second," I yell at the man. He turns around quickly and gets off her. He walks towards me as he pulls up his pants. I glance at the girl, who's lying there, crying. I put my phone in the front pocket of my jeans, hoping 911 is still on the line and can hear everything.

"You bitch. How dare you interrupt me? Did you like what you saw? Is that what you want?" My heart begins to beat fast. I pray the cops show up soon. Why did I come over here and put myself in danger? That's a selfish thing to say, but now I really am in danger.

I look around, realizing I'm on a nature trail in Palmetto Islands County Park. That's why there aren't many people out. Who would walk a nature trail in the middle of the night? I glance at my watch. At 2:00 a.m. to be exact.

"Please don't, by the time you have me on the ground the cops will be here." At least I hope so. It's going to be hard for the cops to find us on this trail. Nothing but trees around us.

"Oh, I promise I'll be quick," he says, smiling. When he smiles, his face shows many wrinkles. This man is not as young as I first thought. His hood is covering his hair, and his eyes are dark and cold.

Oh god, I'm going to have to run, and I don't think I can outrun him. My legs begin to shake with fear. He walks closer to me and starts to pull something out of his back pocket. Before I can think, I kick him in the groin and run. I run as fast as I can. I don't even look back because that would only slow me down.

"You slut, I'm going to catch you." I can hear him running behind me.

"No, no," I whisper out loud as I run. I can hear sirens in the distance. They're going to have to come on foot to find us, and who knows how long that's going to take? I abruptly change direction and run toward the sirens.

Oh God, please let me get there. I can hear his footsteps crushing the leaves. He's gaining on me quick. "Shit." I pump my arms so fast to try and gain speed, but I'm becoming tired. I'm breathing heavy, and my legs feel like jelly.

Then I fall smack down on the paved path, and he's on top of me. "No, no please," I yell. "Help me, someone help me!" I hit and kick at him, trying to get him off.

"You shouldn't have tried to help that girl or you wouldn't be in this situation, now would you?" says the man. Up close, his wrinkles look even worse; his eyes are so dark that they look black. He looks like he's in his early fifties. I'm still kicking and screaming when he hits me hard across the face. My vision blurs. "You were at the wrong place at the wrong time, and now you're going to pay." I start crying and screaming more, hoping someone will hear me. Where are the cops?

"Shut up, you bitch," he snarls and hits me again.

I wake up screaming in my bed.

"Baby, baby, calm down, it's okay." Luke is holding on to me.

"Shhh, it's okay, you're safe." I hold on to Luke tightly, frightened at the thought of how close I came to being raped in my dream.

"I have to call Tom."

"You're not gonna tell me about it?"

I can tell he's upset, so I go ahead and tell him first. He listens closely to me as I talk, looking me in the eyes. He does really want to try and help.

"I'm sorry about the dream. Call Tom and have his men stop him. This is a case where you won't even need to be around because you know exactly where and when it's going to happen."

I stare blankly at him.

"Linda, you're not thinking of going along with him on this case?"

"Well, I was thinking I should go so I can ID the man."

"You can ID him after they catch him! If they catch him raping the girl, you won't even need to ID him." His voice is rising.

"All right, all right I won't go." Even though deep down inside, I want to go and be a part of the action. I sigh and roll my eyes.

"You saw what could happen if you do go; why would you even want to risk that?"

I avoid the question. "I'm going to call Tom now."

His phone rings twice. "Hello, Linda? What's wrong?"

"I had a dream."

"Ok, explain it to me." I tell him the whole story.

"I'm sorry about the dream, but we'll get this guy before anything happens to the girl."

"I know you will."

"And this time, don't even think about going anywhere near the park. I don't want anything to happen to you, and I need to focus on finding this girl and not worry about protecting you." His voice is deep and reassuring.

Why do I get so nervous inside when he says things like this to me? Because he makes me feel safe and I take pleasure in that. Oh God, why am I thinking like this?

Tom notices my pause. "Linda, are you there?"

I catch my breath. "Uh, yeah, sorry. I won't go anywhere near there. Luke already told me not to."

"Good. And about the other day…"

Oh no, why is he bringing this up?

"I'm sorry for what I said and overstepping boundaries. It won't happen again."

I'm relieved that he didn't go into further detail. I don't need any more confusion going on in my head. "It's no problem. Call me when you catch this guy."

"Will do." I hang up the phone and stare at the wall.

Why do I feel an attraction to Tom? I love Luke, but I get a rush of excitement with Tom. It has to be because of his work and how he catches criminals. Or maybe it's the way he feels he needs to protect me? But so does Luke. Ugh, just stop thinking about it!

"Well? What did Tom say?" I almost forgot Luke was lying there right next to me.

"They're going to take care of it. He's going to call me when it's done."

"Good. It's your day off, and it's only seven o'clock. Why don't you try and go back to sleep? You can use the rest."

I shake my head as I yawn. "You're right, I think I'll try."

Before I lie down, Luke grabs my arm and looks intensely into my eyes. "Linda, I love you."

My heart beats so fast, and a smile grows on my face. That's the first time he's said that to me. "I love you too." He leans in and gives me a long, hard kiss. I smile and look into his beautiful blue-green eyes. There's no doubt I love him. I lie back down, and Luke puts his arm around me.

We wake up around eleven thirty and decide to walk to get

some brunch. We go to Kitchen 208. They have a great brunch menu, plus they have a beautiful dining area on their patio.

We start with mimosas. I think we both need to relax a little. We talk about Thanksgiving plans since it's only two weeks away, and to get my mind off the dream.

"My parents always throw a Thanksgiving party at their house. My grandparents, aunts, uncles, and cousins come. This and Christmas are the two times a year where my entire family get together."

"Sounds like a lot of fun. Looks like I'll officially meet everyone then!"

"Yes, you will, but my family is very laid back and a lot of fun. You'll fit right in."

"Good," he says with a smile.

"My mom and dad always do the turkey. My grandparents bring sweet potato casserole. Everybody brings a dish. I figure we can make pumpkin pies."

"That sounds good to me. So two weeks until I meet the whole crew. Let the countdown begin."

I laugh, and my phone pings in my pocket. I take it out to read it. Seriously? It's from Tyler again!

"Who is it babe?"

I sigh. "Tyler."

His face becomes blank. "What does it say?"

"Please talk to me. If I have to come to your house to get you to listen to me, then I will."

Luke's expression turns dark; he's not happy. I don't know why I decide to make the situation worse, but I do. "He texted me that night after he saw me at dinner as well and said he would do whatever it takes to get me back."

Luke's tone is hurt and angry. "Why didn't you tell me?"

"I didn't want to upset you. I never responded to his text, so I was hoping he'd get the picture, but obviously he didn't."

"Give me the phone. I'll tell him myself to leave you alone."

I give Luke the phone with no hesitation. He presses the call button. "Tyler, this is Luke Jackson, Linda's boyfriend. Leave her alone. She doesn't want you anymore; she's with me. If you don't leave her alone, I'll take further actions." He hangs up the phone. I have no idea what he meant by that.

"What do you mean further actions?"

"Well if he doesn't stop, then he's harassing you. Maybe Tom can pull some strings and do something about it."

Tom would not like an ex harassing me, and he probably would do something about it.

"Like a restraining order?"

"Yeah, maybe, and if he doesn't have enough evidence to get one, maybe he can just scare him a little. I know Tom would do that for you. He seems to be very fond of you."

"Luke, please don't start."

"How am I supposed to feel? First Tom, now Tyler. You're mine."

"They know I'm yours. I don't know why Tyler won't stop, but maybe your threat will help."

"And Tom?"

"With Tom, it's business only. He doesn't look at me in any other way." I hate that I'm lying to Luke, but he can't know or else I won't be able to work with Tom anymore.

"He's a man, Linda. I see the way he looks at you."

"I'm not arguing anymore. You have to trust me. We've had this conversation before."

"I do trust you; it's them I don't trust."

Our waiter comes with our check just in time. "Let's go," I say bitterly. I walk out and Luke follows closely behind. We walk home in silence. I'm in front of him, leading the way. We start to walk up the stairs to the front door. Luke grabs my arm and turns me around.

"Listen, I'm sorry. I shouldn't get worked up about it. Tyler texting you set me off. I'm sorry I ranted about Tom. But I'm allowed to be upset about Tyler. I just want to make sure he doesn't cross any lines, and if he does, 'll do something about it."

I have to admit his angry, protective side is very attractive, and I'm getting a little turned on by this. "Oh you will, huh?" I say seductively as I look into his eyes. "What are you going to do about it?"

"I'll do whatever it takes to protect you and show him you're mine." I lean in closer to look him in the eyes. Our noses touching, we begin to breathe heavy. Then he presses me up against the front door and kisses me quick and rough. He puts his key in to unlock the door, and we stumble inside.

We don't even make it to the bed. We strip our clothes off,

and he picks me up and sets me on the carpet in the living room. He's inside me in an instant. Intense, unexpected, make-up sex is always the best. I scratch his back as he thrusts inside me with full force; his hands dig into the carpet, his arm muscles bulging. God, that's so sexy.

I'm moaning at the top of my lungs. Luke says, "Yeah, baby, here it comes." I close my eyes to concentrate on my climax. Our movements are frenzied, our bodies sliding from the sweat. We both yell out with our release, and then Luke gently collapses on me, kissing me softly.

"Wow, that was amazing," I say, out of breath.

He smiles and looks into my eyes. "I love you."

I smile back. "I love you too."

***

As night falls, I start to think about the girl in the park. I picture her eyes closed and tears running down her bruised face. I can't imagine the pain she was feeling. I hope Tom can catch him before he hurts her.

"I don't know if I'm going to be able to go to sleep tonight not knowing what happens."

"I'm sure it'll be hard, but you have to try. You won't find out until morning anyway. I don't think Tom will call you in the middle of the night."

"That's true. Maybe another glass of wine will help me sleep."

"Coming right up!"

After a couple of glasses, the wine is kicking in. We climb into bed, and I close my eyes.

I must have dozed off because I wake up abruptly to the sound of my cell phone ringing. Luke does the same. We both sit up quickly. "I guess I was wrong when I said he'd wait until morning. It's 3:00 a.m."

"Good, I want to know." I pick up the phone.

"Tom, please give me good news."

"Well, we had men all over the walking trails. We captured the man, and he was wearing gray sweatpants and a gray hoodie. Unfortunately, we were too late to completely stop him. He was on top of her when we caught him. I'm sorry, Linda but there were many different walking trails and many different benches. She's in the hospital now getting a rape kit done. The SVU team will now take over the case, but this guy won't be going anywhere.

81

We caught him in action."

"That poor woman," I say as I shake my head.

"I know. I'm upset we couldn't get to her in time. But he might have killed her if we hadn't shown up when we did. We wouldn't have caught him at all if it hadn't been for your dream, so thank you. I'll let you get back to sleep."

"Thanks, Tom for saving her." I hang up the phone and tears begin to form. I picture the poor girl's face slamming into the hard wooden bench. There's no way I can sleep now.

"Are you okay?" Luke asks as he rubs my back.

I nod and tell him what Tom said. "At least you saved her life. Try and lie down and get some sleep."

I lie with my head on his chest, and he rubs my head until my eyes become heavy.

***

Luke and I are watching a movie on the couch. I look outside the tall window. It's dark outside. I can see the streetlights are on, but there's nothing but silence out there. My eyes go back to the movie. All of a sudden, I see something move out of the corner of my eye outside the window. My heart jumps and so do I.

"Linda, what's wrong?"

"I swear I just saw something move outside." We both look outside the floor-to-ceiling window flanking our front door and see a black figure run across our yard. "Oh shit!" I yell.

"Go call the cops," Luke says. "I'm going out there to see who this is."

"No, don't go out there and leave me in here alone! What if there are more men and one comes in here while you're looking!"

"I don't want this guy to get away. He runs upstairs and comes back with two handguns. "Here, take this and lock the door," he says, shoving one of the guns into my hand. "The cops will be here quick, call them now." I'm so scared my legs and hands are shaking, but I dial 911. Luke runs out with his gun, holding it up as he walks around the house. I shut the door and twist the dead bolt to lock it.

After I call the cops, I call Tom right away. I crouch behind the couch, looking at the window to see if I can see anything. I'm frozen and can't move.

"Tom, you need to get over quick. We saw a guy dressed in black run around our yard. Luke is out there now trying to catch him. Please hurry."

"Luke left you alone?"

"That's beside the point. Get over here!"

"I'm already in the car. Stay on the phone with me until I get there." Thank God for Tom.

Then all of a sudden, there's a loud BANG on the window. I scream. My heart is pounding, and my hands are sweating so badly that the phone is slipping out of my hand.

"What happened? Are you okay?"

"I think somebody is trying to break in. I heard a loud bang on the window, as if they threw a big rock. Oh my God, oh my God," is all I can say as I'm shaking.

"Linda, stay focused and strong. I'm almost there."

I hear another loud BANG and a crash. The glass breaks.

My loud, obnoxious alarm goes off. I take a big breath as I quickly sit up in bed. I'm sweating and short of breath.

"It's okay. Tell me what happened," Luke says softly.

I tell him about the dream. "But I only got halfway through the dream. How am I going to prevent it from happening if I don't know how it ends? It's like the fire dream. I need to meet with Tom today to discuss this with him."

"That's probably a good idea."

I widen my eyes in shock. "Really? You actually agree that I should meet with Tom?"

"Yes, because this one puts us in danger. It puts *you* in danger. I need all the help I can get protecting you."

I smile. "I'll let you know what he says. I'm going to call him now and have him come into my shop today."

Luke gets up and goes to the bathroom. I pause before I pick up the phone. Hearing the crashing sound of that window is taunting me. Why would Luke leave me alone? Who's after us and why? And why, behind all of this fear, do I think of Tom?

Chapter 10

Tom walks into the shop as soon as it opens. "Sorry, I'm early. I didn't want to wait to hear about the dream."

"Good morning. It's okay. I want to get it over with anyway."

"Before we start, I checked on the girl from the other night, and she's doing much better. A few headaches here and there, but she's going to be fine."

"Oh, that's great."

He smiles and nods. "Okay, so what happened in your dream last night?"

I tell him the dream with as much detail as I can.

"The problem is I don't know when this guy will try to break in, or what time. All I know is that it was dark."

"Well you can try and dream it again to get a glance at your clock and calendar. For now, I'll get a cop to be on watch near your house at night."

I close my eyes and put my head down. "I'm getting sick of playing the waiting game. Why do people keep messing with me? Do you think this is related to the guy I first started dreaming about?"

Tom puts his warm, soft hand over mine. My skin tingles. "I know, and I wish I could do more about it. I'll make sure one of our best officers is there to keep watch. If anything happens, you call me just like you did in your dream, and I'll come right away."

I look him in his eyes. "Thank you, Tom." He holds my gaze, looking deep into my eyes. My heart starts to beat rapidly. I cough and turn to look around the shop. I move my hand out from beneath his. "Well, I need to get back to work. Thank you for coming down here to help me with this. I'll try and dream it tonight and get a better sense of when it's going to happen."

With a look of disappointment, Tom gets up. "It's no problem. Can I get a coffee to go?"

"Sure." I hand him his coffee and he leaves.

May comes walking in all giddy a few hours later. I feel like it has been months since I've seen her. I give her a big hug. "Aren't you a sight for sore eyes!"

"I know, it has been a while. I've been pretty busy with school and finals are coming up. I've been studying and working hard."

"How are your grades?"

"Good, it's just stressful and hard work to keep them up. How are things with Luke and the FBI?"

I tell her all about the job, Luke, and what happened with Tyler, and Tom comes into the conversation. When I bring up Tom's name, I feel a smile forming.

"Linda, I know that look. That's the same look you had when you first told me about Luke. Same shy smile, same blush. What's the deal with this Tom?"

I quickly remove the smile and shake my head. "Nothing is going on. He's just a business partner."

Her eyes narrow. "I'm your sister; don't lie to me."

I put my head down and sigh. "Okay, but you cannot say a word to anyone." I tell her the things he has said to me in the past, how he has the same dreams, how he's protective of me, and how I feel when I'm around him.

She looks at me with one eyebrow raised. "Sounds a little more than business to me."

"I don't understand it. I love Luke, and it's not the same feeling with Tom. What I feel for Luke is passion and love; with Tom, it's just an innocent crush."

"Whatever you say, sis." Then her eyes get big and she grins. "Hey, I have an idea. Why don't I get this Tom guy off your hands? Maybe set up a meet-and-greet with me and Tom and introduce us. I'm single, and so is he, and he's an FBI agent."

I don't smile even a little bit. "No," I say flatly.

Her smile fades. "Why not? You can't have them both, and it's not fair to Luke anyway. This could help break those feelings for Tom."

I shake my head. "He's ten years older than you and it just wouldn't be a good idea. If something were to happen between you two, it would make it awkward with me. It would be hard to work with Tom knowing he's with you." *Why do I feel so defensive about this? It's almost as if I'm jealous. Why should I be jealous?*

May sighs. "All right, all right, it was just an idea. Don't get so uptight about it." I avoid commenting back. "Well, I just wanted to come and see how you were doing with everything. We need to have a girl's night soon."

"I agree, we definitely need a girl's night; thanks for stopping by. Let me get you a coffee to go."

***

I'm crouching behind the couch, holding the phone so tight I feel my circulation cutting off. Luke is outside, who knows where, looking for whoever is out there. The sound of the glass breaking makes me freeze with terror. "Linda, Linda, what happened? I heard a loud crash."

I stare at the broken window waiting for someone to enter. I barely hear Tom's voice. "Linda, hello, are you there? Fuck, hold on, I'm almost there." He sounds aggravated.

I drop the phone and pick up the gun Luke gave me. I stand up and point it at the window. Whoever comes through won't make it very far. I hold the small 9mm gun straight, my hands shaking as I aim at nothing.

My phone is ringing. I glance down and see that it's Tom. I also notice that the time is three in the morning. I don't answer the phone. Instead, I quickly look at the calendar on my phone. It's Thursday, November, 13th.

I hear the crackling sound of glass being stepped on. I look up and see a man in a black ski mask standing in front of me with a knife in his hand. He's hunching over, ready to attack.

I point my gun at him. Hands shaking, I try to pull it together. Obviously, Luke and Tom won't be here in time to save me. He walks closer to me and begins to smile. His teeth are stained black, probably from smoking so much. "It's time to finally end things, Linda. Even when this is over, you still won't be safe. There are others out there."

Others? What the fuck does that mean?

This could be my one chance to shoot the guy and get this over with! Come on, Linda, stop being a baby and pull the fucking trigger.

I finally gain some courage and smile back at him as I start to pull the trigger.

"Linda, STOP!" It's Tom's voice I hear, but all I see is the man in front of me.

The man turns, and I pull the trigger, shooting him in the arm. He drops the knife and grabs his arm. He slowly gets up and looks me in the eyes. "You bitch."

He jumps at me and knocks me down, and the gun falls out of my hand. He punches me hard. I feel as if I've been hit with a rock. A sharp pain immediately over takes my head.

Tom is trying to get the guy off me, but he's fighting him. Tom kicks him in the stomach, getting him off me, and I roll out and away from the both of them.

Tom is on top of the guy, punching him in the face. The look in Tom's eyes is full of anger. His face is red, and his lips are pressed tight as he beats this guy into the ground.

"How does it feel to be on the other side of a beating?" Tom says in a deep, vindictive voice. Then he gives him one last blow to his face.

Tom turns the guy over and puts cuffs on his hands and then keeps him there. He gets up and looks at me as I'm crouched in the corner.

He walks over to me and puts out his hand. I take his hand as I look him in the eyes. He just saved my life. I feel a rush of gratitude. He puts his hands on my face. "Are you okay?"

His soft tone sends tingles through my body. I nod my head as tears start to fall. Tom hugs me, and I put my hands around his waist, hugging him back.

"You're safe now," he whispers softly in my ear. The soft touch of his breath on my ear brings chills to my body.

"What the hell is going on?" Luke says as he walks through the window into the living room. He looks down at the guy in cuffs and then back at me and Tom.

"What's going on is you left Linda all by herself. This man attacked her after she shot him in the arm. I was here in time to save her," Tom says angrily.

Luke's eyes widen, and he rushes to me and pulls me into his arms. "Are you all right? I'm so sorry I left you alone. I just thought I could catch the guy before he could attack." I rest my head against his chest.

"You shouldn't have left her alone. What were you thinking?"

Luke quickly turns around, his tone angry. "Don't you tell me how I should take care of my family. I was trying to stop anything from happening." He throws up his hands.

Tom gets in Luke's face. "You should have thought about Linda and stayed with her to protect her."

Luke's hands are slowly becoming fists. I move between the two guys. "Please stop, the both of you. You both helped me. We caught the guy, and that's all that matters."

I look up at Tom. "Thank you." He looks at me and sighs and shakes his head. He backs off and calls backup to come help him sweep the scene. I turn back around to Luke and stare up into his eyes.

"I'm sorry, Linda."

My alarm wakes me up, and my whole body twitches. I'm drenched in sweat from my sticky hair to my sticky shirt.

"What's wrong? Did you finish the dream?"

I stare blankly at the wall, not sure what to think of that dream. Luke leaving me and returning just as the guy is caught…it seems obscure, and I have an unsettling feeling about that. It's way too coincidental. But Luke loves me, and there's no way he'd ever be involved in anything that would put me in any danger. Then Tom protecting me and saving me. *What the hell is going on?*

Luke tapping my shoulder brings me out of my daze. "Linda, are you okay?"

I slowly turn my head and look into his soft, friendly eyes. "Yes, I finished the dream, and I'm not sure how I feel about it."

"Tell me." Luke shakes his head in dissatisfaction at what I'm describing.

He interrupts me. "I'll never leave your side. I promise, when this happens, I'll be by you the entire time, protecting you. I don't like the thought of Tom saving the day either, but it's good to know he'd do anything to save you if I wasn't around to do it."

"I couldn't believe you left me. I was devastated and scared to death."

He pulls me into his chest, kisses me on the forehead, and whispers, "I'll never leave you."

I hope you're right. I look up and kiss him. "Thursday is only two days away."

"Call Tom now to let him know." I nod in agreement. I call him and keep it short and sweet.

I sigh as I hang up and look over at Luke. "Well, now the waiting game starts once again."

"It'll be okay. I'm going to get up and put the coffee on."

I watch him get out of bed, wearing only his navy blue boxer briefs. I look him up and down, in awe at the muscles in his back and butt and how tight they are. *I'm overreacting to the dream. I mean, yeah, he left me, but he wanted to catch the guy before anything happened.* I begin to think deeper. *But he was gone for a long time. Wouldn't he come back to check on me?* I sigh and shake my head quickly. *Stop doubting Luke. He's there to protect me, not harm me.*

As I get out of bed to start my morning routine, the feelings of doubt and insecurity overwhelm me.

***

The next two days seem to go by in slow motion. Waiting to be attacked is not an easy feeling to deal with. It's all I can think about. What if the cops don't get him? What if I get attacked? Do I shoot the guy? Will Luke leave? Will the guy even show up? All these questions run through my mind all day and night. Sleep is not even an option.

As soon as Luke and I get home after work Wednesday, the cops are already parked down the street in unmarked cars. Since it will be dark, I hope the guy won't notice the cops and get scared off.

Tom calls as soon as we walk through the front door. "Did you see the cop cars?" he asks as soon as I answer the phone.

"Yes, I did, thank you."

"Don't be afraid tonight. We'll take care of this. Unlike in your dream, I'll be right across the street. I've already talked to one of your neighbors, and they're allowing me to stakeout in their yard and hide behind some bushes. If I see this guy, I'll be able to stop him right away."

That makes me feel safe and comfortable.

"Okay, thank you, Tom."

Luke stares at me, waiting for an explanation. "The cops are set in place, and Tom will be across the street at the Millers'."

Luke rolls his eyes. "I figured Tom wouldn't be far away."

"It's more protection for us, Luke."

"I know," he says coldly and walks into the kitchen.

Luke seems frustrated as he pulls out a glass pan and chicken from the fridge. He slams the chicken on the counter and sighs.

I walk over to him slowly. His back is toward me, and I rest my hands on his shoulders. "Luke, it's okay to be scared. But everything is going to be all right." I honestly don't know why I'm so calm about this, but I feel a sense of strength.

He turns around and looks me in the eyes. He puts his hand

on my cheek. "I'm not scared. I just want to make sure nothing happens to you. That is the only thing that's running through my head: your protection."

I softly graze his lips with a kiss. "I have you. I know I'm safe."

He smiles softly, showing no teeth, and kisses me again. "So what kind of chicken are we having tonight?" I ask to try to change the subject.

After dinner, I have a hard time staying up. The lack of sleep is catching up with me, and my eyes are getting heavy as we watch TV on the couch. "Take a little nap, babe. I'll stay up."

I lay my head in his lap and close my eyes.

After what feels like two minutes, I wake up to Luke softly shaking me. "It's almost time; we need to get ready." I get up quickly. "We need to go ahead and prepare ourselves for a fight. We don't know how this is going to play out."

Luke goes upstairs to get out his two guns and hands me one. Feeling the gun in my hand makes me feel panic and anxiety. My heart starts to beat fast.

"It's okay, Linda. Everything is going to be ok."

I hope you're right.

We crouch to the side of the couch, looking at the door. My entire body is tingling with fear. My hands are sweating, and if I had to shoot someone right now, I don't know if my hands could keep steady. *Stop being so scared. You'll be okay,* I keep telling myself.

Luke decides to look out the window, but he sees nothing.

I glance over at the clock next to the window; it reads 2:58 a.m. My heart begins to beat faster the closer it gets to three.

It is so silent and dark that all I can hear is my own breathing.

Then all of a sudden, we hear people yelling, "Stop right there!" We look out of he window and see figures running across the yard. Luke runs out the door.

"No, Luke, wait!"

Shit, he really left me. I follow him out the open door. I see Luke running after a guy dressed in all black. Then I see Tom running from across the street to chase after Luke. I walk down my front steps.

"Go back inside! It's not safe yet," he yells, but he doesn't stop running.

My body freezes in fear. He's still out there. *Hurry, move your legs back inside.*

I'm so scared because I'm once again alone. I'm walking back up my front steps when I freeze in fear.

"I've been waiting for you," a dreadful, dark voice says from behind me. I immediately turn, and there he is, the same guy from the dream.

I scream as loud as I can, "Luke, Tom!" and start to run back up the steps. I try to shut the door before he can follow me inside, but I'm too late. He slams the door open as I back slowly into the house.

I look around for the gun. I can't remember what I did with it. It must be on the floor somewhere. He slowly walks toward me. "I've been watching you. How can a woman solve all these cases in such a short time? Not once have you messed up. Linda Brown saves the day once again. It's all over the papers. What's your secret? Are you a psychic? If so, then you must have seen me coming. The cops were already here. Nice try, I must say. But I'm still here in front of you, and I'm going to end you."

As I walk back in terror, staring at his nasty teeth, I trip over something. I realize it's the gun. How am I going to get this gun without him attacking me? I don't see this ending well. I'm going to have to fight.

He looks down at the gun, grins, and shakes his head slowly. "Oh no, don't you even think about it. You won't have enough time to get the gun."

Luke, Tom, someone, please help me!

I quickly drop to the floor to grab the gun. I get a hand on it, but the man kicks me in the stomach, and I cry out. "I told you, you wouldn't have a chance to get the gun."

I cradle up in a ball as he bends over me.

"You better stop right there, you son of a bitch." I'm so relieved to hear Luke's voice. The man turns around, and I grab the gun. I stay in the cradle position so the guy doesn't know.

"What do you know, the boyfriend finally comes to the rescue."

"Don't move an inch or I'll shoot," Luke says, full of anger. I slowly start to get into a sitting position so I can shoot if I need to.

"This is working out better than I thought; two for the price of one." I see the man slowly reaching for his back pocket.

I stand up behind him, point the gun at his back, and say, "Not so fast, asshole." I shoot the gun, aiming for his knee. As he falls to the floor, his head smacks the hard surface.

I look up to see Luke staring at me with big eyes. He's in shock that I actually pulled the trigger. I look down at the gun in my hand and drop it to the floor. Luke quickly disarms the man as he holds his knee and moans in pain. Tom walks in then; what perfect timing.

He points his gun at the man, looks at me, then Luke, and then back down to the guy on the floor. Luke points to me and says, "She shot him. He was going for his gun to shoot me. She is so brave." He smiles at me.

Tom raises his eyebrows. "I'm very impressed."

Luke's smile abruptly fades. "I'm so sorry. I was right on his heels, but I lost him on the next street over. He must have circled back around," he raises his hands helplessly. I should tell him that it's not his fault, but part of me is still upset that he left me like that.

Just then, several cops come through the front door. "Let's get this guy cuffed and taken away," he says to them, and then he turns to me. "Linda, you saved the day." He grins at me.

"The guy told me he was following me in the papers. He knew there was something different about me. That was why he was after me. Tom, how could someone put two and two together like that? I mean, how could he make such a big guess as to me being "psychic?" The only people who know about what I can do is you, Luke, Sarah, Bobby, and my family."

Could this mean someone I'm close to is leaking information? Why would anyone leak something that important about my life? And leak it to people who want to hurt me? Why is this happening to me? I get a sick feeling in my stomach.

"I don't know, Linda. He obviously followed all of your cases, but still no one could possibly have that thought run through their mind. But then again, he is crazy."

"It doesn't make any sense," Luke chimes in.

"Well, we caught him, so there isn't anything to worry about now. We'll find out more about him in interrogation. Hopefully, he's got a record so we can keep him in lockup."

"Hopefully?" I feel like I'm going to throw up. "What if they cut him loose and he comes after me again?"

"He'll be charged attempted murder, and to help the case you might have to testify against and tell the jury what he did and said to you."

"Great," I say with a sigh, and tears form in my eyes. "This was hard enough to get through, and now I have to see him again face-to-face?"

"I'm sorry, Linda. If we can find enough evidence with past crimes he's committed, then you won't have to. I'll call you with an update."

I just shake my head and sit on the couch. Luke shuts the door behind Tom and locks it and comes to me on the couch. He holds me in his arms while I cry. I was brave enough to pull the trigger, but I was scared to death. It was my first time shooting a person. It's going to leave a mark for a while.

***

Luke and I both are taking Friday off and going to spend the weekend with my parents. I need to see them and get my mind off everything. All four of us are having conversations about the cases I've solved, about how May is doing, and about Thanksgiving. Then Luke says, "Mr. Brown, do you mind if I speak to you alone for a moment?"

I give Luke a curious look, and he just smiles. I look over at Mom after they leave the room. "I wonder what that's about?"

She smiles and her bright blue eyes light up. "Marriage!" she says excitedly.

"No, really, you think? We haven't even been dating a year."

Marriage? I mean, I've thought about it, but I figured we both were thinking later on, in the future. But then again the thought of marrying the love of my life causes those butterflies in my stomach to go crazy again.

"How many times have I told you? There's absolutely no timeline for love; it can happen whenever and wherever."

"You're right about that." My face brightens as a smile grows big on my face. "Now I'm getting excited! I wonder how he's going to ask me?"

"I'm excited for you! I bet whatever he does, it'll be so romantic."

Just then, they both walk back in with grins on their face. I glance over at Mom, and she winks at me. "So, boys, what was that about?" I ask innocently.

"Oh, just guy talk," Dad says as he smiles.

Later that night, as Luke and I are preparing for bed, my phone rings; it's Tom.

"Maybe he found out something about that man!"

"Hey, Tom, please tell me you found some dirt on him?"

"Actually, we did. Once we ran his fingerprints through the system, we found out he has been arrested in the past for kidnapping. The kids' bodies were never found, so he got out within a few years. We have a warrant and are going to search all the places he has lived since then. If we find those bodies, we're golden. We've been interrogating him for hours. He's slowly starting to break. I think you'll be in the clear about having to testify."

I feel like a weight has been lifted from my shoulders. "Oh, thank you so much, Tom."

"Anything for you, Linda." I smile into the phone and hang up.

I tell Luke what Tom said. "Well, I'm glad he's doing his job."

"Me too." I lie in Luke's arms, trying not to think of all that has happened within the last twenty-four hours, but it's hard.

I shut my eyes and begin to get a sick feeling in my stomach that this isn't over yet. The fire dream has yet to come true. Things just don't seem right, and I think more people are involved. I have a feeling it's someone close to me, someone who knows about my talent.

Chapter 11

It's Thanksgiving Day and one of the best times to spend with family. I've been baking homemade pumpkin pies for the past few hours. The warm, sweet pumpkin spice aroma is filling our house. My favorite part of Thanksgiving is the pumpkin pies.

Luke is upstairs trying on outfits to pick the "perfect" one because he's meeting my entire family. He's a nervous wreck.

"Okay, babe, what about this one? I want to look very clean-cut and respectable."

"Oh, you can do that all on your own with your personality; you don't need specific clothes to show that side of you, it's natural." I smile at him.

He kisses me on the lips. "Thank you, but for real, what about this one?"

He's in khaki pants, a collared, button-up navy blue shirt, and brown dress shoes. He looks like a gentleman and very handsome.

I raise one eyebrow. "You look very good. I like this outfit. It's perfect for this occasion."

He looks at his outfit one more time. "Okay, if you like it, then I like it."

"I'm going to get dressed and then we can head on over!"

"I just want to get this meeting everyone thing over with. Then I can smoothly charm my way into the family."

"You'll fit right in."

We pull up to my parents' house. The driveway is packed full of cars. Luke comes around and opens the car door for me. I was a little nervous myself. I've never brought a boyfriend home to meet my entire family. *I wonder how they're going to act?*

Mom greets us at the door with hugs. The house smells like turkey, stuffing, and cranberry sauce. This house has such a homey feeling. The fireplace in the living room is flickering. I see my some of my cousins over on the couch talking with glasses of wine in their hands.

Luke and I walk into the yellow kitchen, which is full of appetizers and alcohol. I place the pumpkin pies in the fridge. I glance over and smile at May, who's sitting and talking to my cousin Penny.

My sweet grandparents come up first, and my grandma asks, "Who's this handsome man?"

I introduce Luke to my grandparents and aunts, who wanted to eavesdrop. They all begin to talk to him and ask questions. I sneak away and pour us glasses of wine. We then make our rounds around the house, talking to my family. Laughs, smiles, and cheers are all taking place. Football is on in the TV room, where most of the men are. The girls are gathered around the fire talking about boys, jobs, and life.

When dinner is officially ready, we all circle up, and hold hands. I glance quickly around. I see twenty beautiful people and smiling faces. I have such a wonderful family. As is tradition, my dad says grace.

We dig in to all the wonderful food.

By the end of the night, the tone has changed. We're lying on couches and the floor with stuffed bellies and liquor in our systems; we all look like we're going to pass out. People start saying their goodbyes.

***

Monday comes too fast after such a wonderful weekend with family, but unfortunately, we have to keep moving along. Sarah, Bobby, and I start to put up the Christmas decorations in the shop. I'm hanging colored strands of lights around the counter when Tom walks in with a look of concern.

"Hey, there. I hope you had a great Thanksgiving," he says to me.

"It was nice to take a break from solving crimes."

"I'm sorry to put a damper on that, but we need your help with an important case."

I shrug my shoulders. "I figured that's why you were coming in today. What's the case?"

"There's a man who's targeting college girls. He has already murdered three girls within the past three weeks. Each murder occurred at 3:00 a.m. They were murdered in their dorm rooms. Somehow, he's making his way into their rooms. We need to catch this guy before he murders again."

"College girls? My sister, May, is in college! What college is he targeting?" All I can think of is May and how I need to protect her.

"Two from Charleston Southern University and one from," he hesitates before he says the next one, "the College of Charleston."

"What!" Tears immediately start to sting my eyes.

"Linda, this is why I came to you. I need your help catching this guy."

"Of course I'll help. Do you have information on these girls, what they look like, and their names?" We sit down and he proceeds to show me all three girls and gives me the dorm buildings and room numbers they stayed in.

"Okay, I'll try and dream about these girls, the schools, and the time they were murdered to see if I can ID the killer." I can't really think straight; all I see in my head is May's sweet, smiling face.

"That sounds like a good idea. Again, I'm sorry to bring this upon you during the holiday season."

"It's okay. So you don't have one description of this guy?"

"No, we don't. There were no witnesses in any of the murders. None of their family or friends saw anything unusual. Two of the three had boyfriends, but their alibis checked out. One boyfriend was up late studying with a friend for a test, and the other one was in his own dorm with his roommate. It just so happened that one girl didn't have a roommate, and the other two had roommates that were out of town. You are our last hope. We just need something small, anything will help." I can tell he's desperate and really does need my help.

"I'll try as hard as I can. May could possibly be a target. I mean, I know there are a lot of girls on campus, but he has already targeted there once."

"Thank you, Linda. We'll protect her. Call me if you find out anything." I smile and nod, and he leaves.

As soon as I get home I need to research the colleges and get a visual of the campus and their dorm rooms and how they are laid out. You can take a virtual tour on the internet for just about any place nowadays.

Sarah glances over at me and gives me a questioning nod to make sure I'm okay. I nod back and smile.

I call May to see how she's doing. "Hey, sis, what's up?"

"Nothing, just at work and thought I'd give you a call to see how you're doing. Is everything going okay at school?"

"Uhh, yeah, everything is fine. Why?"

"No reason. Is your roommate going to be with you for the next few nights?"

"Yes, as far as I know she is. Why, what's going on?"

"Nothing, just make sure you're not alone, okay? I'm helping Tom with a case, and college girls in the area are being targeted. Please make sure you and your roommate don't go anywhere alone."

"Oh shit, who were the girls?"

"That's classified information I can't share. I don't want to scare you anymore than I have already. I just want you to be safe. Please do what I ask, okay?"

"I will." May sounds frightened. I would be too. Maybe I shouldn't have told her, but I wanted to give her a heads up so she wouldn't be alone.

"If you see anything, and I mean anything out of the ordinary, please call me right away. I love you, May, and I'm going to catch this guy before he hurts another girl."

"I'll make sure a group of us stick together until you tell me he's caught. Thank you for warning me. I'll call you often or send you texts just so you know I'm safe."

I smile into the phone. It's as if she can read my mind. "I was just going to tell you that. I want a text before you go to bed and as soon as you wake up, plus a few throughout the day."

"You've got it, boss," May says.

"I love you. Stay safe."

"Will do and love you too."

To even think there is a possibility May could be in danger makes me sick to my stomach. But it doesn't make me sad. It makes me furious. I'm going to do whatever it takes to help catch this guy, and soon.

I try to act normal throughout the rest of the day, but my customers seem to notice something is wrong. If I had a dollar for every person that asks me if I'm okay, I'd be rich. I keep looking at the pictures, trying to memorize every detail about the girls. It helps my dreams if I really know the details. One blond, one brunette, and one redhead; no similarities there.

I leave work a little early. Bobby and Sarah close up for me. I decide to make dinner before Luke gets home. As the chicken is cooking in the oven, I do some research on the colleges and get familiar with Charleston Southern. I'm already familiar with the College of Charleston campus.

Luke walks in and is surprised to see me home early. "Mmm, something smells wonderful in here." He smiles at me and says, "This is a nice surprise to come home to after a long day of surgeries. What are you doing home early?" I give him a half smile. He can tell by the look on my face that something is wrong. He rushes over to me. "What's wrong?"

All I can do is hug him and cry. I explain everything to him. "I know May's safety is one of the most important things to you. 'll be here for you every step of the way."

"Thank you. It feels so good to know I have your support."

"You'll always have my support, baby, forever."

Forever? That immediately brings up marriage in my mind. I wonder if that's what the talk with dad was about? He still hasn't mentioned it, but I'd totally say yes if he were to ask me.

I smile and kiss him. "All right, time for some good chicken!"

He helps me set the table and we sit down to eat. "So how was work? You said you had a lot of surgeries?"

"Yes, I had to repair two ACLs and do some work on a shoulder."

"Well, they have the best surgeon in town!"

He smiles and continues to eat, but I can't get down much food. Thinking of May and the other girls brings a sick feeling to my stomach.

Luke helps me with the dishes afterward, and I decide to show him the pictures of the girls.

"So how are you planning on doing this?" Luke asks.

"Well, I guess I'm going to think about them and try to put myself in their positions, like I've done with past dreams."

"Good thing I'll be right there for you when you wake up."

I smile at Luke. When he says things like that, I know I'll be okay.

Night falls quickly, and I become tired. Luke and I climb into

“I’m sorry, I didn’t dream about a single thing last night. I’m not going to give up though. I’ll try again tonight. Maybe it will help if I come down to your office today and look at all the information you have gathered? It might give me more insight into what we need to find out.”

“Sounds good. Meet me down here at one.”

***

“Linda, thank you for coming. Are you sure you want to do this?” Tom comes up to me and shakes my hand when I get to the station.

“Yes, I want to help you catch this guy.”

“I have to warn you that we received some new information today that you won’t like.”

My stomach drops instantly. “Please tell me it’s not May.”

“No, there wasn’t another murder, but we got a lead on what the guy looks like.” I feel a little relief but know his next comment isn’t going to be a pleasant one.

“Okay, what’s the new information?”

“We talked to the roommate of Ashley, the last girl murdered. She told us about a guy she saw in their building at 2:00 a.m. the night before Ashley was murdered. She got up to go to the bathroom down the hall and saw a man entering the stairwell. She left to go home for the weekend the next morning, and Ashley was murdered that night. The description she gave us was of a tall man wearing all black. She thought he looked a little old to be there, but it's a coed dorm, and she thought maybe it was a student's father." My head is about to explode and I feel like I'm going to vomit. Tom offers me water and I sip it slowly.

"How is this possible? We've already caught two different men who liked to dress in black and terrorize women. This can't be a coincidence."

"We think this guy was working with the ones we caught."

Again that phrase pops into my head, "There are others out there." *There's no way this is happening.*

"Is there something you're not telling me, Linda?" I tell him about the dream I had awhile back, and how every dream seems to be connected back to me. "The man in my dreams told me there are others."

"Well, that explains the connection to the victims," says Tom.

"Connection, what connection?" I'm almost afraid to ask.

"The names of the victims. The first victim was Danielle Luke, the second victim was Linda Flowers, and the third victim was Ashley Brown."

"Each victim had a connection to my name or the name of someone I love." I start to get light-headed and begin to see black spots, then I feel dizzy and my legs go weak.

Next thing I know, I'm waking up on the couch with my jacket over me and Tom right by my side offering me more water.

"I'm so sorry to get you involved in this. I should have just kept going and not told you, but I was worried about your family. I'm afraid he'll target one of them next."

"May!" I have to call her, but Tom stops me when I try to stand up.

"We'll keep cop cars outside of her dorm and your parents' house."

"Why is this happening to me?"

"Do you have any friends or ex-boyfriends that would want to hurt you? Have you had any past enemies?"

Tyler is the first person that comes to my mind.

I swallow hard, and it feels like I'm swallowing a rock, "My ex, Tyler, was jealous of Luke and told me he would make me his again one day. But Luke called him and threatened him. I haven't heard from Tyler since."

His eyebrows raise and his voice deepens, "What do you mean threatened?"

"He just said something that would scare him away."

"That could have given him a reason to get angry and try to hurt you both. Give me his number and address."

"Tyler is a jealous guy, but I don't think he'd be crazy enough to try and hurt us."

Tom ignores that statement. "Number and address, please." I give him the information.

"We're going to question him. Maybe while I'm at it, I'll rough him up a little bit for being an ass to you," he says with a wink.

I give a half smile and change the subject. "I'll try again tonight with my dreams. I just want this to be over once and for all. I'll call you if I find out anything."

"Thanks, and I'll call you after we talk to Tyler."

It's hard for me to drive home after all that information, but I'm angry more than anything. I want this to be over and that asshole to be caught. I call May and ask her to come over as soon as she can. I make it home before Luke or May. I sit at the kitchen table, gather my thoughts, and get ready to tell them both.

By the time Luke gets home, I have tears running down my face. He rushes to me and pulls me into his arms. He looks me in the eyes and says, "Whatever it is, I'll help you get through it."

"I want to tell you and May both at the same time. She's on her way and should be here in a few minutes."

"What does May have to do with this?"

"You'll see." And that's all I can say. I sit there with my head on his shoulder. I have to stop crying so I can be strong for May. She'll need support.

When May walks through the door, I run up and give her a big hug. "Sis, what's going on? I told my professors that I wouldn't be there the rest of the week because of family issues, so I'm staying here." I sit both of them down at the table and start from the beginning. I tell them how the man who wears black with a black ski mask has been in almost every dream and tied to almost every murder. I tell them there are multiple men involved. I tell them about the murdered girls and their names.

"I seem to be tied to the dreams and murders somehow. I don't know how many of these guys are involved, but they've taken it to the next level with these most recent victims, finding girls with names connected to my life. May, I brought you here because I don't want them going after family next. I need to find this guy and put this to rest. There's something about me this guy wants. He's testing me, sending in different murderers, while he's their puppet master. He's playing some sort of sick game. I'm just afraid of how it's going to end."

"I can't believe this is happening," says Luke. May starts crying.

"May, honey, we'll catch this guy. You'll be safe here with me and Luke."

"It's not me I'm worried about, it's you. I don't know what I'd do if-"

"Shh, don't even finish that sentence because nothing bad is going to happen. The only thing that will happen is this guy is going to end up behind bars, or dead."

"Dead sounds better to me," says Luke.

"Let's have some dinner and then try to get some rest. I need to dream about this tonight so we can catch this guy."

***

I find myself outside of a dorm building at what looks like the College of Charleston. I walk into the dorm building quietly and look at the clock. It reads 2:45 a.m. Shit, I don't have much time. This dorm is huge. How am I going to find who he's going to attack next? I look around for signs, something to point me in the right direction. I look over at the wall and notice the mailboxes.

Each mailbox has the suite number and the names of the occupants. I look carefully at each name to see if I can find something that will lead me to his next victim. That's when I see it, Linda May, suite 214. Both mine and my sister's name, perfect! This has to be it. I rush up the stairs. I find the room number, but the door is shut, and it doesn't look like anyone is here yet. I decide to hide on the other side of the vending machine in the hall and wait. Only a few minutes later, I see him. He's dressed in his famous black outfit. He picks the lock of room 214. I pull my phone out of my pocket to check the date: tomorrow night! Now I've got him, and I really need to wake up because I don't want to see what's coming next. I tell myself to wake up. "Linda, wake up, wake up." I close my eyes and say it again.

I wake up with a deep sigh and sit up in bed. "I've got him!" I say when Luke wakes up and looks at me. "I know where he's going next and who his next victim is. We can get him for good, Luke."

"Call Tom and have the police take care of it. You've done your job. Now they'll do theirs and catch him."

I call Tom right away and tell him the whole story. He tells me they'll clear the girls living in that dorm and post officers in the room to lie in wait. When the murderer walks in, he'll be in for a shock.

Luke and I get up and head downstairs. May comes down just as Luke is finishing cooking breakfast. The three of us don't talk much. We chomp down breakfast as if we haven't eaten in days. Luke's phone pings.

"I've got to head to the hospital now. Emergency surgery for a young boy who broke his leg in a bicycle accident."

"Oh no, poor boy. Drop us off on the way?"

"Of course, babe," he says with a smile.

I glance over at May, poking her fork into her eggs. "I want you to come to work with me today. I'll put you to work and even pay you."

A small smile starts to form on her lips. "Gee, thanks." She sighs and puts her head down.

"Listen, I know my shop is the last place you want to be, but I can't let you out of my sight until this is over."

"I know and I understand. I'm just anxious for it to be over."

"So are we."

We quickly get dressed, and Luke drops us off at work. We're running late, so thank goodness Sarah and Bobby are there to open up.

May and I are cleaning up after the breakfast rush when Tyler comes shoving into the shop. He stalks toward me, face red, lips pressed tightly together. *Oh shit.*

"Really, now you're telling the cops on me? I got the message with Luke and haven't bothered you since. What the fuck, Linda?"

Bobby steps in. "Whoa, buddy, take it easy here. Why don't you two take this outside; we don't want to scare away the customers." I glance around at people staring at us. Good thing Bobby looks like he's a bodybuilder. Tyler doesn't question him when he ushers us toward the door and escorts us outside.

"Look, I'm sorry you got questioned. There's a case going on and it involves me. They're just checking people from my past. Now please leave my shop before I really call the cops."

"Are you in some kind of trouble?" His expression turns to one of concern.

"The cops are handling it; everything is fine."

"If you need anything, you know I'm here. Just please keep the cops away from me."

I nod my head. He walks away, turning back once to glance at me.

"Well, this should make for an entertaining day," Bobby says jokingly. But I'm not in a joking mood today. I smile tightly and walk back inside.

***

Late that night, I wake in a rush when the phone rings.

"Tom, please tell me you caught him."

"That bastard didn't know what was coming when he opened the door and saw us. We've got him at the station."

"Luke and I will be there as soon as possible."

I feel so relieved that this guy was caught as Luke and I rush to get to the station. I hope this is all over now. But in the back of my mind, I can't help but think that this was all too easy.

We arrive at the station, and Tom leads the way to the guy. "His name is Victor Sweep. His fingerprints matched the ones we found at all three murder scenes. He wasn't very careful."

I glare at him in anger through the two-way mirror, but once I get a good look at him, I begin to worry. He's probably in his late thirties, tall, with blonde hair.

"No, no, this isn't the guy. He's too much of a pretty boy to be the real killer."

"Are you sure?"

"No, I'm not sure, but I'm going with my gut instinct. Have you questioned him and asked him why he has been killing people with names that are related to me?"

"I was going to wait and do that once you got here. You all can listen for yourself." I take a deep breath and prepare myself for what I'm about to hear. Tom walks in, shoulders high, back straight, a serious look on his face. He's ready to get some answers. Another detective pushes a button so we can hear inside.

"So, Victor, why did you do it?"

Victor smiles, revealing shiny white teeth. He leans in close to Tom and says, "I like college girls, still a little innocent yet willing to try new things; can't get much better than that."

I shake my head and close my eyes. "This bastard is sick." Luke grabs my hand tight.

"Why those specific girls?"

"Ohhhh, I don't know, I just pick them out. When I see the one I want, I pursue." His tone is smug. He's as happy as a child in a candy store.

"I smell bullshit," Tom says, raising his voice. "Who are you working for?"

"Who said anything about me working with someone?"

"There have been other crimes committed with very similar circumstances. All of the other perpetrators were dressed just like you."

"What, black clothes and a ski mask? They sell those everywhere," he says with a small laugh. "Besides, if I was working with someone, why would I tell you? I'm already going to jail; it's not like you can keep me there longer if I say anything." He leans, back crosses his arms, and smiles.

"He isn't going to say anything," I say as tears burn my eyes. "What if he's working for someone? If we ever find out, it may be too late."

"Have a nice life in jail," Tom says as he gets up.

"Oh, by the way," Victor says as Tom reaches the door, "how is that pretty partner of yours? What's her name? Linda, I believe?"

Tom moves in a blur and grabs Victor by the collar of his shirt, pulling him close. "What did you say to me? What do you know? Who are you working for?"

"That fucker!" Luke yells and storms to the door.

"Sir, please, you can't go in there," one of the officers says and puts an arm out to restrain him. I'm sitting there in a daze, tears running down my face. Pain and fear are churning in my stomach.

The officer walks in and stops Tom before he hits the guy. Victor sits there laughing, his shirt crinkled and cuffs on his hands. Tom walks out quickly and comes up to me. "I won't stop until I find the ringleader." Then he storms off.

Luke and I are standing there in shock. Who would be willing to go through all this trouble to attack me and why? My heart is racing, and I begin to panic.

"Luke, what are we going to do?"

"We're going to keep doing what we're doing. We won't let this man stop us from living our lives. We can't let him scare us and make us show vulnerability. We'll have guns by our side, and we'll always be ready for whatever comes at us."

I put my head on his chest and cry. "I'm scared."

He wraps his muscular arms around me. "I am too, but I won't let anything happen to us or May."

I nod my head. He walks me out of the station. I don't see a sign of Tom anywhere.

We're silent on the way home. As soon as we walk through the door, Luke says, "I can't take this—always watching our backs, waiting, and wondering. You don't need the stress, and neither do I. We're going to get away from this for a while. I'm going to take you on a little getaway so we can clear our heads and try and relax a little."

I'm surprised, but he's right, we do need it. "I think that would be a great idea. But what about your work?"

"I have plenty of vacation days saved up. I have a couple of surgeries on the schedule tomorrow, but after that, I'm taking the rest of this week off. They'll get another surgeon to cover for me"

"I think the shop will be okay without me for a week." May instantly pops into my mind. "But May will have to stay with my parents. She'll be safe there."

Just then, May walks downstairs. "May will have to what?"

"You're going to stay at Mom and Dad's." She sighs and rolls her eyes. "I know you don't like it but, you'll be safe while we're gone."

I call Tom to let him know we're going away. It was a quick phone call. "Tom says he thinks this is a good idea, and he's going to try and work hard while we're gone."

"Good, now we have to figure out where we're going. I know there are some nice bed and breakfast places along the coast."

I smile. "That sounds perfect." We order a pizza while we search online for places to go. We find the perfect bed and breakfast right on the beach. It seems to be nice and private, which is what we need.

We pack and make plans to leave in the afternoon as soon as Luke finishes with his scheduled surgeries. When we lie down to go to sleep that night, I couldn't be more happy or excited, but in the back of my mind, I can't stop thinking about who's after me and why.

Chapter 12

The road that leads us to the bed and breakfast is like a tunnel covered by live oak trees. "Wow, this is beautiful."

We turn into a driveway, and a grand two-story house comes into view. I'm speechless. The pictures we saw online didn't do it justice.

"I can't wait to see the inside," I say as we step out of the car. "And there are no cars here. How nice would it be if we're the only ones staying here this week?"

"That would make this trip even better," Luke says. We grab our bags and make our way to the porch and up the wooden steps. The first thing we see on the cracked white door is a sign that says, "Home Away From Home." I have to agree with that statement so far.

Luke knocks on the door, and we wait eagerly for Judy, the owner, to open it. A few seconds, later a short, white-haired woman slowly answers the door. Her bright blue eyes light up her face. "Well, hello, you must be Luke and Linda," she says with a big smile.

Luke shakes her hand softly. "Yes, we are. It's very nice to meet you. Thank you for letting us stay on such short notice. This is a much-needed vacation."

"I'm more than happy to accommodate the both of you. Here, come on inside." The aroma of cinnamon hits me as we walk in. As we walk along the creaking wooden floors, we're surrounded by maroon and wood-paneled walls. Straight ahead of us is a huge, curving staircase, and beyond that is the kitchen. To the right, we see a living room with sofas, coffee tables, and a big fireplace in the corner. A large window dominates the room, and what I see next is breathtaking. Right outside is a patio with a hammock, and right beyond that is the ocean.

"Oh, my goodness," I say as I walk toward the window. "This is wonderful. I can't wait to feel the soft sand beneath my feet."

It's cold outside, but that won't stop me from being outside on the patio and the beach. "Let me show you to your room so you can unpack, get settled, and then spend some relaxing time on the beach," Judy says.

We walk up the stairs, admiring the paintings of old farms, beautiful woods, and cottages. The paintings make the place come to life.

"Here's your bedroom, and to the left is your bathroom. You're the only guests here, so enjoy the space! Feel free to roam around the house."

"Oh, thank you so much, we'll definitely be doing that." The bedroom has a large, comfortable-looking four-poster bed. There's a large window with a window seat. There's a padded chest at the end of the bed and a tall wooden dresser for our clothes and a huge double-door closet. "This is way better than I expected."

"I totally agree," Luke says with a smile.

"Well, I'll let you two unpack and get settled. I'll have your dinner ready by six o'clock. Any requests?"

Luke and I look at each other with excitement. "I'm sure anything you cook will be great," Luke says.

She smiles. "You've got it."

As soon as she leaves, I wrap my arms around Luke and kiss him. "This was such a good idea," I say. We unpack our bags and spend some time searching around the house, in awe of the vintage furniture and paintings.

We head downstairs into the living room and Luke builds a fire. We relax on the couch and play chess while we wait on dinner. We can smell the homemade rolls from the oven. We head into the kitchen, and there are flower-patterned china plates and crystal glasses set out on the table. "Do you need help with anything?" I ask.

"Oh no, sweetie, dinner is about ready. I'm taking the chicken out in a minute. Go ahead and have a seat."

She pulls out some fried chicken and serves it with mashed potatoes and homemade rolls. "It's like Thanksgiving dinner all over again. Thank you so much for cooking for us."

"Oh, it's not a problem. I love to cook for people." We enjoy dinner and tell her about ourselves, and she talks about the history of this place. She bought the bed and breakfast when she was in her early thirties and has been here ever since.

Luke insists on helping with the dishes. "Well, I'm going to get going. I live right down the road. If you need anything please feel free to call. I'll be over at seven to make breakfast."

"Thank you so much again; we promise we'll be great house guests."

She smiles. "I know you will."

First thing we do when she leaves is head to the beach to take a walk. It's a beautiful evening, and the moon is shining bright in the sky. The reflection of the moonlight on the ocean is mesmerizing.

We walk hand in hand, talking about random things. I can't remember the last time we actually talked about things other than dreams and solving cases.

When we get back to our room, we head to the bathroom and decide to relax in a warm bubble bath in the big, round marble tub. We light some candles and turn out the lights.

"I haven't been this relaxed in I don't know when. Thank you so much for suggesting this and bringing me here."

"Anything for you, babe. You needed this."

After we dry off, we don't bother putting our clothes back on. Luke picks me up and takes me to the big bed. He lies me down and starts kissing my body. He whispers in my ear, "I'm going to make your body tremble."

***

The next few days seem to go by all too fast. We've enjoyed our time here so much. Just the two of us in a beautiful home, on the beach, with home-cooked meals. It's our last night here and we spend it lying on a blanket on the beach. Luke rolls over and kisses me, and then he looks me deep in the eyes. "I love you so much, Linda."

I smile. "I love you too."

He gets up and pulls me up so we 'e both standing. He looks into my eyes with pure passion and love. He gets down on one knee and pulls out a little velvet box. My heart starts racing, and my body begins to tingle. A warming sensation takes over my entire body. I know what's coming and nothing in the world can express how happy I am and how I'm feeling at this exact moment.

"I was going to wait to do this until the New Year, but I can't wait. I thought this was the perfect moment. I want to be here for you for the rest of your life. I know it's soon, but we have a special connection that can't be broken. I love you, and that's all that matters, not the time or how long it's been. Love doesn't lie. Linda Brown, will you marry me?"

Tears begin to form instantly. I smile so big and my heart is still pounding. "Of course I'll marry you." He puts the beautiful square-cut diamond ring on my finger and stands up, picking me up and kissing me.

Back inside, he opens a bottle of champagne to celebrate. We drink the entire bottle and make love—the perfect way to end our last night. I'm lying on his chest, tracing his arm muscles with my finger. "I never want this trip to end. But I can't wait to go back and tell everyone the good news!"

"I already got your father's permission."

"I knew it! That's what you all talked about when we were over there a few weeks ago."

"Yup," he says with a soft laugh. "I made it too obvious, didn't I?"

I smile. "Actually, my mom was the one who suggested it."

"She's a smart lady."

"They're going to be so excited." I yawn and it triggers Luke to yawn. I look up into his eyes and kiss him good night. "I can't wait to marry my best friend."

"Neither can I," he says as he kisses me again.

***

I see May tied to a chair in what looks like an old basement. There are mice around and spider webs. The only light comes from a single bulb hanging above May's head. I'm trying to reach her, but it's as if I'm stuck and can't move. I can see her, but I can't help her. Her mouth is gagged, her head is down, and her eyes are closed. She's dirty from head to toe. Her long brown ponytail is messy and filled with mud. Her face is bruised as if she has been beaten.

My worst nightmare is coming true. Someone took May to get to me, and now I have to do to whatever it takes to save her and keep her alive. Then I hear an eerie, raspy voice, so close it's as if he is whispering right in my ear. "I'm finally going to get you, Linda. It's only a matter of time." My stomach turns and my throat tightens; this has to be the man who's controlling everything. His final act is about to take place.

I wake up crying, shivering, and so frightened. I look at Luke and begin to cry. He holds me tight and tells me everything will be okay, but I know deep down inside that nothing is going to be okay, not for a while.

"What was the dream?" he whispers as he holds me.

"It's May," I say as I swallow. "I found her in an old abandoned basement tied to a chair. She was passed out, dirty, and looked like she'd been beaten."

"Oh my God."

"I need to call her now." Then I look at the clock. It's 6:00 a.m.

"Want to wait a little bit? She's probably sleeping?"

"No, I don't care if I wake her up."

I grab my cell phone from the nightstand. The phone rings once and then goes straight to May's voice mail.

"This isn't good." I try again and get the same result.

"She's probably sleeping; that's why she isn't answering."

"Yeah, but it only rang once. If her phone was on, it would ring multiple times until it goes to voice mail. I'm calling Mom."

"Linda, honey, it's six in the morning," Mom says groggily when she answers. "What's going on? I thought you and Luke were out of town."

"We are. Listen, is May still staying with you?"

"Yes, she's sleeping right now."

"Are you sure? Please go and check her room."

"Linda, what's this all about?"

"Just do it, Mom."

"All right, I'm going to look now." I wait anxiously until she responds.

"She's right here, sound asleep." Relief floods into me.

"Okay, good. Don't let her leave your sight until Luke and I come back today. We'll come and get May and bring her back to our place to stay."

"You still haven't told me what's wrong."

"I'll explain later. Luke and I have a lot to tell you."

"Safe travels back, honey. I love you."

"Love you too."

"She's fine, but I'm not. I have no idea when or where or if this is going to happen. All I know is I'm not letting May out of my sight. The man who I think took her is the man that has been involved in most of my dreams. He's the one who sent in all the other killers and the one who has been playing games with me. He's slowly making his way to me. He told me he was close in the dream."

"We need to call Tom and tell him. We need this to end once and for all," Luke says in frustration.

Tom doesn't answer. But I'm sure he will call back.

We get in the car and head home. "It was such a wonderful week," I sigh. "I'm so sorry it ended badly."

"It's not your fault. Right now, we need to focus on keeping everyone safe."

"I want this fucker caught and put away forever. I want this nightmare over."

"I want to see this guy burn more than anything."

We finally arrive at my parents' house after about an hour-and-a-half drive. As soon as we walk in, the smell of grilled chicken and sweet potato pie warms me, but I'm not sure I'm going to be able to stomach good food after what I'm about to tell them. *Maybe I shouldn't tell May about the dream? I don't want to freak her out even more.* I grab Luke's arm to stop him from walking any farther. "Go along with me; don't say anything about the dream." He shakes his head. We walk into the kitchen where my parents and May are sitting around the island having lunch.

"Hey, you two, how was the trip?"

I smile and look at Luke. I hold up my hand and say, "We're engaged!"

Mom and May jump up and scream with excitement. "Oh my God, this is so exciting! Let me see the ring!" May shouts. She grabs my hand and looks at it. "Wow, good job, Luke!"

"Let me see!" Mom says as she pushes past May. "Wow, Luke, this is a lovely ring!"

"Well, thank you."

"I love it," I say as I admire it again. "It's not too big, and it's simple, not overbearing."

"Congratulations to you both," says Dad.

"Well, have you started talking details yet?" asks May.

"No, it just happened last night," I say with a smile.

"Well, whatever you guys decide, I want to help in any way I can!"

"Will you be my maid of honor?"

She screams and jumps up and down. "Of course I will! I can't wait to start planning."

We grab a couple of plates and talk about how wonderful the trip was as we eat. May says, "Mom told me you called this morning worried about me. Sorry, my phone was dead and I forgot to put it on the charger. So what was wrong?"

"I had another bad dream, and I'm worried. I want you to stay with us again until further notice so I know you'll be safe." I decide not to go into detail about the dream.

"What was the dream?"

"I don't want to say. All I know is that we're going to get to the bottom of this." And I leave it at that.

"Well, good thing is we can get a lot of wedding planning done while I'm staying!" I know she's going to drive me crazy, but I don't care. What I care most about is her safety. "Can you stop by my dorm so I can pack some things?"

When we leave Mom and Dad's, we take her to her dorm, and I have to explain to Katie, her roommate, why May is staying with us. By the time we get back to the house, it's late and we're all exhausted. Just as Luke and I are getting into bed and ready to fall asleep, my phone rings.

"Finally, it's Tom calling back," I say to Luke.

"Hey, Linda, sorry I missed your call earlier today. We've been very busy. Is everything okay?"

"No, I had a really bad dream about May."

"Oh no. I'm sorry. Come down to the station tomorrow and tell me about it. I also need your help on another case."

"All right," I say with a sigh.

"I know you don't need to take on anything else, but maybe this case will help with the one with May since there have been connections."

"I'll be down tomorrow after work."

"See you then."

***

"Linda! How was your trip?" Sarah asks when I walk in the next morning. Bobby comes out from the back to listen in. First thing I do is show them the ring.

"I'm so happy for the both of you. I need to tell you something that happened while you were gone, but I don't want to worry you, especially after such a great trip," says Bobby.

"Oh, I'm already back to work with Tom on some cases, so go ahead and tell me."

"There's a man who has been showing up at the shop a few times a day. He seems a little suspicious," says Bobby.

"What does the man do to make you feel suspicious?"

"We can show you. We have him here on the surveillance camera, if you'd like to look."

My heart drops into my stomach because I have a feeling I'm about to see the man who has been in control of this entire nightmare.

"Yeah, let's go take a look at it." We go to the monitor in the back office, and Bobby fast forwards to the times when the man was there.

"There doesn't seem to be a pattern to when he comes, but it's pretty often. He just walks by, pauses, looks in, and then walks away. He's maybe there for a minute or two before moving on."

The camera got a close-up of this guy's face, and I freeze. I feel like my world has just turned inside out along with my stomach. I'm so scared and disgusted. The guy looks up at the camera like he knows he's being watched and smiles, revealing big yellow stained teeth. His black greasy hair is parted right down the middle. His nose is long, thin, and overbearing. His smile is abnormally wide, almost stretching from ear to ear. He looks like something you'd see in a circus, only a very dark and ominous circus. I run to the bathroom and throw up.

"Linda, are you okay?" Sarah comes in behind me.

"No, I'm not. This is the same guy that keeps reappearing in my dreams. He's the one who has been after me since the beginning. He set all those other guys up so it would throw me off track. I've been dreaming bad things that have to do with May. Now that he's presenting himself, he must be almost to his conclusion. He wants me, and he's going to do everything in his power to make sure that happens, including hurting the ones I love." Sarah and Bobby don't know what to say, but they both hug me. I stare off into space, stiff and scared for a minute before I run to get my cell phone.

"Luke, I need you to come to my shop right away. It's an emergency." He doesn't even respond before he hangs up. I'm sure he's already halfway out of the hospital. Next person I call is Tom.

"Change of plans. Come to my shop right away."

"I'm on my way."

While I wait for both Luke and Tom to get here, I keep looking at the tape. I freeze it on that yellow smile. He's getting closer and closer. I just wish I knew when he's going strike. I hear the morning rush kicking into gear in the dining room and decide working while I wait will help get my mind off of things. I fill coffee and pastry orders. Not even twenty minutes later Luke arrives. I walk from behind the counter and hug him. I'm crying on his shoulder when Tom walks in.

"Uh-oh, this isn't good," says Tom.

"What happened?" asks Luke.

"Both of you need to come and take a look at this." They follow me into the back, and I show them all the times he has shown up in the past week. "Remember me telling you about that guy I keep dreaming about, the one who has been after me?"

"Are you sure this is the guy?" asks Tom.

"Am I sure? Who else would it be? He has been very good at not showing himself in my dreams, but this has to be him. I know he was the one who hurt May in my dream; he's making his way closer and closer to me. I heard his deep, raspy, eerie voice in my dream, and that voice matches this deformed, dirty man. It has to be him."

"Well, Tom, what are we going to do about this? He's showing up at her work almost every day waiting for her. We need to take care of this immediately," says Luke.

"What has he said to you in the dreams?" asks Tom.

"This was the first dream I had where he actually showed up. I didn't see him, but he spoke to me for the first time. My last dream was May tied to a chair in an old abandoned basement. He told me he's finally about to get me." Luke puts his hand over mine and rubs it gently.

"Well, at least we know what he looks like. We'll make copies of this image and put them all over town. I'll have his picture put on the news as a person of interest. We will find him."

"This guy is smart. He probably wants this to happen; he has probably already planned everything. And what happens if we do catch him? He hasn't committed a crime; you can't just throw him in jail."

"Linda, I know you're frustrated, but this is our only hope.

What do you want to do, wait around every second of every day, wondering if he's going to take May or hurt you? We have to do this, and we're going to need your help." I know exactly what that means: using my dreams.

"He's probably watching us right now, loving that we're having a hard time figuring him out," I say. "I don't know where to even start dreaming about him. I don't have any place or time to put myself in."

"Just try to dream about him. Maybe see if you can follow him in your dreams. Throw him off track," says Tom.

"This is what he wants. He wants a cat-and-mouse chase, and I'm going to give him that, but the ending won't be what he is expecting. I want this son of bitch dead so I don't have to worry about him ever again."

"I want every little detail and update. I'll go ahead and take this camera tape to the station and have them make copies."

"What's the case you need my help with?"

"Linda, you don't need to take on anything else right now," says Tom.

"I know, but this guy seems to have a connection with almost every case, like you said over the phone. I think this is part of his game. Maybe this next case will lead me closer to him."

Luke is pretty quiet during this conversation, and I don't blame him. I know he's worried, but I just want all of this to be over. Tom begins to tell me about the case and pulls out the folder he brought along with him.

"There have been three cases of preteen abduction: three girls, all age thirteen. The girls went missing exactly two weeks apart on the exact same day and time each week. They all attend Middleton Middle School, and all three disappeared right after school let out. We talked to the principal and the girls' teachers, but they haven't noticed anything out of the ordinary. We've got officers outside the school every afternoon now."

"Well, if this deformed man has anything to do with it, he's not going to leave behind any evidence. But I should be able to dream about this. What day of the week and time does the kidnapping occur?"

"Wednesdays at 3:30 p.m."

"How the hell do they kidnap kids in plain sight without anyone seeing anything?" asks Luke. I nod in agreement.

"There's a lot of traffic, and buses, and kids walking home. It's a busy scene."

"If this man has anything to do with this, he'll show up in the dream at some point, at least I hope he will. Have you found the girls that have been kidnapped?"

"No, we have no idea where they are."

"Oh gosh, I hope they're still alive."

"Me too," says Tom.

"Well, I'll keep you posted with my dream tonight."

"Do you want me to stay close by, just in case he shows up?"

Luke chimes in, "No need, I'll stay here for the rest of the day and help Linda work."

"Are you able to stay away from the hospital another day?"

"I'll have another doctor cover for me. They know a little about what's going on. If they really need me, they'll call."

"It'll make me feel better if you are here. It's a long way to closing time."

Tom glances at me as he walks away.

Chapter 13

I *find myself about a block away from Middleton Middle School. I arrived early so I can stakeout the school and look for suspicious people. I'm wearing an oversized sweatshirt, and my hair is tucked up under a ball cap. I walk toward the school, my eyes swiveling in every direction.*

I've been walking around for about thirty minutes and haven't found anything out of the ordinary. I decide to sit on a bench across the street from the school and wait.

I notice an unmarked navy blue van parked on the street. I find it a little suspicious, so I walk toward the van. It has black tinted windows. First thing I look for is the license plate number. I find it odd because it's only three numbers long: 214. That number seems familiar to me. At least I'm able to get that information. I walk past the van and circle back around.

I head back to my bench. It's almost time for school to let out.

From across the street, on the other side of the van, I see a man. He's in blue jeans and a plaid shirt. He's an average height white male, but I can't see his face clearly. He looks at the van, nods his head, and gives a thumbs-up to the driver. The van pulls away from the curb and slowly moves toward the school.

The man turns to follow the van's movement, and I catch a better glimpse of the guy. It's him! I didn't recognize him because he isn't in all black, and he looks normal, but when he smiles as he watches the van drive off, I recognize his wide, clown-like smile. I knew he was in on this! He's behind this whole thing. I start to cry.

"Snap out of it!" I say to myself. Just then, the school bell rings, and hundreds of kids start pouring out of the school. I search for the van and see it parked down the street on the other side of the school. I notice a girl with long red curly hair wearing blue jeans, brown boots, and a white dress shirt walk up to the van.

"No, please don't get in there," I whisper.

When I see the girl get into the van, I start to run. No one else seems to notice the girl. Where are the police officers who are supposed to be watching the school?

The van pulls way, and I run to follow it. Good thing there's a lot of traffic, or else I wouldn't have been able to keep up.

I follow for seven blocks before the van pulls down an alleyway. The alleyway leads to a parking lot behind an old rusted warehouse.

I plaster myself to the wall of the building and peek around the corner so they can't see me. I see four men in all black carrying the same girl into the building. She's out cold. "Got ya," I whisper as I begin walking toward the warehouse. Suddenly, someone comes up behind me and clamps their hand over my mouth and says," I knew I'd find you here. Perfect plan, isn't it?"

I know that voice better than my own. I fight against him with all my might, and then I hear my alarm clock going off.

I wake with a start. I look over at Luke, who's already up sitting in bed.

"Did you find anything out?"

"Yes. I need to call Tom." Luke listens as I explain the dream to Tom.

"Excellent work. We'll need you to be there to ID him. Even though we've seen him on camera, you know him better than we do. If we can catch him and prove he's in on the kidnappings, he'll be put away."

"Okay, I'll be there."

"I'll bring extra backup. Now that we know where they take the girls, we can stop this girl from getting taken and hopefully find the other three there and alive. We're tracking down that license plate now. Linda, we'll get them all, I promise."

"I know we will. I'll come down to the station so we can go together." I hang up, and for once, I'm not scared. I'm angry. For once I feel strong and confident that we're finally going to get this maniac.

***

As we walk into the station, we see Tom sitting at his desk and he waves over to us.

"Are you ready to catch this son of a bitch once and for all?" he asks.

"Hell yes, we are," I say

"I have some good news. We've gotten a few phone calls from people who saw the posters we put up and have seen him. One person saw him go into a Lowe's, so they waited for him to come out, and all he had was rope. We went into that Lowe's and that idiot used his credit card. So we now have his name. Walter Glass. Tons of stuff came up on him in the system. Kidnapping and assault. He was in jail for ten years but got out on good behavior."

"Good fucking behavior? What, do they think this asshole can change after ten years?"

"Things like this happen. His address came up when we searched his credit card. I sent cops down there now to check it out, I should be hearing back from them soon."

Well at least now I can put a name to that ugly smile, Walter Glass.

We go over the plan. "There will be cops standing outside the school looking for the girl with your description and get to her before she even gets off campus. There will be an unmarked car close to the van so it can be chased. There will be people standing near the warehouse, and people between the school and the warehouse looking for Walter."

Hearing his name gives me chills. "What do you want Luke and I to do?"

"You're going to be watching for Walter. That's the only thing you're going to do. We'll get the girl and hopefully find the others in the warehouse. Here's an earpiece so we can communicate back and forth." He goes to put the hook around my ear when Luke steps in.

"I've got this."

"You can talk as if I'm right next to you, and I'll be able to hear you."

I'm getting anxious about this.

Tom gets a call and looks at his phone. "My officers. Maybe they found Walter at his house before he could even leave."

"I highly doubt that."

After a few "yeahs" and "okays," he hangs up the phone. "Looks like no one has lived in that house for a while. I should have known he wouldn't be stupid enough to stay there." He puts his head in his hands, and I realize how much this ordeal is taking out of him. He's pretty much been working nonstop.

"You look tired," I say.

"I haven't been sleeping well, and I had a dream last night. I haven't had a dream about seeing things in a long time, almost since we've been working together. I think you working with me took the pressure off my dreams."

"What was the dream about? Anything to do with these cases?"

"I'd rather not say. It's been so long since I've dreamt that it probably won't even happen. Let's just focus on today. It's time to make our move."

We get to the school and there's no sign of the van yet, but it's still early. I feel the rush of adrenalin and excitement, but I'm preparing for the worst. We take our position on the bench where I was sitting when I saw the van and Walter.

About an hour later, the van pulls up to the exact same spot I'd seen in my dream. I feel a little relief, only because so far my dream is correct with the same van and license plate number, 214. I can hear one of the police officers in my ear, telling the team that the van is in place. There's no sign of Walter yet, and no movement from the van.

At quarter after three, Tom says, "Get ready, everyone!" I know who signals that van to move and I should see him any second now. But when the van moves, there's no sign of Walter.

"Shit! This isn't good," I say nervously.

"What's wrong?"

"In my dream, Walter was standing right there. He's the one who motions for the van to move, but there's no one there! What's going on? Where is he?" The bell rings, and students come pouring out of the school, just like in my dream. I'm scanning the crowd for any sign of Walter or the little girl, but I don't see either of them. A school bus pulls in between us and the school, blocking my view of the van.

When the bus finally pulls forward, I see the van pulling away from the curb, and the unmarked police car pulls out behind it. "Something's not right." Luke and I make our way over to the school, but there's still no sign of them.

We've already started to head toward the warehouse when Tom comes on the radio. "Come to the warehouse. We got the girl before she made it to the van. We followed the van and caught them here at the warehouse."

"Thank God," I say. Luke and I jog the remaining blocks to the warehouse. When we turn into the alley, there are blue and red lights everywhere. Three men are handcuffed and sitting in the back of cop cars. I look at one of the guys, and he smiles at me.

Tom comes up to me. "Did you see Walter?"

"No, and I'm really worried. Why hasn't he shown up?"

"Don't worry, we've got enough here to find him and arrest him. These men all said they're working for Walter. They'll all go to jail."

"That's good, but the most dangerous one is still on the run." Just then, paramedics with three stretchers come out of the warehouse. All of the girls are alive—injured, but alive.

"Thank you, God," I whisper. An officer approaches Tom and hands him a piece of paper. Tom reads it and glances at me. This can't be good. Tom brings it over to me.

"Linda, this was left next to the girls who were tied up."

He hands me the note and my knees buckle as I read it. *I finally got you now, Linda. Well, maybe not you, but someone very precious to you. My plan worked out perfectly. See you soon.*

I fall to my knees. "May, he's got May. This was his whole plan all along, and we fell for it. He tricked me, and we left May all alone at our house. How stupid can I be?"

Luke has to lift me up. I can't even stand on my own feet. I feel lifeless and empty. The one thing I was trying so hard to protect, I basically gave right to him.

We're halfway home before I even realize I'm inside a cop car with Tom and Luke.

"We're going to find her. We won't stop day and night until we do," says Tom. A few other cop cars follow behind us; they want to check the house to see if there was any sign of a struggle. May had classes today, but he could have gone in right after we left.

When we finally arrive at our house, the first thing I notice is that the front door is wide open. I start to sprint up to the house yelling May's name. Tom stops me. "You can't go in there; we need to go in first and collect evidence."

"Seriously?"

"I'm sorry, but we can't have you compromising the scene. Call forensics and get them out here right away," Tom yells to one of the officers.

From what I can see peeking through the door, the house is a mess. Furniture is tossed around—May put up a fight. I can just imagine how scared she was. This is all my fault.

I sit outside on the steps of my porch while they search the house for any kind of evidence. Luke sits next to me. "We'll find her." I just lie my head on his shoulder and cry.

Tom comes up. "Tell me about the dream again when you saw May in a basement."

"It was a very short dream. I have no idea if it was a basement; that was just a guess. I don't have the slightest clue where it is. All I know is the room was dirty, and there was only one light bulb lighting the room. There were mice and spider webs everywhere. It was just her tied to a wooden chair. I'm going to have to dream about it again. It's going to be hard, but I need to fight hard, and I won't stop until we find May."

Tom nods his head when the head forensic investigator comes out.

"We didn't find any blood or any other kind of physical evidence, but we did find some fingerprints on the door knobs; we'll run those today and see if any match Walter Glass."

"All of our fingerprints are on those door knobs. Even if they're his prints, we have no idea where they are," I say as tears fall.

"We'll be doing whatever we can down at the station. Call me if you find something out. There will be a cop out front on guard at all times."

I nod in response as I stare blankly into nothing. All I can picture is May in that chair in that disgusting basement.

Luke puts his arm around me. "We'll contact you, Tom."

He just nods, and everyone leaves.

I walk into the house as if I'm a zombie and stare at the couches flipped over, lamps broken and on the floor. "How are we ever going to clean this up?"

"Don't worry about it. I'll do it. You go on upstairs and run yourself a hot bath."

I sit in the tub and stare blankly at the ceiling. I realize that I need to call my parents to let them know. Shit, that's the last thing I want to do right now.

I grab a towel and put on my robe. I sit on the bed and call Mom from my cell phone.

"Hi, honey, how are you?" Mom asks with her sweet voice.

God, I'm about to break her heart.

I'm going to find you Walter, and I'm going to kill you.

Chapter 14

I'm staring down a dark and eerie alley way. There's graffiti sprayed all over the Dumpsters. The smell of rotten trash overtakes my senses, and I have to fight the urge to throw up. There are rats running along the alley. There's barely any lighting, only a dim streetlight. I figure if there's any place that's home to that abandoned basement, it would be somewhere around here.

Before I begin to search the buildings, I check the street signs to see where I am because I don't recognize this area at all. I walk out to the main road, and it literally looks like a ghost town. There are a ton of old abandoned buildings. "Where the hell am I?" If I'm in Charleston, I've never even heard of a place like this.

It's hard for me to get a clear look at everything in the dark. All the buildings are boarded up and covered with graffiti. I have no idea how long this place has been run down. As I'm walking around I pay close attention to as many details as I can. I swear I've seen hundreds of rats. After walking around for a little while, taking very small breaths of air because the stench is so strong, I find a street sign.

It's barely hanging on to the pole, and it's scratched up. Luckily, I'm able to read it. Opal Street. I don't think I've ever seen an Opal Street for as long as I've lived here. Well, at least I have a street sign to go by. I'm looking through all the windows to see if there are any lights coming from any of the buildings to at least give me a starting point. I haven't had any luck. If May is anywhere around here, Walter has done a great job of hiding her.

I decide to go back to the creepy alleyway and start with those buildings. There are a ton of back doors, and I'm hoping I can find something. As I turn down the street, I brace myself for the awful garbage smell. Then I start to get the weirdest feeling in my gut; the feeling that someone is watching me. I turn around and look up into a broken window and see what looks like a camera of some sort.

Chills instantly run down my spine, and I get a sick feeling in my stomach.

I go up to the door, and I'm not surprised it is locked, but it seems pretty shaky, so I decide to try and kick it in. Turns out I'm stronger than I think because I'm able to kick it open. I could really use a flashlight right now because all I see is darkness coming from inside. Then it dawns on me that I have my cell phone in my back pocket.

I open up the flashlight app, and as soon as I turn on the light, I instantly regret my decision. It looks like a slaughterhouse. There are bones all over the place, and there are cut-open pigs hanging up. I'm praying that none of this flesh belongs to any humans. I instantly think of May and how scared she must be if she is stuck in this building.

I know these are Walter's tactics to scare me, and honestly, it's working, but it isn't going to stop me from searching. I carefully make my way through this mess of flesh and begin searching the building for a staircase. Someone has to be here because I saw that camera, and it can't just be a coincidence that I had the gut feeling someone was watching me. Trust your gut is what everyone says.

After a few minutes of searching, I find a staircase—or what's left of one. But this one goes up, not down. The steps that remain are broken and crooked. I know I'm going to have a hard time climbing up these things. Then that's when I hear a loud noise coming from upstairs, a scraping sound, like furniture being moved. I quickly yet carefully step onto the first step, and then I jump over two missing steps to land on the next step. I finally make it to the top and shine my light into a big open room.

Oddly, this room is completely spotless— just wooden floors and peeling white walls. I notice there are three other doors. This is definitely a sign of Walter, him playing all his sick games with me. I take my chances on the first door. I slowly open it. My heart is racing. All that's in there are a bunch of dead rats and nothing else.

I move on to the second door. The room is empty except for a noose hanging from the ceiling; again, I have to stop myself from throwing up. I'm just glad nothing was in the noose. Before I open the third and final door, I realize that I'll probably find something in there and I have to brace myself for it. Then that's when I hear, "Linda, help me, please!" I quickly open the door to find a TV sitting in the middle of the room.

"No, this can't be," I cry. On the screen is a shot of May tied up in the chair. She looks dirty and bruised. She's crying. How can this be

happening? Then his face fills the screen.

"Looks like I've fooled you once again, Linda. Hurry, your precious baby sister needs you. I wasn't going to kill her, but if it keeps taking you this long to come to me, then killing her will just have to do. I'll give you until tomorrow by midnight to come find us, and if you don't show, May is going to have to pay the price. But you'll be able to find us. After all, that's your special talent, isn't it?" He laughs an evil laugh. The look in May's big, wide eyes is straight-up horror.

I jump up and begin to cry, my body trembling. This is worse than I thought. What I saw in my dream is something out of a scary movie. Something I never thought could ever be real, but it's very real, and it's happening to May.

***

When we pull into the station, a little relief comes over me because I know we will be able to start the search. As soon as Tom sees me, he gets up.

"Tell me everything." I tell him about Opal Street, the abandoned ghost town, the boarded up buildings, and the sick camera and TV.

"Sounds like we've got not only a smart one but a seriously fucked up guy to deal with."

"Thanks a lot; that's very encouraging," I say sharply.

"But we're good at finding guys like this and putting them away," says Tom. "I'm going to put a search in for all the Opal Streets in South Carolina," he says as he goes to his laptop. About twenty of them show up in the search results.

"We can work with this. I've dealt with a lot worse," he says.

"Are there any somewhat close to our area?" asks Luke.

Tom points his finger to an area on the map and says, "Actually, yes, this Opal Street looks like it's about twenty-five miles out from downtown Charleston." He zooms in on Google Earth to see the actual street. "You weren't kidding about it being abandoned."

We can see the empty town—no cars, no people, but May is there somewhere.

"Let me Google it and see if we can find any info on it." The first story that pops up is about a small town called Quiet Lake that was an industrial town until the Great Depression caused the factories to close and the town to become abandoned.

"A perfect place for a killer to make a home where no one would even think to look," I say.

"But we've nailed him, Linda. This has got to be the place where May is. That whole town is probably his laboratory," says Tom.

"Oh, that's the right place. I recognize a building from the map on Google Earth."

"All right, it's time to make a quick plan. We've got to make it hard for him to know we're coming or to even know we are there. Going in at night would be the best thing."

"But also hard for us to see all his little tricks."

"We're the FBI. We have plenty more tricks up our sleeves."

"He's right, Linda, we need to trust him. This is the only way we're going to get May back. This is what Walter wants. He wants to play a big game with you and the FBI, and he wants to win. But he won't win because we're smarter," says Luke.

"Then let's start the process and come up with a plan. The hours are counting down," I say.

***

The rest of the day is spent hashing out our plan and going over every single detail until we all have it memorized and mapped out to the second. I finally feel a ray of hope because we have planned for every contingency.

It takes us about thirty minutes to drive out there, and then we stop a mile outside of Quiet Lake. We're going in on foot to prevent him from seeing us, and we're wearing black clothes. Ironic, I know, because that's Walter's signature. *What goes around comes around.* Cops have the entire town surrounded, so it would be hard for anyone to get out. As we get closer, the smell of rotten eggs and dead meat assails us.

"Yup, we're heading for the right place. I can tell by that god-awful smell," I say with disgust.

"I'm afraid to actually see what's in this place," says Luke.

"Brace yourself because this will be like nothing you've seen in the hospitals." It feels like we're walking on a dirt road leading to hell, which I guess is the closest thing to it. The dark shapes of the buildings loom ahead of us.

We make a detour and head into the woods to approach the town since Walter probably has camera everywhere. Tom has his gun out and ready to go.

Here goes nothing. I'm beyond scared, but I won't show it. It's time to put on a strong front and find my sister.

As we near one of the buildings from behind, Tom bends over, gagging. The burning, rotten stench of animal flesh isn't something anyone is prepared for. "I told you it was bad."

"You weren't kidding," Tom says before he gags again.

"Come on, you have to pull it together. You're a detective for goodness' sake!" I say in fury. I turn my attention back to the town and see the creepy building. "There—that's the building I saw in my dreams. That's the one where I found all the dead animals and the TV that showed May! We have to get over there." We start walking slowly. It's very quiet and eerie.

"I'll warn you before we go in, it's going to smell even worse." Tom and Luke pull their shirts over their noses. Again, I see animals hanging that have been dead for a while, and straight ahead is the broken staircase.

I nod toward the stairs. We tiptoe our way up the creaking stairs. I go straight to the room where I saw the TV. I open the door and prepare myself for what I'm going to see.

Even though I know what's coming, the feeling in my stomach I get when I see the TV with May on it is like a punch to the gut. I feel nauseous, nervous, and achy all at once. I walk over to the TV and touch the screen as tears form in my eyes. *Stop, fight it, be strong.* I wait for Walter's face to fill the screen and taunt me, but he never appears.

Luke walks over to me. "We will find her, Linda. Let's examine the room she's in to see if we can get any leads." All I can see is a dirt floor and a dim background. There's one light bulb hanging right over her. She's tied up with dirty rope.

"There's nothing specific here. All the buildings around here are dirty and rundown; it's all the same. She could be in any one of them. It's like we're in a big maze," I say in frustration.

"Then we'll check every building, starting with the one right next to this one," says Tom. He relays the order to the officers outside through his earpiece. Then he turns to me. "We aren't leaving until we find them." Once again, I get that sick feeling in my gut that tells me this isn't going to end well.

The next building is empty. Dirty and broken down, but no blood and guts. This is just all too weird. "He has everything set up for a reason. We have to be smarter than him. Look for trapped doors; look for odd spots in the walls," says Tom. We search floor to ceiling and are just about to move on to the next building when I see something. A square spot on the wooden floor looks different from the floor surrounding it.

We drop to our knees and pull up on the floorboards. Several of them are connected, forming a trapdoor. We slowly pull it open and discover a ladder leading down. "This has got to be it! Why else would there be a secret door leading down to a basement?"

"Let me go first," says Tom. He slowly makes his way down and takes a little jump at the bottom. He pulls out his flashlight.

"What do you see?"

"A long dirt hallway and a ton of spider webs."

"I'm coming down," I say without any hesitation. Luke holds on to me and slowly helps me down. Then Luke jumps down as well.

Tom leads the way down the hall. There are very small candles placed in little nooks along the walls. It's a creepy place!

We finally come to the end of the hallway to a small dirty room. I see the same light bulb and chair, only the chair is fallen over, the rope is on the floor, and May is nowhere to be found. I run to the center of the room. "This sick bastard is playing fucking games with us. I'm here, Walter, come and get me! Leave May alone!" I shout.

Then I hear the sick voice.

"Linda, you're too slow. We've already left." We look around to see where the voice is coming from. Up in the corner is a black speaker. *Seriously? This is so messed up.*

"No, you haven't. This is just a trick. You want me and I'm here, so come and get me."

"Aww, playing tough, Linda? I like it. Walk outside." And that's all he says. We all look at each other in confusion, but we do as he said and walk outside.

We see him standing in the middle of the street. To see him in person is terrifying. A rush of anger flows through my veins, and I go straight for him. I run at him so fast he doesn't even have time to move. I hit him hard, and we fall to the ground. He isn't fighting back. He just lies there taking the blows. I'm going crazy, screaming, "Where's May? What have you done with her, you bastard?"

He lies there, laughing while I hit him. Blood runs down his face, but he keeps that wicked looking smile on as if it's painted on. Luke and Tom run over and pull me off of him. Tom turns

Walter around and puts handcuffs on him, then stands him up.

"Where's May?" asks Tom.

He laughs vindictively. "Well, I don't know, Mr. FBI agent. It's your job to find her, now isn't it?"

I lung forward, but Luke catches me. "You sick bastard, tell me where my baby sister is." He laughs. "Guess you'll never know. I had to find a way to hurt you. You didn't see this one coming. How does it feel knowing you can't see what's coming or how I got here or how I got May? I was able to totally throw you off track. What's your secret anyway? Can you see the future?"

"What's it to you, and why are you so interested?"

"It's so unusual. I find you amusing. I've been researching you, but I want to know more about you. I want you, Linda."

"That will never happen, asshole," says Luke.

"Oh, you have no idea how close I am. You'll never see me coming, Linda. So close to you yet so far away," Walter says as blood drips down his face.

Luke punches him, and Tom intervenes before he can punch him again. "Tell us where May is and you might just live."

He shakes his head and smiles.

I fall to my knees in agony, fear, and pain. Tom calls in his team to search the premises.

Tom puts Walter in the back of the cop car. "We're organizing search teams now to go through all of these buildings and search the woods."

I can't speak; I'm frozen in time. I close my eyes, hoping to wake up in my bed. I want this to be a dream more than anything. But when I open my eyes, I'm still standing in the abandoned town, surrounded by blue and red lights.

***

Tom drops us off at the house.

"Anything little thing you find, call us," says Luke.

"I will, don't worry. I won't stop working until I find her."

I still don't say anything. I feel like a zombie; no feeling, just numb, walking without a purpose.

Luke draws a bath for me. I sit there lifeless while he washes me. He kisses my forehead. "May will come home to us, Linda, I just know it." *No feeling, numb inside.*

He dresses me in my nightclothes and lays me down for bed. He holds me and rubs my head while I cry until my eyes become so heavy and swollen and tired they begin to shut on their own.

I'm tied to a chair with rope. I have a gag in my mouth, and I'm surrounded by earth. I look up and see sky, but I look left and right and all I see is dirt. I realize I'm in a huge hole in the ground. There's a thick rope ladder leading to the top of the hole. I struggle to try and get loose. "Linda, can you hear me? Please help me. I know you can see me. I don't know how much longer I can hold on. Forget the emotions and focus on the dream. Think straight, Linda. He has you trapped, right where he wants you. He's in your blind spot. Think hard and search. I don't have much time left. I'm wasting away from his beatings and lack of food and water. I know you can do this. I love you.

I wake up in a panic. Luke gets up as soon as he hears me. "I saw her, I mean it was like I was in May's body, but she was also talking to me. May is sending me a message, and I think I know where she is. We were literally right on top of her. We were so close, and we just left. She has to be somewhere in the ground in the forest surrounding the abandoned town. She's still alive, but she's suffering and won't make it much longer. He has beaten her badly, and he's leaving her there to rot. I have to tell Tom."

"If May is there, then the search team should have found her by now," Luke says.

"Not if she's underground; they might have missed her. It's a big forest. I have to be sure," I say as I dial Tom's number.

Chapter 15

Luke and I quickly go to the station. Tom is in a room questioning Walter. I storm in and open the door. Cops try to stop me, but it doesn't work. After having that dream, I'm so close to finding May. I go up to Walter, who's handcuffed, and punch him with all my might.

"Where's my sister, you fucking asshole? I had the dream; I saw where she was. You have her tied up and buried like an animal! Your life is over now. You'll rot in jail for the rest of your life. Tell me where May is."

He laughs. Tom pulls me back and tries to talk to me, but I'm not hearing it. I just stare Walter in the eyes.

"You really think I'm going to tell you where May is? Don't you think this was my plan the whole time? If I can't have you and your special little talent, then I want to make you suffer for the rest of your life. You'll have nightmares about May tied up and suffering; you won't ever be able to live a normal life. You'll be searching for May forever."

I jump at him again, but Luke quickly pulls me back. "You sick bastard, you'll burn in hell!"

"Take her out of here now," says Tom. Luke has to drag me out of there.

"How can you sit here and not get anything out of him? Make him suffer to the point where he'll tell you!" I scream into Tom's face.

"Linda, it doesn't work that way. We have him finally, after all this time. He won't ever be after you again."

"But what about May? She's suffering, and he's the only one who knows her exact location."

Luke jumps in, "Linda tell him about your dream." I almost forgot about the dream because I was so angry when I saw Walter.

I tell Tom everything I can remember.

"The search team searched all night and couldn't find anything."

I become even more frustrated. "Then fucking send them out there again! I'm telling you she's out there!"

"All right, I'll gather as many people as possible with search dogs. Do you have an item of clothing of May's, for the scent?"

"I have her sweatshirt in my trunk."

"Get the sweatshirt and meet us out front."

On the way to Quiet Lake, I shut my eyes and picture May. It hurts so bad to think about it. *May, hang in there, we're coming.* I pray to God the whole drive there. I hadn't realized how big this forest surrounding the town is until we're standing in it in broad daylight. I'm not giving up hope.

After hours of searching the forest and deserted town, we come out with nothing. It's almost dusk, and we all agreed to meet back at the town when it turns dark, but I'm not going to stop looking no matter how tired I am.

Then I hear someone shout. "Linda, get over here now!" It's one of the search team members, and I run as fast as I can, jumping over fallen trees.

"What? What is it?" He doesn't say anything; he just points down to the leaf-covered ground. That's when I see her. I can't believe my eyes. I'm so relieved yet so scared. May is still tied to the chair and her head is down; she's not moving. She's in an open hole in the ground, exactly how it was in my dream.

"Someone get over here now and get her out!" I scream. Everyone makes their way over, including Tom.

Tom climbs down into the hole. "There's a stab wound in her abdomen," he calls out. "We have to remove her carefully."

"Oh my God, no!" I burst into tears. They cut off the rope and take the gag out of her mouth. She still isn't moving. They slowly get her out of the hole and then put her in Luke's arms. I gently touch her bruised and bloody face.

"It's okay, May, you're safe now." I kiss her on the forehead. Luke carries her all the way to the ambulance. They put her on a stretcher, hook her up with an IV, and we all go to the hospital. We found her just in time. She has lost a lot of blood from the stab wound, and on top of that, she hasn't eaten or drank anything in the past few days.

I close my eyes and say, "Thank you, God."

She's asleep the whole ride to the hospital. I can't take my eyes off her. I'm so happy that this crazy nightmare is over. Walter will be locked away, May is alive and safe, and things are finally starting to look up. No more constantly looking over my shoulder. Now our family can truly relax.

Once we get to the hospital, they take her into surgery to repair the stab wound. The doctor tells me that she'll more than likely sleep for at least twenty-four hours after the trauma she went through. Just the little glimpse I saw in my dream about what happened to her makes me feel awful, but going through the torture for days, I can't even imagine.

When they move her into a private room, I sit in the chair right beside her bed; I'm not going to leave her side until she wakes up. Luke knows not to ask me to go rest or go home because he already knows what my answer will be. Instead, he offers me coffee and a pillow.

"I called your parents. They're on their way."

"I never got the chance to thank you, Luke."

"Thank me? For what?"

"For being by my side through everything, for never giving up on me or May, for taking care of me and being so strong. I don't know if I'd have had the strength to look for May or fight till the end if it weren't for you."

"She's your sister. If I wasn't in the picture, you would have found the strength. You did it on your own; I was just the motivator."

"I'm still confused as to why Walter fought so hard for me. He wanted me for my talent, or so he says. He's infatuated with what I can do and became obsessive. But obsessive enough to do everything he did? It doesn't make sense. And is it just me, or did it seem like Tom didn't want to fight hard to get answers?"

"Walter is crazy. Maybe it was all just a major obsession. Many killers become fixated on certain kinds of people, and they won't stop until they have them or kill them."

That makes me feel a little unsettling. "Yeah, I guess you're right. It's just...something doesn't feel complete about all this."

"Tom has been working night and day since this nightmare started. Maybe he's using a different tactic to get answers. He's been trained to do this, and we have to trust that he knows what he's doing."

I know something still isn't right, but I can't put my finger on it, and the unknown is going to drive me insane.

Luke leans over in his chair and puts his hand on my thigh, "Babe, it's over. Time to let it go."

I take a deep breath and shake my head, as if to jar the unhappy thoughts loose. "I can do that." I look over at May lying still, eyes shut, bruised face, covered in white sheets, and tears start flowing all over again.

***

My parents arrived during the night, and we all ended up sleeping there, waiting for May to wake up. When she finally does, she sees us all there and starts crying. We all crowd around her bed. "It's okay, May," I say as I stroke her hand. "You're safe now."

"Is he dead?" she asks with a raspy, worn-down voice.

"No, but he'll be in jail until he dies. We have nothing to worry about now."

A look of relief flashes across her face and she gives us a small smile. "Thank you for coming and saving me."

"Don't thank me for that. I wasn't going to stop until I found you."

Dad tries to make a joke to get her to laugh, but she grabs her side in pain instead.

"Okay, enough with the talking. May needs more rest."

The doctor comes in a few minutes later to check her vitals, and he tells us she's looking good and should make a full recovery. He gives her another dose of pain meds, and it makes her sleepy.

Satisfied that May is out of the woods, we decide to go to my parents' house since it's closer to the hospital to get some rest ourselves. After we've had a few hours of sleep, we head back to the hospital.

The doctor is in the room with her when we arrive. May is laughing at something the doctor said. She's definitely feeling better.

"You'll be very sore for the next few days, and we're going to keep you here for another twenty-four hours to make sure everything is fine, then we'll send you on your way," says the doctor. "These pain medications will pretty much make you sleep for that entire twenty-four hours, which is exactly what you and your body need."

"We can stay with you if you'd like," I say to her.

"What, to watch me sleep? I'm okay now. You guys go home and get some sleep yourselves and I'll see you in twenty-four hours!" We all give her hugs and kisses and then we leave feeling a bit better knowing she's going to be fine.

Luke and I spend the next couple of days basically doing nothing but lazing around, enjoying each other's company, and trying to put the events of the last few months behind us. After everything that has happened, this is what we truly needed. May leaves the hospital and stays with our parents so they can take care of her as she recovers. She's getting better every day and is already making up her schoolwork so she can graduate on time.

Our family is back and everyone is safe. Life is good.

Chapter 16

A New Beginning

It's amazing how fast the next few months fly by. Spring is here, and my sister is about to graduate from college. May is finally healed mentally and physically. She had a lot of nightmares and went through a lot of counseling, but it helped her. She can finally put it in the past and move on as a college graduate stepping into the real world.

As for me, I've been dreamless for a few months now, and I'm not complaining. I told Tom I didn't want to help with any more cases. I know that's selfish of me, but I'm enjoying being "normal" for once.

We've been planning our wedding for October 10th since fall is our favorite time of year. We found the perfect place for it too: a country club surrounded by beautiful trees. The ceremony will take place in a big open room that has huge windows so we can see the trees and the colors of fall. As I walk down the aisle, the view of the vividly colored trees will surround me. Everything is turning out perfectly. It has been a long year of pain and fear, but I can't wait to make a new beginning with Luke officially.

I'm finally able to walk by myself to work again without any worries, and it feels so good. When I arrive this morning, Sarah and Bobby are already setting out pastries for the day.

"Hey, guys, I'm throwing a graduation party for May next Saturday evening at our house. Would you like to come?"

"We'd love to! Do you need us to bring anything?" asks Sarah.

"Could you make some of your awesome red velvet cupcakes for the party?"

"Absolutely!" Bobby says.

After a normal, busy day at work, I head to the party store to pick up decorations for the party. When I get home, Luke already has dinner on the table.

"Mmm, something smells wonderful," I say. "What are we having for dinner?"

"Chicken parmesan and broccoli."

"One of my favorites! You're going to be one hell of a husband. You're the best. I love you, baby."

"I love you too." He kisses me sweetly and gently on the lips. It makes me ache for more, but I control myself—at least for now.

"How did decoration shopping go?" he asks.

"Good. I picked us up a bottle of wine to enjoy with dinner. And I got May's gift." I show him the gold angel necklace with a halo made of diamonds.

"That's beautiful. She'll love it! Oh yeah, I invited Jeff to the party."

"That's fine. We have plenty of room, food, and drinks. We may have a house full of overnight guests. I don't want anyone drinking and driving, so I'm telling them they can stay the night."

"Sounds like it's going to be a great night. May still has no idea?" asks Luke.

"Nope. She just thinks she's coming back to enjoy the night with you and me. Boy, will she be surprised!"

***

Saturday comes quickly. We have a wonderful lunch before the graduation ceremony, and Mom can't get through it without crying. I'm saving my tears for when I see her walk up on stage to get her degree.

Even though May tries to put on a front, I can tell she's emotional as well. I don't know why she tries so hard to hold it back. "You know it's okay to cry," I say to her. "This is a big day for you and a turning point in your life; it's normal to be emotional about it." She looks at me with sad eyes, and then she starts to tear up. I give her a big hug and rub her back while she lays her head on my shoulder and says, "I love you."

Of course I start to cry as soon as she says that. "I love you too, sis, always and forever."

We all drive to the college together. I help May get her cap and gown on, and she looks beautiful. She meets up with Katie and the rest of her friends, and then we take our seats.

I'm so proud of her as I watch her walk across the stage, shake the president's hand, and take her diploma. Mom and I are both sobbing. Dad has tears in his eyes, but he's always the strong one.

The ceremony is finally over, and we all take pictures and then we're on our way home. I can't wait to see how surprised May will be. As we pull into the driveway, the house is dark. It doesn't look like anyone is here. We walk up and open up the door, turn on the lights, and everyone yells, "SURPRISE!"

"Oh my gosh, this is amazing! Thank you, everyone, so much!" A few minutes later, all of her friends storm through the door. May is shocked, and this is the happiest I've seen her in a long time.

"We're college graduates! Let's get this party started!" yells Katie. We turn on some music, set up the taco bar, and serve the drinks. May is having a blast, the food is great, and everyone is happy. The night couldn't have gone better.

After another night of dreamless sleep—which is becoming a real treat for me—I wake up and see everyone still asleep on the floors and couches. Luke and I make some pancakes, sausage, and bacon. Everyone needs some good hangover food.

After all of the guests have left, I pull May aside. "I wanted to wait and give this to you when I had you alone."

She opens her gift and starts to cry. "This is the most beautiful gift I've ever received. I'll wear this every day. You're the best; thank you so much."

"You deserve it. You truly are a special person," I say and give her a big hug.

May heads back to her apartment and Luke and I spend most of the day getting out house back in order. Night falls quickly, and we're lying in bed watching TV when I get a text. *Weird, who would be texting me at this hour?*

It's Tom. I haven't heard from him in a long time. It reads, "I miss working with you. I hope everything is going well. I hope we can work together again soon. You've been on my mind a lot lately."

My eyes widen, and my heart beats faster. *Shit, play it cool. Act like nothing is wrong.* I delete the text and put the phone back down.

"Who was it?" asks Luke.

I have to lie; I don't want to start a conversation that could lead to a fight. "It was May, thanking me again for the party and the gift."

Chapter 17

I'm standing in front of Walmart at three in the morning. "What in the hell am I doing here?" I see something in the distance. It's a girl who's stumbling. I walk closer to get a better view. She appears to be in her twenties with long brown braided hair, and she's by herself. I can tell she is drunk. I start to run up to help her when a blue van comes out of nowhere, tires screeching as it speeds up toward the woman. "No! Watch out!" I yell.

The girl puts her hands up as the van races toward her. She tries to jump out of the way, but the van is too fast. The van runs right into and over the girl.

As she lies there, a tall, thin, lanky, man comes out of the van and starts walking toward her. He's dressed in jeans and a black leather jacket. I can see her moving her legs, trying to get up. But he comes around and punches her in the face, which knocks her back down. Then he pulls out a knife and holds it to her neck. I walk closer and I can hear her say, "Please don't. Take what you want."

"Oh, I'll get what I want," says the man. Then he picks her up and throws her in the back of the van. I try to get a quick glance at the license plate. It reads 214. That number sounds familiar.

Then it dawns on me. I've seen that license plate and van before, and it brings back the horror.

I open my eyes when the alarm buzzes and just lie there, staring at the ceiling. I thought the nightmare was over with this guy. They arrested all the people that were involved with that van already; how is it still in use?

Luke turns over and sees me staring. "What's wrong? Did you have a dream?"

"Oh, I had a dream all right. Just when I thought everything was back to normal and the nightmare was over." I tell him about the dream.

"It might be the same van, but there's no way those people have anything to do with what happened to you and May."

"Then why in the hell is that man using the same van with the exact same license plate?"

"I don't know, but we need to find out. Let's go and see Tom," says Luke. We don't even bother to call him; we drive immediately to the station.

When we walk in, Tom hugs me and says, "Aren't you a sight for sore eyes."

I smile awkwardly, still feeling weird after the text I received from him last night.

Luke glares at Tom. Tom backs away when he sees his defensive glare.

"So what brings you in here today?"

"I had a dream." He looks up quickly, and his eyes widen with surprise.

"Really? It has been awhile. Tell me about it." He records me on tape so he can document all the details.

"214?" asks Tom. "Are you serious?"

"Yeah. That's why I came down here instead of calling. I thought you picked up all those guys involved with Walter?"

"We did! All the guys that were driving the van or involved at that building. We took the van to the impound lot, and the tags were removed."

"Then how in the hell is the van on the loose? And involved in committing crimes again?"

"I don't know. Either someone found a copycat van or someone went and got the van and got license plates to match."

"Can people do that?"

"Maybe. How about we pay Mark a visit at the Holiday Car Impound Lot?"

I nod. "Let's go." On the drive over, we formulate possibilities of how this happened and why.

I ask the obvious question that Luke and Tom are avoiding. "You don't think Walter has more men involved?"

"I don't know. I guess he could. He's a smart man," says Tom.

"Great," is all I can say. We turn into a gravel parking lot. The sign is crooked and looks like it was painted by a seven-year-old.

"Wow, out of all the impound lots, you decide to put the van in this sketchy one?"

"We have several we use," Tom replies.

"What a lovely choice," I say sarcastically. We walk up to a guy who has "Mark" stitched on his shirt. He's short and heavy with yellow teeth, dark, greasy hair, and he's very dirty.

"Howdy, folks, how can I help you today?"

"We're here to talk about who purchased the blue van we brought in a few months ago."

"Oh, I don't know officer; there are a lot of people that come through to buy these cars."

Tom gets out his wallet and shows him a twenty. "Are you sure about that?"

"Well, now that you mention it, there was a man wanting that van specifically."

"What was his name and what did he look like?"

"Um, you know I'm not that smart and can't remember that well." We all roll our eyes. Tom shows him another twenty.

"His name was Scott and he was wearing blue jeans and a black leather jacket. He was really tall and had some scruff on his face. Here, I can show you on camera."

"You have a camera in this place?" I ask.

"Yes ma'am. Even though we're cheap, we still like to be safe." It takes him a few minutes to find the footage from so long ago. He shows us the video of the man.

"Yes, that's the man I saw in my dream."

Tom takes a picture of him with his phone. "Did he pay with a credit card?"

"Yes, he did."

"Did you save the receipt?"

"Actually, yes. Let me find it."

"Great, thank you for the help," Tom says as he hands him another twenty.

"Anytime!" he replies and smiles, showing his stained yellow teeth. He gives me the creeps.

"This is a great start. We'll run this credit card through the system and see if he has a record," says Tom.

"Is it just me, or is it weird that he specifically wanted that van?" I say.

"It is strange, but we'll get to the bottom of it."

When we get back to the station, Tom runs the credit card right away.

"Scott Lewis, thirty years of age. All he has on his record is a couple of burglaries from convenience stores."

"That's it? So he goes from burglary to kidnapping and possibly murder?" I ask.

"Or he just hasn't gotten caught yet," says Tom.

"Well, let's put an end to that. Look, it even has his address. Let's go and get him now," I say eagerly.

"And arrest him for what exactly? We can't just pick up someone unless they have committed a crime and we have a warrant," says Tom. "We'll watch his house and follow him where he goes; that way we can catch him in the act or right before something happens."

"And if you happen to miss him, the cops will be at all the area Walmarts until they're given orders to leave, correct?"

"Yes, and don't even think about going anywhere near the crime scene—before or after—because if this guy happens to be involved with Walter, I don't want him seeing you."

"I'll make sure she stays away," says Luke.

"Good. I'll call you when we make the arrest."

***

We decide to stop over at my parents to see how May is doing. We arrive just in time for Mom's awesome cooking. Cheesy baked spaghetti, garlic bread, and green beans.

May walks into the kitchen as Luke and I are talking about the new case with my parents. "Hey, guys, what are you doing here?"

"Hey, sis, just stopping by to see how everyone is doing."

"I'm glad you're here. I have something to tell you." My heart starts beating fast, and I get a little nervous about what she's going to say.

"What is it?"

"I got a job! I'm going to stay here with Mom and Dad for a few months and save up, and then find my own place!"

"That's wonderful news! What's the job?"

"I'm going to work for Crystal's Fashion Design. They saw my portfolio, and they loved my drawings!"

"May, that's wonderful. I'm so happy for you! Soon enough, you'll be your own designer and have your own store."

"Well, that's my dream, one step at a time."

We all enjoy dinner and wine. We talk about the wedding and

May's new job. This is the happiest I've seen my family, and I'm happy myself.

When we get home, we watch some TV. I lie down on Luke's chest and end up falling asleep.

Six o'clock comes pretty fast the next morning, and I have a voicemail on my cell phone. I know it has to be from Tom.

"Hey Linda, I have some good news. We caught the guy just as he was pulling the knife on the girl, and he's at our station right now. The van came out so fast we didn't have time to get the girl first. The girl is in the hospital with bumps, bruises, and a concussion, but she'll be fine. Call me when you get this."

"Oh, thank goodness," I say. I call him back right away.

"Hey, I'm so glad you got him. Luke and I are on our way to the station; don't start questioning him until I get there. I want to hear if he's involved with Walter myself. "

"Don't worry, I won't." We quickly put on some clothes and head out. The station is starting to seem like our second home.

When we walk in, Tom and a few others are standing outside the interrogation room, and Scott is sitting there with his head in his arms on the table inside. His body is so much longer than the height of the table.

"Do you want some coffee?" Tom asks.

"Yes, that'll be great." Tom nods at one of the officers to get some for us.

"Stay out here and listen in on us while I ask him questions."

My heart is racing. I don't want him to be involved; that will mean there are more guys involved with Walter, and the nightmare will continue. He'll continue to direct his work from jail and make my life a living hell.

Luke rubs my back as we stand there and listen.

"Do you like abusing and kidnapping women, Scott?"

"I don't know what you're talking about. She was drunk and ran out in front of my car. I didn't do anything."

"So holding a knife to a half-unconscious woman and threatening her life if she wouldn't go with you isn't kidnapping? How many women have you captured, tortured, and killed, Mr. Lewis?"

"What are you talking about? I've never killed anyone in my life. I made a mistake with this girl. I don't know what got into me."

"Mm-hmm. We've got you in action ourselves, and you're going down for attempted murder. When we find more women you've killed, you can expect to have a long life in prison."

"You won't find any murdered women because I've never murdered anyone!" Lewis's tone becomes loud and angry.

"We'll see about that. You'll serve some time behind bars for what you did tonight; that should clear your mind up a bit."

"It was my first offense, so we'll see how well this holds up in court."

I look at Luke with worry.

"I'll make sure you spend a lifetime locked up, just wait and see. No one hits a girl and holds a knife to her neck like that just one time. You knew what you were doing."

"Whatever you say, detective."

"Where did you get the van?"

"What does that have to do with anything?"

"Just tell me where and why you got that van."

"I went to a few places looking around for the perfect van and came across this one, and the guy told me he'd sell it to me cheap."

"So you had no prior knowledge of that van?"

"No, I didn't, and I want a lawyer." Tom proceeds to walk out of the room.

"Well, you heard him," says Tom.

"He's obviously a good liar and knows what he's doing. He could be lying about the van as well!" I say angrily. "And now he wants a lawyer? He'll get out if you don't find more victims."

"He's allowed to have a lawyer; that's how this works. We're going to keep digging for information until we find something to nail him with. Until then, he's still going to be locked up here."

"So what am I supposed to do?"

"Well, he didn't name you or your family, he doesn't seem involved with anything in the past, and he's here, so you have nothing to do or worry about. Leave it to my crew to put him in prison for good. I'll keep you posted on anything I find. Until then, relax and continue with your normal routine."

"Easier said than done," I say, annoyed.

"This case has nothing to do with you," says Luke.

"Nothing except I dreamt it, and it's the same van and same license plate as past dreams and cases."

"Try not to worry about it too much. You have work, your family, and our wedding coming up soon." I know Luke is right, but it's always easier for someone else to say it when they aren't going through it themselves.

Luke drops me off at work after we leave the station. I'm grateful for work because it keeps my mind off things.

"So how are the wedding plans coming along?" asks Sarah.

"Everything is great! Actually it's all planned. We just need to send out the invitations when the time comes."

"That's awesome! May is doing a good job planning your wedding shower and bachelorette party."

"I can't wait. I'm sure May is going to make them good."

"Oh, she is, for sure," says Sarah, and we both laugh.

The rest of the day is nice. We have lots of costumers, and we stay busy.

Luke comes back to pick me up. "Hey, babe, let me help you close down."

"Thank you. How was your day at the hospital?"

"It was surprisingly light. I had two scheduled knee surgeries and no emergencies."

"That's nice for a change!"

It only takes about ten minutes to close down. Having extra hands always helps. We don't feel like cooking, so we decide to pick up Chinese.

We walk into the Chinese restaurant and run into Tyler of all people. He turns around after paying for his food and looks at me with big eyes.

"Hey," he says.

I nod and smile and walk past him. He puts his hand on my arm as I walk by. I turn around quickly, about to become angry. "Are you doing ok? Has everything been taken care of with that case? The cops haven't come to me since the last time. Thank you for taking care of that. I felt bad after getting angry with you."

"Take your hand off her," Luke says, low and menacing.

"Luke, it's okay," I whisper. He sighs and walks forward to pay for our food.

I look back at Tyler. "I'm doing better, and the case is getting there." I don't know why I feel like I should tell him these things.

"Well, if you need any help, please don't hesitate to call." He glances down at my hand. "Engaged, huh? Well, congrats and I wish you the best, even if it's not with me."

I smile as Luke makes his way back to us. "Are we finished here?"

"We are," says Tyler. Luke nods, and we walk away.

Luke slams the car door shut. "Did you have to talk to him about the case? That's a personal issue, and after the past situations with Tyler, I don't think that was a good idea."

"I didn't go into much detail, and I think he's finally over me." I don't know if that's true, but I'm hoping it'll help stop the argument.

"I highly doubt that."

We get home and begin to eat in silence; I have to break this tension. I bring up the wedding because that always smoothes things over. "We need to start working on the guest list," I say with a full mouth.

"Sounds perfect to me," Luke says with his amazing smile.

It takes awhile to hash out our list. We both want to keep things small and intimate. As we're lying in bed, about ready to fall asleep, I get a phone call. It's Tom. I know if he's calling this late then it must be important.

"Hey, Tom, what's going on?"

"I have some good news. We've been digging up information all day and found some old cases that have never been solved. Five cases about women who all had the same injuries and the same things happen to them."

"So how does it involve Scott Lewis?"

"We went to talk to the forensic pathologist who did the autopsies on their bodies and she pulled out the files. Each girl was run over by a car, and they each had knife marks on their neck. They were kidnapped and murdered. Their bodies were found in an abandoned farmhouse right outside Charleston. They were never able to find who did it, but with your help, we just caught the guy. We had a warrant to take his DNA, and it matched some of the DNA they pulled from the bodies."

"That's great news. Did he confess to the murders?"

"He did. He said he had nothing left to live for, so he admitted to all of them."

"That seems all too easy," I say nervously.

"Well we got lucky because guilt overtook him. By putting this guy away, you just saved many lives. Thank you for your help."

"Of course. Did Scott confess to knowing anything about the van?"

"He said he had no idea the van had a criminal history. He just wanted a van for his kidnappings. He said the tags were still on the van when he found it."

"But you said you had them removed."

"I ordered them to be removed. I don't know if they ever were."

"That still seems fishy to me. Is there something you're not telling me, Tom?"

"No, that's everything," he says with a slightly higher pitched voice than normal.

This doesn't sound like the confident Tom who's always right; this sounds like an uncertain Tom.

A few moments of silence go by while I wait for him to come out with the truth.

"Well, sorry for calling so late. I'll talk to you later," he says quickly then hangs up the phone. I look at my phone with my eyebrow raised.

"There's something Tom isn't telling me. I can tell by his tone."

"Why would he withhold something from you?"

"Maybe to keep me from worrying, but I'm more worried because he wouldn't tell me."

Luke yawns. "I'm sure it's nothing."

I kiss Luke and lie down. "I guess you're right," I say and close my eyes. But I know deep down inside that something isn't right. Tom is withholding information from me, and I want to know why.

Chapter 18

The rest of the summer passes without incident, and the date of our wedding approaches. We spend my bachelorette party at Prohibition. Our fancy limousine pulls up, and when we walk in, they're playing some loud music and the bar is lit up in bright neon flashing lights. The DJ says, "Welcome Linda, the bride to be!"

All of my friends scream. This just keeps getting better. We have shots and drinks, but if I want to truly remember this night, I can only have a few more. The night is full of dancing, laughing, telling funny stories, and alcohol. Just when I think things can't get better, I see Luke and his friends walk in the door.

"Luke!" I yell and run over to him. I jump on him and he catches me, and I kiss him hard.

"The lovely couple and soon to be newlyweds," says Bobby. I have a bachelorette shirt on that's bedazzled in rhinestones and glitter, and he has on a plain bachelor shirt. We're probably the most obnoxious group of people in the bar, but we don't care. We're drunk and having too much fun.

Luke and I can't keep our hands off each other on the dance floor. No one seems to care because everyone else is dancing and having a good time. I whisper in Luke's ear. "How about we move this to the limousine?"

He raises his eyebrows and smiles at me. "Oh, you got it, babe." We sneak out so no one sees, but they aren't paying attention anyway.

"This is a first for me," I say with a huge grin.

"For me too," says Luke. We start kissing and take each other's clothes off in record time. By the time we're done, we're sweaty and out of breath. "Wow, that was amazing."

"Yeah, it was. I can barely breathe." We sit there and laugh as we cool off before we get out. We put our clothes back on, and I try to fix my hair as much as I can, but it's pretty messed up.

When we walk back inside, we find everyone sitting around a table. "And where have you two been?" May asks with a smile.

"Oh, you know, we just decided to take a break from dancing," I say with a wink. We all laugh. We order one more round of drinks and grub on some mile-high nachos.

This turned out to be one of the best nights of my life. I've had so much fun with my friends and the man I'm going to marry. I glance around the bar as we're getting ready to leave and do a double take. Standing in a corner is a man who's staring at us. He's tall, light skinned, wearing black pants, a red t-shirt, and a baseball cap. He isn't smiling. His expression is blank, as if deep in thought, and he's staring right in my direction.

I figure it's just my imagination and the alcohol, making me see things.

"Babe, are you okay?" asks Luke.

I shake it off. "Yes. My stomach isn't feeling the best."

"Let's get you home."

The limousine takes us all home, stopping at our house first. Luke and I make our way to the bedroom and pass out. Darkness takes over immediately.

***

I'm standing on the sidewalk next to our house, but it's nighttime and I'm alone. I don't know what I'm doing out here, so I start to walk back inside, but something across the street catches my eye.

There's a man standing on the other side of the street, right across from my house. He's standing under the streetlight, so I'm able to get a look at him. He doesn't move at all, he just stands there staring at me. I try to move, but I'm scared. Something about his eerie, still stance is frightening me.

I squint my eyes to see if I can get a better look, and I realize that I recognize him. He's the same man I saw in the bar that night. He's wearing the same clothes, but I can't see his face. It's hidden by the shadow of his baseball cap. I turn around and run inside, and when I look back, he's gone. I shut the door and lock it quickly.

Then I wake up. I sit up and shake my head. I walk into the bathroom and splash some warm water on my face. This has got to be one big coincidence.

Luke walks in a few minutes later.

"What's wrong? Are you okay?"

"No. I don't know. I thought I was seeing things in the bar last night because I had too much to drink, but I just dreamt about the same thing."

"What was it?"

"It was a very scary man. I saw him standing in the corner of the bar just staring at us. Then he was in my dream. He was standing across the street from our house, under the streetlight. He never moved and never said anything, he just stared."

"What did he look like?"

"I couldn't see his face, only his clothes and baseball cap. I have a sick, weird feeling that he seems very familiar to me."

"Do you think it's just nerves about the wedding?"

"Since when have my dreams not meant something or predicted something?" I ask him. "Plus this feels different than anything else that has happened. It's like I can see this guy, but not really, and I can't see him do anything. So if something were to happen in real life, I wouldn't know it was coming."

"Well, let's keep a close eye out. We're always ready for something. We each have a gun, we keep the house protected well, and you have me. Do you want to tell Tom?"

"No, I don't want it to seem like a big deal since I haven't seen much."

"Come back to bed for a little bit." He takes my hand and leads me back to the bed and rubs my back until I fall asleep.

I wake up to the smell of bacon and pancakes. A smile instantly forms on my face, and I crawl out of bed and get my robe. I look at the clock: 11:00 a.m. I walk downstairs to see Luke hard at work in the kitchen. "Why did you let me sleep that late?" I ask him.

"Well, you had a rough night, so I figured I'd let you sleep."

"Thanks for cooking, babe. It smells delicious."

We're eating breakfast when my cell phone rings.

"Linda, it's Tom."

"Hey, what's going on?"

"I'm so sorry to bother you. How have you been? Have you had any dreams recently?" Funny how he asks me that after what I dreamt last night; for some reason, I feel the need to lie to him.

"I've been doing great, finishing up last minute touches for my wedding. And no, I haven't had any dreams. Why do you ask?"

"I'm working on a case, and I thought maybe you'd have seen something because I did."

"Really? It has been awhile since you've seen things in your dreams, right?"

"Yes, that's why I wanted to see if you dreamt anything as well. I can't seem to finish the dream or know what is going to happen next. This is where I need your help."

"What's the case?" I ask, wondering if it has anything to do with the tall man in a baseball cap.

"A drug addict stole his two kids from their mom during the night. I need to know where he's taking the kids so we can capture him."

"Okay," I say with relief. Nothing to do with my dream. "I'll help you. I'll be down to the station in a few minutes to get details and take a look at the family."

"Are you sure you want to do this?" Luke asks when I hang up.

"The case isn't that bad. One dream and it'll be taken care of. A dad who's addicted to drugs stole his two kids from the mom's house while they were all asleep. I just have to figure out where the guy is taking the kids so they can find him."

When we get to the station, Tom has all the information out and ready. He explains the whole story and how this dad could be dangerous and possibly harm the kids.

"So in my dream, I should put myself near the house before the kidnapping and follow him?" I ask Tom.

"Yeah, that should work. Thank you again, and I'm sorry." Tom seems to be acting different today. He's quiet and almost shy. He shows me the picture of the dad and the kids he took. He gives me the address of their house.

"I hope I can find out information tonight."

"Yeah, me too," Tom says as he puts his head down and walks away.

Luke and I walk out of the station. "Is it just me, or is Tom acting weird?" I ask.

"Yeah. I wonder what's going on with him."

"I think he really feels bad for asking me to work on a case so close to the wedding."

"That might have been it. Oh well, just concentrate on this case tonight, and then hopefully tomorrow it'll be taken care of."

"Let's hope it's that easy." After we get home, we decide to go on a long run together. It helps us relax and clear our heads. I like to have a clear head before I go to sleep so I can concentrate on a case.

When we get back, I cook good old spaghetti. We have some wine and watch TV to relax. We both have to go back to work tomorrow after this fun-filled, crazy weekend, so we decide to go to bed early.

I lie in bed and think of all the images Tom showed me today. I've got the address in my head, and I think of those poor kids, and then I get angry thinking about the dad injuring them. I imagine myself standing in front of their house and shut my eyes.

***

I'm sitting in my car outside of the exact house Tom showed me. I hear a car door shut and I slowly glance over at a van parked on the street. A man has just gotten out of it, and I can't believe my eyes. The license plate is 214. What the fuck? This can't be happening. I try to focus on the dad, but my mind is in another place. There's no way this is just a coincidence.

Then I hear kids screaming and crying. I turn my head and see the dad carrying the kids over his shoulder, one on each side, into the van. The kids are hitting his back and screaming. He slams the doors. I turn on my engine, ready to follow. The mom comes running out.

"Get back here with my kids, Daniel!" she screams and begins to chase after them. But the van takes off fast. I pull out and follow the van. I imagine the crying faces of the kids. I have to help them somehow. I follow him for about ten minutes until he pulls into an old and boarded-up Ray's Famous Pizza. This place has been closed for years, and no one has ever rented it or changed it into something else. It's completely locked up.

I watch him carry his kids, who are no longer fighting him. Their limp bodies hang over his shoulders as he walks through the back door of the old pizza place.

I get out of the car and walk up to the door. Of course, it's locked. I look around at specific details so I can tell Tom where they are.

That's when I see him standing across the street under a streetlight. Same black pants, red shirt, and baseball cap. I try hard to look at his face, and I can't see a thing. Then everything goes dark.

I wake up in a panic. Shaking my head, tears begin to fall. "Not again, this can't be happening." Luke wakes up right away like he usually does.

"Did you find out anything?"

"Yeah, I know where the kids are. I need to call Tom now so he can go find them and hopefully save their lives."

Tom answers tiredly.

"I know where those kids are. You and your officers need to go now before any more harm is done."

He seems to have woken up at that and raises his voice, "What? Where are they?"

"At the old Ray's Famous Pizza place. Go in the back door. And Tom, he was driving the van."

"Van? What do you mean?"

"I mean the same damned van that has been in all these stupid dreams, that involved Walter and his guys. The 214 van!" I scream into the phone.

"Okay, calm down. We'll take care of it." He hangs up quickly. I throw the phone on the bed.

"Something weird is going on, and I don't have a good feeling about it. I mean, the same van that has been linked to all these cases in my dreams? That guy was in the dream again, standing under the streetlight."

"I swear I'm going to kill this guy if I ever come across him."

"I'm scared he's going to come out of nowhere and at any time. Remember my fire dream? Doesn't this seem coincidental? It's like he's waiting to make the perfect move."

"Then we'll prepare ourselves. Never walk out of the house without your gun, and I'll take you to and from work. I don't want you to be alone."

I just lie my head against his chest and whisper, "Why now, when there are only a couple weeks till our wedding? I thought Walter was the only one who was trying to kill me, but now there's another?"

"We don't know that for sure. It could possibly be a coincidence or a figure made up in your dreams."

"The people in my dream have never been fictional before."

It's only 5:00 a.m., but I know I won't be able to sleep for another hour, so I get up, put the coffee on, and take a shower.

I have to act normal at work because I don't want them thinking anything is wrong. I have a wedding to get ready for, and this should be the happiest time in my life. I'm going to do my best to not worry about anything but that.

The day goes well. The thing I love about working with Bobby and Sarah is that they can make me laugh and forget my worries.

My cell phone rings. It's Tom. I step outside for a few seconds to talk to him.

"Hey, did you catch him?"

"We did and just in time. When we walked in he had them chained to walls by their hands. They were bruised and passed out from drugs when we found them. They're in the hospital now and seem to be doing better."

"Okay, good, and the van?"

"It wasn't the same van. You read the license plate wrong. It was GFHT-1214. You must have only seen the 214 at the end."

"Oh, thank goodness. I feel so much better now. Was there anyone else that seemed out of the ordinary when you were there?"

"No, why?"

"Just wondering. Thank you for saving those kids."

"Thank you for all your help. I won't bother you again for a while. Enjoy your wedding." While I'm relieved that the kids are safe and I misread the license plate, I'm still terrified of the man in the baseball cap. I have to promise myself I won't let it ruin my wedding. But I know he's going to show himself at some point.

Chapter 19

The Wedding

It's my wedding day and I wake up so happy. Luke stayed with Jeff for the night because we aren't allowed to see each other until the wedding. It's hard sleeping without him, but it does make it more exciting. May and Sarah are on their way over. We're going to eat a big breakfast and then go to the salon to get our hair and makeup done. I'm cooking scrambled eggs, bacon, and sausage when they walk in.

"Heyyyy, it's your wedding day!" they both say in sync. They run over to me and give me a big hug.

"I'm so excited! This is going to be the best day ever!"

"It's supposed to be, it's your WEDDING DAY!" May says.

"I'm starving! I brought some orange juice and champagne to make us mimosas as we get ready," says Sarah.

"Thanks, I'll need some of that to calm my nerves as the time gets closer."

We eat, laugh, have a few mimosas, and then head off to the salon. Good thing Luke and I packed yesterday for the honeymoon because I'd have no time today. I'm super excited to go on a cruise to the Caribbean—our first vacation as a married couple.

"Only a few hours to go and I'll be Mrs. Luke Jackson." It sounds so good.

"I know! You're going to be the most beautiful bride ever," says May.

When we get to the salon, my hairdresser, Missy, has already set up four chairs around her area. She has decorated the seats, and one says "the bride."

The girls are looking through magazines to see what they want their hair to look like. I already know mine.

"Okay, miss bride, how do you want your hair?"

"I want it down with lots of big curls, but I want a strand of hair on each side to braid together in the back. So it kind of looks half-up and half-down." I show her a picture of what I want.

"I think that's perfect, and you'll look beautiful."

One of the other hairdressers brings us all glasses of champagne.

They turn up the music, and we all sing and laugh. When our hair is finished, we start on our makeup. I realize this is the last step before putting on our dresses. My heart begins to race. I don't know why I'm so nervous.

"Well, you girls are all finished!" says Missy. We all look at each other and smile.

"Thank you so much! I can't believe how close we are to the wedding!"

May rented a limo to drive us around for the day. We all have a glass of champagne on the way back to my house. When we get back to the house, we get our dresses out and lay them on the bed.

"Wow, this is it. Once I put this on, it's wedding time," I say nervously.

"Here, this will help," says May as she hands me a glass of champagne. I down it like a shot.

"Phew, okay, here we go." I help the girls get dressed first. The medium-gray dresses turned out perfectly. They're short in length, right above the knee.

"You girls look beautiful."

"Thanks, but it's your turn now."

My dress is tight in the bodice and then flows from my hips down. It has straps but the back of the dress is cut deep and stops right above my lower back. The bodice is sparkly, but not overbearing. My heels are white with silver and orange sparkles. The final touch is the veil that covers the back of my head.

I stare at myself in the mirror. I've never seen myself look this beautiful before. I start to get teary eyed because my dream wedding is coming true. I turn toward the girls and see that they're silent with tears.

"Linda, you look stunning. Luke is totally going to cry when he sees you," says May. We all laugh.

"Are you ready for the limo to take us to the country club?" asks May.

After I see myself all dressed up, I'm more than ready. "Yes, I'm so ready to get married."

The drive is about thirty minutes long, and we all have one last glass of champagne. May decides to make a toast.

She raises her glass, and we follow suit. "Cheers to Linda, who's about to tie the knot with her soul mate."

As we pull up to the country club, my mom and dad are standing outside waiting for us. I wasn't ready to see them, especially my dad. I know he's going to cry again. The girls get out first. I get out and look at Mom and Dad.

They both smile, and then the tears come down. "Please don't cry because then I will and I don't want to ruin my makeup."

"I can't help it. You look so beautiful it's hard to put into words," says Dad. That totally makes me cry. I give them both a big hug and a kiss on the cheek.

"Now go and marry that special man of yours," says Mom.

"See you soon." Dad comes with us since he's walking me down the aisle. I think he's having a rough time knowing he has to officially give me away. We've been so close my whole life, but I know that he's beyond happy for me.

The ceremony is about to start. We all line up in the room adjacent to the main ballroom. "The room is beautiful, and Luke looks very handsome," says Dad.

The rooms are decorated with fall leaves, pumpkins, and white and orange candles. It looks just as I have dreamed.

Dad turns to me and grabs my hands and says, "Linda, I'm so very proud of who you are and what you have become. I'm so happy that you found your soul mate, but just know you'll always be my little girl."

I smile, and my eyes begin to water, but I hold it back. "I love you so much, Dad. You'll always be my number one man in my life." We both face forward, and I grab onto his arm and we begin walking.

"Here we go," he says.

My stomachs is in knots, but when I enter the room and see Luke standing under the beautiful alter with the beautiful fall foliage in the background, my nerves turn into excitement and comfort. I know I'm marrying my best friend.

Luke smiles at me the whole time I'm walking, and I see a few tears fall from his beautiful eyes. Nothing else matters right now. The only person I see is Luke. It's like everything and everyone else in the room has disappeared.

When my dad hands me off, I kiss him on the cheek and then I stare at Luke and whisper, "I love you."

"I love you," he whispers back.

The wedding is more beautiful than I imagined. We exchange our vows, put the rings on each other, and when it's time to kiss, we give it all we've got. Everyone is cheering and crying.

The reception is so much fun. The food is amazing. The alcohol is good, and there's a lot of it. Everyone is dancing and having a good time. May's maid-of-honor speech makes me cry. Good thing the ceremony is already over because my makeup is screwed after that.

It's time for the father-daughter dance. It's so sweet, and neither of us cry because we both are so happy. Then Luke and I dance the night away.

We change into our traveling clothes, and as we walk out of the country club, everyone is standing there, and they all throw glitter up in the air. It's as if we're walking through a rainbow shower of glitter. We get into the limo, and we're off to the airport for our honeymoon.

Luke and I kiss each other, and then we look into each other's eyes. The feeling of true love is better than life itself.

"You looked so beautiful today. I really had to hold back the tears when I saw you."

I smile shyly and say, "You looked so handsome up there, almost took my breath away."

Luke kisses me again. "Mrs. Jackson."

I smile. "That has a nice ring to it."

"Yes, it does, and finally being able to call you my wife sounds even better." We kiss until the limo driver stops driving and opens the door for us.

He helps us carry our bags to our terminal. "Thank you, sir," says Luke.

"You're welcome. I hope you have a wonderful honeymoon."

"Thank you," I say.

When we're sitting on the plane, Luke whispers in my ear, "I can't wait to get you out of those clothes."

"I can't wait until you take them off me," I say as I kiss him.

***

Unfortunately, the honeymoon has to come to an end. We

have to leave paradise and go back to our normal lives. At least I can now call Luke my husband. This whole week has been the most relaxing week of my life, and I'll never forget it.

"Are you ready to go back to the real world?" Luke asks me.

"No, I don't ever want to leave," I say with a sad face.

"Just think, we have our whole lives together. We can travel and do so many things."

"You always know how to put me in a good mood." I smile and kiss him.

It's definitely a long flight back to reality. When we land, we have to get a taxi back to the house.

"I'm spoiled after all that. I want the limo," I whine. Luke shakes his head and laughs.

When we get back to the house, we unpack and start doing laundry. Luke looks through the mail.

"Um, Linda, there's a letter addressed to you, but it only has your name, not our address. Which means someone had to hand-deliver this." He sounds a little worried.

I shrug it off like it's nothing. "I'll read it later. Let's go get our pictures printed."

"We haven't even sat down yet."

"I know, but let's get it done before we sit down and don't want to move," I say, smiling.

Luke shakes his head and smiles. "Always have to get things done right away."

"Hey, that's why you married me; I keep you on your toes."

"You're right about that one." He winks.

Two hundred pictures later and they're all printed. Yes, two hundred. We wanted to capture each moment so we wouldn't forget. When we get home, we're officially drained. We order pizza for dinner and have a glass of wine.

I decide to open up the letter I received. It's just one sentence: "It's almost time for you to finally be mine."

I get chills over my entire body. I start to shake and hand Luke the letter.

"What the fuck is this? Who would write something like this?"

"I don't know. Just when life is perfect, I now have another stalker."

"And he knows where we live. This is sick. I'm calling Tom now."

I have the most sickening feeling in my stomach. I didn't see this coming. I haven't had any dreams. What else is going to come without me knowing? A new nightmare has begun. And all I can picture is the man standing under the streetlight with the baseball cap. I know he's the one who's after me.

Chapter 20

"Tom is on his way over now. Do you want to write down your description of the guy so he can have it drawn?"

"I don't even know what this guy's face looks like, just the clothes he wears."

"Well, it's a start. Any man matching that description must be caught and brought in for questioning."

"They can't go around arresting guys wearing ball caps. I just have a bad feeling that this one isn't going to be as easy to solve as the others. All I ever see is him standing across the street under the streetlamp. He never talks or moves. I have no clue what he's going to do."

"If you dream about him again, maybe try to go up to him to get a good look."

"I'll try, but it isn't as easy as you think it is," I say with frustration.

"I'm not saying it's easy, babe." He sounds hurt at my tone of voice.

"I'm sorry, I'm just frustrated with everything."

"I understand."

Just then, Tom knocks on the door.

He comes in with a straight and serious face. "What happened?"

I show him the letter. "So this guy knows where you live."

"That's why I called you. We both have an eerie feeling about this," says Luke.

"Do you have any leads? Have you noticed anyone following you recently?"

I tell him about the guy in my dreams.

"And you never see his face? He never talks to you or threatens you?"

"No, that's the weird thing. He wants to stay hidden so I don't know who he is. I can't see what he's going to do or if he'll even do anything."

"Maybe he won't attack. Maybe he's just a weirdo who likes to watch."

"And that makes its okay?" Luke says angrily.

"We'll assign an officer to follow you at all times, and if a guy shows up with that description, we'll take him in."

"Thanks, Tom."

He leaves with the description of the guy. Twenty minutes later, there's a cop car sitting outside our house.

"I do feel safer with a cop here," I say to Luke.

"Yeah, me too."

"I'm super exhausted, and we have to get up bright and early for work in the morning. And we're also doing dinner at my parents' house tomorrow to show them the pictures and tell them about the honeymoon. Let's go to bed."

"Okay wifey," he says with a smile.

***

I get to the shop a little earlier than normal, so I start all the coffeemakers and get out all the pastries. I take a cup of coffee out to the officer who followed me to work. It's not too long before Sarah and Bobby come in together.

"What's with the cop car across the street?" Bobby asks. I didn't even think about explaining the situation to them. I was kind of hoping they wouldn't notice the cop car.

"Um, well, it's a long story. They're just following me around for a little while."

"What kind of trouble are you in this time? You just got back from the honeymoon," Sarah says with a raised brow.

I tell them how we came home to the letter.

"Oh shit, that's scary. I'm sorry Linda," says Bobby.

"It's okay. They're taking extra precaution just in case."

As soon as we turn the sign to OPEN, our regular customers start coming in for their morning coffee. I know just about every order by heart for most of them.

While I'm ringing up one of our customers, I glance over at the door and am shocked to see Tyler walk into my shop.

"What are you doing here?"

"What? I can't grab a cup of coffee from the best coffee shop

167

Megan Johnson

in town?"

"You know better than to come here."

"I know, but I heard about the wedding, and I wanted to congratulate you. So congratulations, I hope you two have a happy life together." I'm bewildered. A feeling of anger automatically sets in. *What's he really doing here?*

"Mm-hmm, you came way out of your way to congratulate me, and that's it? You usually want something, so what is it?"

"Well, of course I want something." He pauses for a second, and my heart races. "I want a cup of coffee."

"Okay, whatever you say." I take his order. Is it a coincidence that Tyler shows up when I've been seeing, but not really seeing, this guy in my dreams and after receiving that letter?

He leans toward me as I hand him his coffee and whispers, "What I really want is you. You should have been my wife." My stomach drops. The look in his eyes isn't comforting; it's cold and obsessive. His eyes are big and eerie.

"You need to let this go, Tyler. I'm married and you need to move on with your life and leave me alone," I say quietly.

He begins to walk around the counter toward me. *Oh shit. Should I call for help?* His eyes are still big and crazy as he comes closer. I should move, but I'm scared and my feet seem to be rooted to the floor.

"If I can't have you, then he can't either," he says and grabs my arm.

I try to shake him loose and finally find my voice. "Get off me!" I yell. Heads turn and stare. He takes me to the ground with his arm around my neck.

Bobby comes running out of the back. He grabs Tyler by the neck and shakes him like a rag doll when he pulls him off me.

Sarah runs by us. "I'm going to get the cop!" Then she turns to the staring customers. "Everyone out now!" They scramble to their feet and run out the door. Meanwhile, Bobby has Tyler in a headlock so he can't go anywhere.

I rub the back of my head as I stand up. My head hit the floor as I fell, and he choked me pretty hard.

The cop comes in and puts handcuffs around Tyler's wrist and walks him out. I sit down and shake my head. I don't know why I didn't think of him before. I knew he was jealous of Luke, but I didn't think he was crazy enough to hurt me. That goes to show

168

even that though you think you may know a person well, they can turn out to be the complete opposite. That's a scary concept to think about. *What if Luke and Tom aren't who they say they are? What if deep down inside, they're capable of hurting me?* I shake my head. *That's nonsense. Stop thinking like that.* I married Luke because I know who he is, and I've worked with Tom for a long time now. I don't know much about his personal life, but I do know he'd do anything to protect me.

Sarah comes up as I'm gazing up at nothing and puts her hand on my shoulder. "Are you okay? Do you want me to call Luke?"

"I can't believe he actually hurt me. I thought he was going to kill me. I don't understand it. Yes, please call Luke for me. I'm in no shape to even try to describe what happened over the phone."

I sit there still in shock, scared and helpless. Sarah comes back a few minutes later with coffee.

"Luke is on his way."

I take the coffee. "Thank you." Sarah sits down and rubs my back as we wait.

Luke rushes through the door. When I see him, I get up, and he runs over to me and takes me in his arms. "Are you okay? That fucking bastard, I knew there was something wrong with him. I could kill him!"

"The cops arrested him."

"It's a good thing they did before I got here." I squeeze him tight. I don't want to let go. The comfort is what I need.

"Let's take you home," Luke says softly.

That night, he cooks me dinner and brings it to me in bed. We eat together as we watch TV. I have to take small bites because my throat and neck are still sore. Luke is trying hard to get my mind off what happened. It's working a little bit. As we watch TV, my phone rings. It's Tom. I forgot to call him about today, but I'm sure he found out soon enough.

"Hey, Tom."

"Hey, are you doing okay?"

"I'm doing all right, a little better now."

"I've been here with Tyler. I don't know what you ever saw in him. He's a nutcase."

Ouch, not the right thing to say to me right now. I'm silent because I don't know how to respond to that.

169

"But unfortunately, Tyler isn't your guy. He admits that he's jealous of Luke and what the two of you have, but he claims he isn't the one who wrote the letter or the one who's stalking you."

"And you believe him? He attacked me and tried to choke me to death!"

"I know, but my team searched his place and found nothing. He doesn't even own a red shirt."

"So because you didn't find the clothes the man wore in my dream, Tyler walks?"

"No, I want you to file a restraining order so he can't come anywhere near you. He's going in front of a judge in a few days, but more than likely when the jury sees how he's mentally unstable, they'll send him to a mental hospital for testing and treatment."

"A restraining order doesn't make me feel safe."

"I know, but it's the best we can do. He has never committed any crime, not even a speeding ticket. We did some research on his family history and bipolar disorder runs in the family. We think that's what is wrong with him."

"When I dated Tyler, I never saw any bipolar symptoms or signs. He seemed normal."

"It can be triggered by a big event or traumatic situation. I believe Tyler was so obsessed with you, that the wedding triggered this behavior."

"But he cheated on me and screwed me over!"

"But he also saw what he lost and became obsessed with what he couldn't have."

"Do you really think he won't come near me with a restraining order?"

"If he goes and gets the treatment he needs and is put on medication, I think you'll be okay."

"Well, I hope you're right. So if it's not Tyler, then there's still someone out there who's trying to get me."

"And we'll keep working on that until it is solved. The cops will still watch over you."

"Thanks, Tom."

"You're welcome. I'm sorry about all this, and I know I've said this before, but we'll end this once and for all. You'll be able to live your life without fear, I promise."

"Don't make promises you can't keep."

"Don't worry, I don't." He hangs up.

Luke has a blank look on his face. "A restraining order? That's it?"

I tell him everything Tom told me.

"This is bull shit. If Tyler isn't the man after you, then who is it? Tyler has the perfect MO for it. He has to be the guy."

"I agree, but Tom said there's no evidence to prove it."

"I hope I come in contact with whoever this man is first. I won't hold back. This has been going on way too long. We have to live in fear every day because of this asshole. This has got to stop."

"You're telling me. I want this to end more than anyone."

He hugs me. "I'll protect you. I'm going to do whatever I can to keep you safe."

***

We postponed dinner with my parents for a few days. When we finally made it over, Dad cooks some amazing barbeque chicken. We have it with mixed vegetables and sweet potatoes. The moscato wine goes perfect with dinner. Luke and I do most of the talking. We show them all the pictures and talk all about the honeymoon.

After a second glass of wine, I decide to tell them what happened with Tyler. Mom begins to tear up and Dad becomes angry. "Tyler? The same Tyler you dated? How could he do something like this?" Mom asks.

"I guess bipolar disorder can make someone do that."

"I'm so sorry you had to deal with that. Let's hope he doesn't show his face near any of us from here on out," Dad says. "I'll step in if I have to."

"I'm hoping it should be okay now." I change the subject. "So how's May doing? It has been a little while since I've seen her."

"Her job is going great, and she has started apartment hunting. She wants to be out in about a month."

"Wow, that's so soon. You think she can handle being on her own?" I ask.

"She seems stable enough, and she wants to move on with her life. I think she's ready. She is looking for a place close to you guys."

"Good, the closer she is, the better I'll feel. I'm surprised she's not here tonight."

"Oh, she has a new man in her life."

My ears perk up at that. "A new man? Is she ready to date? I mean, after what happened, I don't know if that's a good idea." I'm freaking out for some reason.

"Linda, calm down. That was months ago. She's fully recovered. This guy is supposed to be very nice, and she feels safe and comfortable with him."

I'm being the over protective sister as usual. "Well, I want to meet him first before it gets too serious."

"She already knows that. She's inviting him over here for dinner this weekend, just like you did with Luke."

"This guy better be ready to answer some questions. So where did they meet?"

"I'll let them tell you the story," Mom says with hesitation. She sounds concerned.

"Mom? What is it?"

"Nothing, just keep an open mind about the guy."

"How can I keep an open mind when I haven't even met him yet? What is his name?"

"I'll let May tell you." Mom is acting weird about this. I don't understand why she won't tell me.

When we leave my parents' house, I call May right away. "Why haven't you told me you're dating someone?"

"I didn't want to take away from the wedding and honeymoon, so I just decided to wait and tell you when you got back."

"How long have you been dating?"

"A few months."

"What! A few months and you kept it from me for this long? How could you?"

"Linda, calm down. I knew if you found out I was dating, it would have taken your mind away from the wedding, and I didn't want to do that. Please just relax and don't give the guy a hard time. I really like him, and I don't want you to scare him off."

"Scare him off? I'm not that bad." Luke looks over at me with a "yeah, right" kind of look.

"Okay, I am that bad, but it's only because I care about you. So who is it?"

"I know you care, and I'm not telling you anything about him until you meet him this weekend. I don't want you having preconceptions already in your head."

"All right, whatever you say. I'll support you, even if I'm not happy about it," I say with a joking sigh.

May laughs. "I love you, sis. See you in a few days."

"Okay, what's going on with this guy?" I turn to Luke when we hang up. "Why can't they even tell me his name?"

"I don't know babe, but we'll find out."

The next few days couldn't have gone by any slower. I keep imagining what this guy will be like. It's good that I have something to keep my mind occupied. I've almost forgotten that I have a stalker out there somewhere, watching and waiting for the perfect moment. I get chills down my spine thinking about it.

I can't find the right outfit to wear. I mean, this is a big deal meeting a boyfriend of May's. She hasn't really had a serious one, so this is weird and different for me.

"Babe, you've tried on ten outfits; just pick one. You look great in all of them. We're already late."

"I'm doing that on purpose so the guy has extra time to get nervous," I say with a wink.

Luke laughs and shakes his head. "You're bad, babe."

On our way over there, I begin to get a little nervous myself. I mean, why can't they at least tell me the guy's name? We park and walk in. Everyone is sitting around the table: Mom, Dad, May, and the man holding her hand. And now I see why they waited to tell me.

"TOM!"

Chapter 21

"Sis, don't freak out. This isn't just a fling. Tom and I really have feelings for each other."

"Don't freak out?" I yell. "It's Tom!" I turn on him. "After everything that happened to May, I can't believe you'd even pursue her!" Tom can't even look me in the eyes.

I remember May making a joke about hooking up with Tom awhile back, but I thought she was only joking. Tom and my sister? I'm not sure how I feel about this. This has got to be why Tom was acting a little standoffish the past few times I've seen him.

He finally speaks, "I really care for May. I'm not going to hurt her."

"You better not, or you'll be the one getting hurt. You're like ten years older than her!" I say indignantly. Everyone sits silently at the table; even Luke doesn't say anything. I think he's in just as much shock as I am. "So how did this all happen?"

"Well," May says as she smiles sweetly at Tom, "he was just so nice and sweet to me after everything that happened. He came and checked on me while I was in the hospital. Then after that, we started talking more and more. It just happened. We both fell for each other."

"This happened in the hospital? You didn't give her any time to heal?"

"Linda, stop. I'm glad he didn't. It was nice to feel comforted and safe."

I stand there and cross my arms. Yeah, Tom can be a good guy, but I just don't like the fact that they have been hiding this from me the whole time. I don't know if I truly trust Tom, especially after some comments he has said to me in the past.

"He's a detective for the FBI; he'll keep her safe," says Luke.

He's probably just happy Tom found someone else to fawn over instead of me.

"I'll do whatever it takes to protect her," Tom says.

I let out a huge sigh. "All right, I guess I have to just get it over it."

"What's your problem? Why are you acting like this is about you? Can't you just be happy for me, please?" May asks desperately.

"If you're happy, sis, then I am." A little white lie, but who cares?

We sit down to eat, and I try to enjoy dinner. It's a good meal, but I'm still a little sick inside after finding this out. I hope Tom doesn't share what happens at work with May. I don't want her to get involved at all, especially after what happened to her.

We leave as soon as dinner is over. I need time to digest this information and get it through my head that my younger sister is dating Tom.

"Linda, it really will be okay. You've been working with Tom for over a year. You know he's a good guy."

A *good guy who likes to flirt, at least he did with me.*

"I know, but I have an unsettling feeling about this whole thing."

"That's only because you haven't had time to really think about it."

"Yeah, I guess." Luke decides to take me to Bay Street Biergarten so I can have a few drinks and relax. It feels good to let loose. I haven't done it since the honeymoon. We stay for a few hours and then head home.

We make straight for the bedroom when we get home. Luke picks me up, throws me on the bed, and climbs on top of me. "Lie back and relax, let me take care of you," he whispers in my ear.

***

I'm inside the library at the College of Charleston around midnight. I didn't even know the library was open this late. I look around and see only one other girl, who looks like she's studying. I'm here for a reason, so obviously something is going to happen, and I have to be ready for it. There's someone working the counter; he's wearing glasses and has his head deep inside a comic book. He isn't going to notice if anything happens.

I decide to sit down and wait. Then all of a sudden, someone walks into the library. When I see who it is, I almost let out a scream. He's tall, wearing blue jeans, a red shirt, and a baseball cap. I know exactly who this guy is. I try to move a little to get a look at him, but I still can't. It's the weirdest thing because I can never see his face, not even a little bit. He wears the cap down as low as it can go. The librarian has fallen asleep with his head on the comic book on the counter and doesn't even see him walk in. The guy walks up to the girl from behind, puts his hand over her mouth, and drags her out of her chair.

He pulls her behind a bunch of bookshelves in the back of the library, and I really don't want to know what happens next. I expect the worst. I quickly yet quietly walk over to the section of shelves. I'm scared, but I think of the poor girl and how she needs help.

I turn the corner, and there he is, standing there, thrusting his hips forward with the girl's face shoved into the bookshelf and her pants around her ankles. She's crying and trying to move her head to breathe, but his grip is too strong. This is my chance to get a look at his face. He starts to look up at me. My body is shaking with fear. My heart races, and I freeze. Then there is darkness.

I wake up to the sound of my alarm. "Shit!" I yell out. I'm so pissed that I woke up right as I was about to get a look at the guy.

"I had another fucking dream about the guy." I tell Luke what happened.

"It sounds like he's getting closer to revealing himself. I hope he does it in your dream and not in real life." His comment scares the shit out of me. What if this is building up in my dream, and then it happens in real life, and I won't be able to see it coming? But who's doing this and why? I feel a panic attack coming on, and I break out in a sweat.

"I've got to call Tom and let him know about this. He needs to save the girl. Hopefully, he can catch this guy as well."

***

Luke drops me off at work again. I wish I could walk like I used to. Always having to watch every move I make is getting tiring. I can't wait until this is over, but who knows how long that will be?

Work is going well. No exes or weird guys. Sarah and Bobby can tell I'm preoccupied but decide to keep their mouths shut and not ask any questions, which is good because I don't feel like talking anyway.

May comes in right before closing. "Work is kicking my butt today. I figured I'd come in and get a coffee to keep my mind sharp."

"Sounds like a tough job. How do you like it?" As we talk, I make her favorite latte.

"I love it. I love designing clothes and having the models try them on. Seeing my stuff on the runway is a pretty satisfying feeling."

"I'm very proud of you." I don't want to talk about the elephant in the room, but May has other plans.

"I know that you don't approve of Tom and don't agree with my decision, but it's my decision, and I really do like him."

I raise one eyebrow and look at her. "I remember my first love; obviously, it didn't work out in the end. Most first loves don't end up working out anyway."

"Ouch, that hurt."

"I didn't mean for it to come off that way. I hope that this works out for you. I can see that you're happy. I'll kill him though, if he hurts you in anyway."

"Oh I know you will, and so does Tom." We both start to lighten up a little after that.

I hand her the coffee. I never charge family members.

"Thanks, Linda. Back to work. I love you."

"I love you too, May." I watch her walk out the door, happy as can be. But I get this horrible feeling in my stomach. Something about May and Tom honestly has me worried. It's not just because I'm the big sister and I'd worry about any guy she dates, but something isn't right here.

***

I wake up the next morning to my alarm. I'm surprised I slept through the whole night without any interruptions. I feel refreshed and ready for the day. I roll over to check my phone for messages. I didn't get any calls from Tom. I begin to worry, so I call him to see what's going on.

"Tom, I didn't get a phone call last night. Did you catch the guy? Is the girl okay?"

Once Luke hears me talking, he sits up in bed. "Is it Tom?" he whispers. I nod my head.

"Linda, nothing happened at the library last night. There was no girl in there. There was no attack and no sign of the baseball cap guy."

"What?" I'm so confused. This is the first time my dream was completely wrong. I've gotten some details mixed up before, but never has the crime I've dreamed not occurred. What does this mean?

"Nothing happened."

"Are you sure? Because I remember everything about that dream, and I'm usually never wrong."

"I'm sure. Maybe it was just an ordinary nightmare. There's a first time for everything," Tom says, shrugging it off.

"A nightmare about the guy who's after me, whom I've dreamed about many times before, and I'm wrong? Are you saying this doesn't mean anything and maybe there's no guy after me?" I'm starting to get angry at this point.

"Linda, did I say that?"

"No, but the tone of your voice implies it. I know there's someone after me. I can feel something bad is going to happen. I don't know how he's doing it, but this guy is interfering with my dreams and what I can see. I can't see into the future with this guy. He's taunting me."

"We'll keep surveillance on your house. I'm sorry, Linda, but there's nothing else I can do at this point." I hang up, aggravated.

"Something isn't right here, Luke. My dream was wrong. This guy is totally messing with me and knows how I dream. He must have been following me for a long time to know me this well."

"We'll be ready for this guy when he comes," Luke says. He seems to be getting frustrated with this whole thing as well. I know he wants it to be over as much as I do. We both just want to live in peace.

"I don't know how I'm going to be able to function at work after all this," I say.

"If you take off work, then you'll be sitting around driving yourself crazy trying to figure this out. The last thing you need right now is to be alone."

"You're right."

We both start getting ready for work. It has to be someone who knows what my dreams are like and what they usually consist of. There are only a few people in my life who know me and my dreams that well, and they're all very close to me. That's what scares me the most.

Chapter 22

A few weeks pass, and nothing out of the ordinary happens. No man in a baseball cap has come after me. I haven't had any more dreams about him. Maybe it's just a character in a dream; maybe I just worry too much. I can't figure it out but I try to stop worrying about it. Thanksgiving is tomorrow, and I want to be in a good mood and enjoy time with my family. I'm thankful for everyone and that everyone is safe.

Thanksgiving dinner will be held at my parents' house, like usual. I'm making the pumpkin pies. Luke is going to help mom with the turkey. This is going to be the first family event where May has brought a boyfriend over to meet the family, so obviously this really is a serious relationship. I've finally started to come to terms with it.

I'm finishing up the pumpkin pies when Luke walks in from work.

"Mmmm, something smells good in here." He tries to put his finger in one of the pies to get a taste. I slap his hand away and laugh. Luke always tries to eat the desserts I make ahead of time.

"NO! You can have some of the pie tomorrow with the rest of the family."

We eat leftover pizza from the night before and then relax for the rest of the night.

My stomach hasn't been feeling all that good today. The last thing I want to be is sick for tomorrow's dinner. "Babe, I haven't been feeling good today. I'm going to go to bed now and get a good night's rest. I don't want to be sick at the biggest family gathering of the year."

"Do you need me to get you anything?" He's always so sweet.

"No, I just think I need some rest. I love you."

"I hope you feel better in the morning." He kisses me good night.

***

I'm running to the toilet, and when I get there, I start puking. I don't feel like I have the flu or anything. Maybe it was something in the food I ate. I throw up one more time and then sit on the edge of the tub with my head between my knees.

My head pops up quick, and I realize why this could be happening. I think back and realize that I'm more than a month late with my period. I actually can't remember the last time I had one. Then I get a huge smile on my face. Maybe I'm pregnant!

I go to the store to pick up pregnancy tests and hurry home. I excitedly take the test and set it on the counter as I wait for the results.

Two minutes later, I look and a pink plus appears on the test. "I'm pregnant!" I yell to no one. This is the greatest feeling. I smile and rub my stomach. I can't wait to tell Luke.

I wake up to the sun shining in my room. I look over at the clock: eleven thirty. I can't believe how late I slept. Then I think about my dream. The feeling of being sick and tired could be symptoms. Maybe I really am pregnant!

Luke is making breakfast, so I walk down there all smiles. "Good morning, sleepyhead," he says.

"Good morning. I think there's a reason why I've been so sleepy and why I haven't been feeling my best." At first Luke raises in eyebrow in concern. I walk up to him and look him in the eyes. "I think I might be pregnant."

"What! Really? This is the best news I've ever received!"

"Now I'm not a hundred percent sure. I had a dream about being pregnant, and then I woke up this morning realizing I'm over a month late. I guess I didn't realize it with everything that has been going on. I'm going to the store to buy a pregnancy test."

"I'm going with you."

"Okay, but first I'm going to eat this yummy breakfast because I'm starving."

"And you might be eating for two!" Luke says with a wink.

"If I'm pregnant, we can tell the family today!"

We drive to the closest drugstore and buy a pregnancy test. I'm nervous because I do want to be pregnant and will be disappointed if I'm not, but my dreams are usually accurate—besides the one before last, of course. When we get back home, I go straight upstairs to the bathroom. Luke is standing right outside waiting for me.

I set the test on the counter and open the door for Luke to come in. I look at him and put my arms around his neck. "This is it, baby. We could be starting our family." I turn around and look at the test with butterflies in my stomach. Then I see the pink plus.

"Baby, we're pregnant!"

Luke picks me up and twirls me around, and I can't stop laughing.

Luke sets me down and takes my face in his hands. "I love you so much, and I can't wait for our baby to be born. I know the baby will be beautiful because it'll have your genes." I swear he always knows the right thing to say.

"I love you so much too. And it goes both ways. That baby is going to be one good-looking child." I smile, and he pulls me close again.

We get ready to go to my parents' house, and I grab the pumpkin pies on our way out. On the drive over, I think about the pregnancy. I must have been pregnant for a few weeks. "Hey, what if me being pregnant is what's causing all the weird and inaccurate dreams? Maybe that's why I can't see things anymore or why my dreams have been wrong."

"I guess it could be. You do have another person growing inside you. It could be affecting the dreams."

"That would make me feel better because I thought I was going to lose this ability or I was just going crazy seeing weird men in my dreams."

"It could be a lot of things. The baby and how Walter was after you for so long. It could be the fear coming out in your dreams."

"Yeah, I guess you're right." I suddenly feel as if a weight has been lifted from my shoulders. When we arrive at my parents' house there are already a ton of cars parked down the street.

We walk in to the aroma of wonderful food. The smell overtakes all of my senses and makes my stomach growl. Luke helps Mom with the final touches on the turkey while I mingle with the family. It's loud in the house, but it's so nice to have everyone in the same place. I find May and Tom, and they look happy.

Every time I turn the corner, there's food and alcohol available.

Usually, everyone is already tipsy by the time dinner is actually ready. Looks like I'll be the sober one making fun of everyone. Finally, dinner is ready, and everyone circles up to say grace. I think this is the perfect time to tell everyone. Once Dad has finished saying grace, I decide to tell them. I'm super nervous.

"Everyone, Luke and I have an announcement we would like to share with you. We're having a baby! I'm pregnant!" A mass of loud cheers echoes through the house, and I'm stormed with hugs and kisses and congratulations. It's a wonderful celebration. Mom and Dad come up to me last and give me a big hug and kiss.

"Why didn't you call us right away when you found out?" asks Mom.

"We just found out today! We thought it'd be nice to tell the whole family."

"I'm so excited to become a grandparent," says Dad. Then Mom begins to tear up with joy.

"Aw Mom, don't cry."

"I'm just so happy for the both of you. Have you picked out names yet?"

"Mom, we just found out today! We haven't even had time to discuss it yet, but I'm sure we'll come up with the perfect name."

Mom smiles. "Sorry, I'm just so excited!"

I smile and look over at Luke. "So are we."

"All right," Dad says. "Let's go and enjoy this wonderful food and give thanks to God for the precious gift he has just provided us: another member of the family."

The rest of the evening is full of family fun. We're starting to get exhausted. Everyone starts to leave around the same time. Surprisingly, I didn't get to talk to May and Tom that much. I think they're still leery about me and how I feel. But only a few minutes later, May and Tom both come up to me and Luke as they're getting ready to leave.

"Sis, I'm so excited for you both. I can't wait to become an aunt." She gives me a big hug and then walks out the door. Tom walks by both of us on the way out.

"Congrats to you both," he says with a smile and a nod.

"Thank you," Luke and I say at the same time.

On our way home we're still glowing and smiling. As we pull up to our house, I notice something in the distance that looks all too familiar.

My heart drops into my stomach. "Oh shit, there's no way." "What, babe? What is it?"

"Do you see the van parked down the street?"

"Yeah, looks like a normal van," he says, confused.

"No, Luke, that isn't an ordinary van. That is the van Walter and his people used for the kidnappings."

"Are you sure?"

"Pull up behind it and check out the license plate." I get out my phone ready to take a picture so Tom will know I'm not making this up.

"Oh my God, you're right, 214," Luke says in shock. I snap a picture of it and send it to Tom.

"I told you! Maybe that guy with the baseball cap really is after me."

I dial Tom's number. "Did you get my picture?"

"Yeah, I did. Where's that van?"

"It's parked right outside my house. I bet it has something to do with the guy in the baseball cap. There's no fucking way this is a coincidence."

"Okay, relax, I'm sending some of my officers over right away to check it out. Sit there in the car with the doors locked. I don't want you going inside; someone could be in there."

I hang up and turn to Luke. "He's sending cops over now and says to stay put."

We keep looking out of the car window until the cops arrive. They park near our house and step out. Two of them give us a head nod and proceed to the van. Two others are checking the surroundings of the house. I look at Luke with worried eyes.

One of the cops opens the door of the van, and it instantly explodes, sending the cop flying back, huge flames lighting up the night around us.

"Oh my God! Whoever did this is sending us a message. He's getting closer, Luke." The other cops come running to check on the officer. He's injured, but it doesn't seem serious. They call in an ambulance and fire truck. People in the neighborhood start coming out of their houses to see what the commotion is.

Luke starts to get out to check on the injured officer when one of the cops tells him to stop and get back inside the car. "Stay here," I say anxiously. "This guy is after us and we don't want to put ourselves out there for him to see. Plus, I don't want you to leave me alone." I'm terrified.

"I won't ever leave you." He wraps me in his arms to help my shaking. About ten minutes later, a news crew shows up, and Tom comes knocking on our window.

"I'm so sorry this happened. We had no idea."

"Well, maybe if you would have kept the officers following us like before, this wouldn't have happened," Luke says angrily.

"You're absolutely right. After we get this all cleaned up and get the press out of here, I'm going to sit outside and watch the property myself. I owe it to you both."

"Thank you, Tom." He nods, and Luke rolls up the window. It takes about an hour to get everything cleared and for the reporters to leave. I'm so tired, but I'm not sure I'm going to be able to sleep. I know deep down inside this was a warning. And the worst part is I didn't see any of it coming.

***

As we lie in bed, Luke holds me tight like he'll never let me go. Despite my nerves, I'm exhausted, and I soon fall asleep. I wake up some time later to a strange smell. I'm still half-asleep, but I quickly realize what it is. Smoke!

I shake Luke awake. "Get up, our house is on fire!" A strong sense of déjà vu comes over me. The clock reads 3:15 a.m. This is my dream about the fire coming true, the one where I didn't survive.

"Luke, we need to hurry. In my dream about the fire I fall through the floor," I say frantically. We both rush to put our shoes on. I don't bother checking the doorknob or try to leave the room because I already know the flames have engulfed the first floor. "I need to call 911!"

"No time, plus Tom is out there. I'm sure he sees this is and is calling it in. We have to get out now!"

The only way to get out of here is to climb out of the window. Luke and I look at the window and then at each other. We know what we have to do. My stomach is in knots and my heart is pounding. I begin to worry about my baby and if we're going to make it.

"I'll go first, and once I'm on that tree limb, you'll grab my hand and I'll pull you over. We'll slowly climb down the tree."

"Okay, I can do this." I glance outside at the tree and see a figure standing across the street wearing a baseball cap, long pants, and a t-shirt. "Luke, look over by the streetlight." He takes a quick glance but doesn't pay much attention. He's too focused on getting us out of the house.

The flames begin to lick up our bedroom door, and the heat becomes unbearable.

"We've got to go now!" shouts Luke. He leaps to the tree and barely makes it. I scream as he falls and latches onto the limb, pulling himself up. I step up into the window. I've never been so scared in my life. If I miss Luke's hand and fall, I'm risking not only my life but our baby's.

"Linda, grab my hand! I'll not let you go, I promise." He's standing on the big thick limb of the tree, holding on to another limb with one hand and holding the other hand out for me. I finally get the courage as the flames get closer to me, and I leap onto the tree and grab Luke's hand.

His grip is so strong there's no way either of us is falling off the tree. "Good job, baby," he says as he presses a kiss to my forehead. "Now we have to slowly climb down the tree." Luke makes his way down first. Once he's on the ground, he talks me through it and guides me down. As soon as my feet hit the ground, a huge BANG comes from the house, as if a grenade went off, and the entire house is taken over by the fire. Luke pulls me out into the street, and I stand there in shock, tears falling down my face.

"All of our belongings are gone," I moan.

"At least we're safe, baby." He looks around. Our neighbors are running out into the street, but there are no emergency personnel. "Why in the hell aren't the fire trucks here yet? Tom should have called and taken care of it."

I look around too. "Wait, where is Tom? He said he wouldn't leave. Do you think something happened to him?" I look over to the streetlight and tug on Luke's hand. The man in the baseball cap is still standing there, like he's waiting for us to come over.

"That asshole put my family's life in danger and ruined our home. I'm going to fucking kill him." Luke runs toward the man, and I follow. To my surprise, the man takes off running. Luke and I keep following. I have to know who he is and what he wanted with me and my family.

He runs down the street and then turns into an alleyway. He's fast, but Luke is faster. Luke catches up to the guy and tackles him to the ground. I finally catch up with them as Luke is struggling to get the guy to turn over so we can see his face.

"You're gonna pay for everything you've put my family through, you son of a bitch! I want to see your fucking face before I kill you."

That's when the man finally twists around. Luke is kneeling over him with his fist poised to strike, but he freezes and stares at the man in shock. "What the fuck?"

The light in the alley is dim, but I can see the man's face, and I can't believe my eyes.

Chapter 23

"TOM? It has been you all along?" Luke's shock is quickly overcome by anger, and he punches Tom in the face.

Tom is able to block Luke's next punch and shoves him off. Luke falls over to the side, and Tom gets up quickly with his fists up, ready to fight. "I wouldn't try to hit me again," he says as blood drips from his nose.

Luke stalks forward when I interrupt. "Stop. Tom, what the fuck? Why would you do something like this? After all the good work we've done together, and after seducing my sister...you asshole! You got to know myself and my family like it was your own. You knew I was pregnant and still put us in danger. We all trusted you."

I throw my arms up in supplication. "Why?" Fear, pain, and shock are all I feel right now. Deep down, I knew there was something strange about Tom, but I always thought it was because he had a thing for me. I didn't know he'd turn out to be crazy.

Tom smiles a vindictive and hateful smile. Luke stands guard, ready to make a move if needed. "It was you all along, Linda. You were meant to be mine. We were supposed to fall in love and become the famous couple who could solve crimes. No one truly understands your talent but me. I helped you bring out the dreams and evolve into something even greater, something out of this world. I helped you to see the future clearer. I knew you better than you knew yourself.

"I've followed you for a very long time. Remember me telling you how I was able to see things in the future with my dreams as well? Well, I saw you coming. I saw us as a couple, in love, sharing our gift, becoming the heroes of the town. When I heard about you from the other cops, at first I thought it was a coincidence. But when I saw you in person, I couldn't believe my eyes. My dream came true. But this asshole," he points to Luke, "got in the way of our love, our adventure, and our life together."

My stomach is sick, my heart racing. I let him into my life, I trusted him, and I even had some sort of feelings for him. What was I thinking? How could I not have seen it?

I look at him in shock. "You're sick, Tom! Look at yourself! And May? How could you?"

"She's your sister and the closest I could get to you. But she doesn't even compare; she isn't like you at all, Linda. You're special, and I had to get closer to you somehow."

"I'd watch what you say," Luke snarls.

The horror of the situation and the lengths he must have gone to start to sink in. "You used your position to call off the officers watching out for me whenever it was convenient for you."

"I orchestrated this entire plan," he says with sick satisfaction. "I recruited Walter Glass myself, and all of the other people involved. I choreographed the kidnappings and the van. I wanted to make you think and make your dreams stronger. I knew what got to you and what didn't. I was able to keep myself hidden this whole time by putting your mind in other places."

"Oh my God, Linda's right, you're fucking sick. Why in the world are you telling us this?" Luke spits out.

"You caught me, which is what I wanted in the end. It doesn't matter now what I say. I don't care how I end up as long as you know the truth. That it was supposed to be you and me, Linda, forever, and just the fact that you know and will never be able to forget me will satisfy me enough."

"Just wait until the FBI finds out about you," I tell him.

"They'll never find out. I've covered my tracks well. You think they'll believe you, who has been working for me all this time, over me?"

"Oh, they will, you better believe it," says Luke.

I hear sirens in the distance.

"It's time, Luke. We need to bring him in." Luke shakes his head, lunges forward, and punches Tom so hard in the face it knocks him straight to the ground. Blood flies from his mouth as he hits the concrete. Luke stands over his body with his fist raised. "Linda, bring the cops over here. I'll stay with Tom." I nod my head and run back over to our house. I stop dead in my tracks when I see the firefighters putting out the fire. The house is burnt to a crisp; I'm surprised it's still standing. The front of the house is completely black.

I walk up to an officer who's standing by his car. I glance at his name tag. "Hello, Officer London."

"Hello, ma'am, is this your house?"

"Yes, it is. My husband and I were able to escape just in time."

"You're very lucky; do you know how the fire got started?"

"Yes, it was started by a man who has been stalking me, and my husband has him trapped in an alley down the street."

He gives me a funny look, his unibrow scrunched together. "Explain the story to me as we drive over there."

I tell him the story but don't give him Tom's name. I want the cop to see Tom first for himself.

When we get there, Luke is still standing over Tom's limp body. He shakes the officer's hand and introduces himself. "This is the man who burned down our house. He was standing outside when we escaped, so I chased after him."

"Good work. Let me take a look at him." Officer London squats down to get a closer look at his face.

He stands up quickly. "You have the wrong man. This is FBI Detective Tom Walker, one of the best in town."

"No, we have the right man. I have proof," I say proudly. Even Luke looks surprised. I pull out my phone. "I recorded everything!" I say with a smile.

"You never cease to amaze me," says Luke.

I hit the play button, and the officer listens to everything.

"Wow, I'm shocked," Officer London says. "Tom was always an outstanding detective. Talk about being completely wrong about someone. Time to take this son of a bitch away."

"You better lock him up and make sure he never gets out. He knows a lot of people, and I'm sure there are still some out here willing to work with him," says Luke. "I want to talk to his FBI superiors right away."

"I'll put the call in right now. And don't worry, we'll take serious precautions. It'll be up to a jury now, but I don't think you have anything to worry about. Thank you for helping us catch him. I'm glad you weren't hurt." He calls for backup to help him take the still unconscious Tom away.

I shake my head. Luke takes me in his arms and holds me. He

kisses me on the forehead.

"It's finally over, Linda, once and for all."

"I still can't believe it was Tom this whole time. He got so close to our family. May is going to be so hurt. Our family has been through hell."

"Yes, we have, but we're all safe now and there's a baby on the way we need to focus on. Where are we going to stay until we can find a new place to live?"

"We can stay with my parents or even May. She has her own place now."

"Do you think May would mind?"

"I don't know how she's going to react when we tell her about Tom. But regardless, she's going to need our support. I don't know how I'm going to break it to her."

"Once she finds out what he did, I think she'll be more angry than heartbroken."

"I hope you're right, Luke. I hope you're right."

"We might as well search through the house to see if anything is salvageable," he says. I walk in and immediately tear up. I carefully pick my way through the still smoldering black ash. Everything is gone. The burning stench fills my nostrils, and I have to hold my nose.

"Oh my God! Everything is gone, Luke. There's nothing left."

Luke sifts through a pile of rubble. "Everything but these," he says and hands me our wedding and honeymoon photo albums, which, miraculously, are untouched.

"I can't believe it." I was already crying, but now they're tears of joy. Our memories have survived, and this has to be a sign that good things are coming our way.

"I told you good things were going to happen for us," Luke says as if he read my mind. He kisses me, and I hold the photo albums close to my heart.

We go outside, and I call May, telling her we need her to come over right away. We sit out on the porch step, watching the fire crew and the police canvassing the scene, waiting for May, trying to figure out what in the hell we're going to do. Thank goodness we still have months until the baby will be born. That gives us plenty of time to find a new place and get new things. And we have insurance. They should pay for all the damage.

"Don't worry, babe, everything will work out. After all we've been through it's about time something good comes our way."

Just then, May pulls up. She rushes out of her car and runs over to us. I stand up, and May throws her arms around me.

"Oh my gosh, are you okay?"

"We're okay, but all of our belongings are gone. We're going to need a place to stay for a few months until we can get back on our feet again and find a new place to live."

"Oh, come and stay with me! I need the company anyway, and I'm sure Tom won't mind."

Here it comes; I have to tell her. I look over at Luke with concern. He gives me a nod of encouragement.

May notices something is going on. "What is it? Is Tom okay? Is he here?"

"Well, not really, he…he was the one who did this to us. He was the one who set the house on fire and tried to kill us."

"What?" May yells. "Are you serious?" Her face turns red, and her eyes begin to sparkle with tears. "You're lying! I know you can't stand the fact that we're together, but I never thought you'd stoop so low!"

"I'm not lying, May," I say gently. "Tom has been after me since the beginning. Here, listen, this will tell you everything." I play the recording on my phone, and she starts to cry harder.

When it's finished, Luke puts his arm around me in support, and May just stands there, silent and staring into space.

It's a long time before she speaks. "I-I had no idea he was crazy. He was so sweet to me, and so kind. I can't believe he'd do something like this. I feel so awful and dirty. I can't believe he played me like that."

I rub her back. "I'm so sorry, May."

She shakes her head. "I can't believe it. I actually loved him, and it was all a lie."

I put my arms around her, and she doesn't push me away. I let her cry on my shoulder. I don't say anything else; I just let her get it all out.

After a few minutes, she wipes her tears and then glances back behind me to the house. "Linda, your house, your things, did anything survive?"

I show her the photo albums. "This is it."

"I'm so sorry. Let's head back to my place."

"I wish we could. I'm so exhausted." And to prove my point,

I yawn.

"We have to stay here to give our statements, and we're waiting for Tom's superiors at the FBI," Luke says.

"Then I'll wait with you," May says.

Chapter 24

A New Beginning
(For Real This Time)

It has been about five months since the fire, and our sweet Michael Bradley Jackson will be here in two months. The insurance paid for most of the damage and we were able to get a new house and new furniture, still downtown so we can be close to work.

The house we bought is a classic Charleston single house with white piazzas on both floors that run the whole length of the house. We chose pale yellow for Michael's room. Yellow is a happy color and very soothing. I think it's a perfect fit. Michael is healthy and I'm healthy. What more could we ask for?

I'm still working and will continue to work up until the day I have Michael, then I'll take some time off. I haven't had any worries about anything. Tom is in prison, and I haven't had any dreams. I think the baby has something to do with that, but who knows. All I know is that I'm grateful.

Luke and I are enjoying our new home, our work, and enjoying life free of madmen and psychos. I did talk to the guys at the FBI, and they want me to continue to work for them. I told them I if I have any dreams, I'll let them know, but for them not to contact me until after I have the baby. The last thing I need is added stress.

May has a new boyfriend named Charlie, and he's a pretty good guy. I had the FBI do a background check on him. I had to make sure he was okay for my sister, especially after the whole Tom thing.

Charlie treats my sister the way she deserves to be treated. I think he might be the one. He fits in well with our family. My parents are overly excited to have a grandchild on the way, and they keep buying stuff for Michael. He's going to be one spoiled baby.

I'm finally able to walk to work without the fear of someone watching. When I arrive on this beautiful spring day, Sarah and Bobby are already hard at work. "Guys, you really don't have to open and close every day. I know I'm seven months pregnant, but I can still work."

"We know. We just want to help out as much as possible," says Sarah.

"Well, I truly appreciate it."

"How's the new house treating you?" asks Bobby.

"It's everything we ever wanted in a house. Luke even put a swing on the tree in the backyard. It feels like home."

"We're so happy for you," Sarah says as she hugs me.

We're having a great day. The lunch rush has just died down when I start to feel some pains in my stomach.

"Ouch," I say as I fall to my knees holding my belly. "Oh my God!"

"Linda, are you okay? What's wrong?" Sarah says as she rushes over to help me.

"I don't know, I'm having weird pains." I grit my teeth to keep from crying out. The pain isn't going away; it's only becoming worse.

"I'm going to take you to the hospital right now."

"Take me to MUSC, where Luke is."

Sarah calls Luke on the way over to the hospital. We pull up to the emergency entrance. Sarah rushes in and comes back with a nurse pushing a wheelchair.

The nurse helps me get settled in the chair and wheels me into a cubicle in the emergency room. Luke runs in with a look of fear in his eyes.

"I can't be delivering yet! I'm still two months away. This is too early!" I cry out.

He grabs my hand. "Everything will be okay, Linda, I promise."

They place me on the exam table and a doctor comes in pushing a portable ultrasound machine. "Hello, Mrs. Jackson. Can you describe the pain for me and point to where it is?"

"It's right here," I say as I point to my upper abdomen. "It feels almost like a burning sensation. I've never felt anything like this before, and it hurts so badly."

"Okay, just relax and let me take a look." He uses the ultrasound wand to do a thorough examination.

"Everything seems to be fine. The baby is in good shape, and so are you."

"Then what's causing this pain?"

"I think it's a bad case of heartburn."

"Heartburn? Seriously? Now I feel like an idiot."

The doctor laughs. "Don't feel like an idiot. Many pregnant women deal with serious heartburn. Be careful of what you eat and drink, and when you feel the pain coming on again, take some over-the-counter antacid medicine. I'd cut back on work as well, if you can. You don't want to push yourself in your final stages of pregnancy."

Luke looks at me and raises an eyebrow. "You heard the doctor, no more work"

"I can't just sit around all day and do nothing!"

"She can work as long as she takes many breaks and sits often throughout the day," says the doctor.

"See!" I say to Luke and stick my tongue out at him. He laughs and winks at me.

"You're good to go, Mrs. Jackson. Remember, take it easy."

"I will doc."

"I'll make sure she does," says Luke. "No more walking to work. I will drop you off from now on."

"Yes, sir," I sigh.

***

I wake up feeling rested but feel something wet underneath me. Luke is already out of bed. I lift up the sheets and scream in horror at what I see: blood and lots of it. "Luke!" I scream. I'm sobbing uncontrollably and can't catch my breath. He runs up the stairs and stands in the doorway, shocked at what he sees. "What's wrong with me?" I cry.

"I don't know, babe; let's take you to the hospital." I slowly get up and change, still freaking out the whole time. "I know you're scared, but you have to try and relax so we can get you taken care of." I know he's right, but I'm so scared that something is wrong with Michael.

He rushes me to the hospital and gets me right in. The same doctor I saw before quickly runs some tests to see what's going on.

"Luke, Linda, I'm so sorry to have to report this information to you, but you're experiencing a placental abruption."

"What the hell does that mean? You said we both were as healthy

as a horse the other day!"

"It's when the placenta peels away from the inner wall of the uterus. Your baby is not getting the oxygen and nutrients he needs. We're going to need to do an immediate C-section to get the baby out and give it a chance to survive."

The doctor and nurses rush in to get me prepped. Fear, sickness, pain, and worry all run through my body and mind. The nurse starts to give me an anesthetic, and my mind begins to fade.

I wake in horror. I quickly check my sheets, but there's no blood. I let out a sigh of relief. This is the first time I have dreamt in months. This has to be a sign.

"What's wrong, babe?"

"I had a dream that I had a placental abruption, and they had to do an immediate premature C-section."

"Honey, it's just a dream. Pregnant women dream bad things about their babies all the time."

"But I haven't had any dreams in months, then all of a sudden I have this dream?"

"You were just at the hospital and he told you everything was fine. Do you feel okay?"

"Yeah, I feel fine, but I'm freaking out!"

"Want me to take you back to the doctor in the morning?"

"Yes, please. It'd make me feel so much better."

"All right, try and go back to sleep. You need as much rest as you can get." He kisses me and I lie down with my head on his chest. He rubs my head until I fall back asleep.

The next morning, I wake up anxious and ready to go to the doctor. We don't even eat breakfast. Luke knows I want to go as soon as possible.

Once we get there, I tell the doctor about my dream. "Mrs. Jackson, women have these dreams often because they worry about losing their child. This is normal and nothing to worry about."

If only he knew about my so-called gift and what my dreams can really mean.

"I'll go ahead and check everything out." I know I am probably overreacting but I want to make sure.

When he finishes his examination, he says, "Just as I thought, he's fine and so are you. You have nothing to worry about."

"Thank you, doctor," I say as I get up from the table.

"I'll see you back here soon when you're ready for a good and safe delivery." We both smile at him.

"I told you everything was okay," says Luke.

"Yeah, yeah. You're not the one who is pregnant here." Luke shakes his head and smiles.

He drops me off at work, which he isn't happy about, but I can't just sit around all day with a huge stomach and do nothing. It'll drive me insane, so I demand to go to work.

But work turns out to be annoying because Sarah makes me take breaks like every half hour. I know it's for my safety, and I'm being bitchy, but I blame it all on being pregnant. My mood swings are pretty bad, and not to mention my cravings. Sarah makes my favorite muffins because she knows how badly I crave them. I'm lucky to have such a great group of friends and family. They have been supporting me and taking care of me, and I don't know what I'd do without them.

The rest of the day goes by smoothly, with no stomach pains and no crazed killers coming to get coffee. I'm not going to lie, I am pretty tired after work. Sarah drops me off at home because Luke is stuck in surgery. As soon as I get home I turn on the TV and lie on the couch. Before too long, my eyes become heavy and all I see is darkness.

***

I wake up in a strange, all-white room. White walls, white floors, there's nothing in this room but white. I stand up quickly and begin to panic. I touch the walls and start hitting them. "Where am I?" I yell. I walk around so many times I can't keep count. I don't know where I'm at or what I'm supposed to do. Is this a trap? Is this hell? And most importantly, how did I get here?

I lie down in a fetal position, cradling my head and rocking back and forth. "Someone, please help me." I close my eyes tight, hoping I'll wake up from wherever I am.

My prayers are answered, and my body twitches as I awaken. I open my eyes and stare at the ceiling. It's still dark outside. *What the hell was that?* I think to myself. *What does it mean?* That dream was very different than anything I've dreamt before. I lie awake for the rest of the night, eyes wide open, thinking of some sort of explanation.

Chapter 25

The next two months fly by, and I'm as big as a freaking beach ball. I'm more than ready for Michael to come into our lives. No unusual pain since the heartburn and Michael and I are healthy. It's only a matter of days now.

I haven't been working because I can barely move. I don't mind though because I'm always tired, and what I need the most is rest. Luke is so sweet to me, making me dinner every night and taking good care of me.

It's the night before my due date and Luke makes my favorite meal as a good luck charm. "I can't believe after nine months Michael is finally about to come into our lives and make us a family," Luke says.

"I know, I'm so ready for him to come out! I can't wait to hold my baby boy in my arms. I think he'll love his nursery."

"I think it's perfect; I think everything is perfect."

"Me too," I say as I kiss my husband and soon-to-be father of my child. After dinner, we rest on the couch and watch TV. All of a sudden I feel a sharp pain. I cry out, and then the pain goes away. Then I feel something wet running down my leg.

"Luke, my water just broke!" But then I look down and see that it's not just water running down my leg, but blood. *No, God, no! Please don't do this to me. Please let my baby be okay.*

"It's finally time!" Luke says excitedly, but then he looks at me as I cry and looks down on the floor. "Is that blood?"

I nod my head as the tears fall.

"Oh my God, let's get you to the hospital now!"

Luke quickly grabs my packed bag and helps me out the door. My contractions are seriously painful. I wish I would have been expecting this. I call May and Mom on my way to the hospital. They both scream with joy when I tell them the day is finally here.

I don't tell them about the blood because I don't need anyone else freaking out.

Luke rushes me into the hospital, and they get me in a wheelchair. They move me into a private room and set me up on the bed. I'm a little nervous because of the pain, and I know it's only going to get worse.

"Doctor, when her water broke, there was also blood," Luke says worriedly.

"Okay, let's take a quick look with the ultrasound to see what's going on inside."

I look at Luke through my tears.

He takes my hand. "It'll be okay, baby, I promise."

"Okay, Mrs. Jackson, it looks like you are experiencing a placental abruption, and because it's happening now during labor, this is what is causing the loss of blood. We need to perform an immediate C-section." He presses a call button and moments later, his team of nurses walk in with bags of liquid and needles.

"Mrs. Jackson, we're now going to give you the epidural. It'll take away some of the pain."

"Luke, I'm scared." *Please, God, let my baby be okay.*

"I'll be with you, don't worry."

The sharp pain of a needle enters my back.

"What about my parents and May? I don't want them to see me like this."

"Don't worry, they can't come in here right now. We'll worry about them after we have our beautiful little boy to show them. Everything will be okay. I love you so much baby; you are such a strong woman. You can do this, and I'll be right here."

He takes my hand, and I look up and see many faces around me. Time and sight begins to fade away. I'm getting light-headed, and my vision is dimming.

"She's losing a lot of blood. We have to hurry," I hear the doctor say faintly.

"Help her, please!" Luke cries out. "Linda, baby, hang on!"

Darkness and silence take over.

***

I open my eyes to a bright light and a white room. Is this heaven? I look down and see my body lying on the table in a pool of blood. I see the baby in the doctor's hands and Luke hovering over my body, crying.

I try to listen to what the doctor is saying. "She lost a lot of blood. She's alive, but barely. She's in a coma."

A coma?

My baby is so beautiful. I try to yell out that I'm there, I can see them, but suddenly, everything disappears. I'm surrounded by white—no walls, no floors, no doors, no existence.

No, this can't be happening! I want to go back; I want to see my baby! I close my eyes and shake my head. "Linda, wake up this is just a dream. Wake up!" I open my eyes, but nothing changes.

"What the fuck is going on?" I keep shouting out loud like someone is going to hear me. I pinch my skin hard, hoping it will wake me up. But I'm still here. I'm stuck in whatever the hell this is, and I have no way out. I panic, I cry, and I can't stop shaking.

I look up and down, left and right, it's all the same. I'm going to go crazy in here! I'm still in my hospital gown. I close my eyes one more time, hoping to wake up in that hospital bed, but that doesn't happen.

I am stuck in this dream—if it even is a dream—and I don't know how long I'll be here. I sit down, cradle myself, and start crying harder. Stuck in a dream, with no one and nothing, no time limit, nothing but fear and loneliness, nothing but the sight of white walls everywhere…this has to be some sort of hell. Will I ever get back to my family? My darling husband, my beautiful baby boy? In the hope of waking up somewhere else, I close my eyes tightly and pray.

To be continued…

About the Author

Megan Johnson is an Elementary School teacher from Charleston, WV who has a passion for writing. Her dream has always been to become a published author. She is happy that with hard work and dedication this dream has now come true. She loves crime/mystery novels and she hopes that this 'dream trilogy' will have everyone sitting on the edge of their seats. She will continue with her writing career and hopes to continue making readers happy.

www.ingramcontent.com/pod-product-compliance
Lightning Source LLC
Chambersburg PA
CBHW071237250626
47163CB00001B/214